NADI

Loren Walker

Octopus & Elephant Books

PROVIDENCE, RHODE ISLAND

Octopus & Elephant Books
www.oandebooks.com

Publisher's Note: This is a work of fiction. Names, characters, places, and incidents are a product of the author's imagination. Any resemblance to actual people, living or dead, or to businesses, companies, events, institutions, or locales is completely coincidental.

Book Layout ©2015 BookDesignTemplates.com.

Cover by Deranged Doctor Designs.

NADI / Loren Walker. -- 1st ed.
ISBN 9978-0-9973922-2-7

For the ones that I love.

PART ONE

I.

The body was identified as Dasean Renzo Byrne, fifty-seven years old. Hair: gray. Skin: brown. Eyes: gray-green. Death was attributed to a single stab wound to the heart, severing artery and ventricle: heart failure due to internal bleeding. Defensive wounds on the knuckles of both hands. As per policy, anti-rigor serum was administered at the death scene, but blood had still pooled in the corpse's back, the spine framed in purple.

Wife: Lora Byrne, deceased.

Next of kin: Renzo Raeden Byrne, eldest son.

The funeral was small and private, with hardly any attendees, just a few older men who shuffled into view and then faded away. A second cousin here and there, waiting for permission to escape the overwhelming cloud of white and black flowers, strategically placed to conceal the emptiness.

Renzo Byrne slipped into the reflection room, adjacent to the viewing space. Locking the door behind him, he pushed his glasses to the top of his head, rubbing his face with a deep, long sigh. Then he shrugged off his stiff jacket and undid the collar flap.

Across the room, the parlor's public Lissome was perched on a dusty pedestal, projecting a picture slideshow. Old photos, when Dasean still had brown in his hair. With a flick of his fingers, Renzo disabled it. Then he brought up a new screen and the Bounty-Track database, moving through rows of mugshots.

There he was, Denn Acelin. Still framed in green. The retrieval bounty was still live.

Come on, Renzo groaned inwardly. *You two aren't finished yet?*

There was a knock at the door. Renzo collapsed the screen, though he didn't bother to reinstate the mourning display.

"Mr. Byrne? It's time."

Outside the home, the casket was being prepared for transport. Renzo stood by, watching the process. He still didn't quite know how to feel about the death of his father. There was a weird, sickly feeling in the center of his chest, true. But he didn't feel anything that resembled emotion. There should be sorrow. Or relief, if nothing else. But there was nothing but flat, frank observation.

The hatch to the carrier closed with a hiss. Propulsion engines ignited, and the tiny funeral procession stepped back as the hearse lifted into the air.

Next to Renzo, the woman held her blue jacket closed, the backdraft rippling at the hem. Sydel had insisted on accompanying him. His sister, Phaira, and younger brother, Cohen, were two districts over, completing a bounty retrieval, their first ever as a team. They knew about their father's sudden death, but neither volunteered to come back. So it was left to Renzo to sign every form, arrange every detail, and sort out the remnants of Dasean Byrne's dismal life. It was kind of Sydel to offer to come along, though he still felt discomfort around her: the former resident of a cult-like commune, Cohen's somewhat girlfriend, and the fourth person living in the *Arazura.*

The hearse disappeared behind a low-lying cloud. It was quiet now, save for the sounds of traffic in the far-distance.

"It's done," Renzo told Sydel. "We can leave."

"There's...." Her words trailed off as she turned, facing east, staring into the horizon with a puzzled look on her face. Her dark copper-brown braids, piled on top of her head, reflected the sunset. Then she nodded. "Someone is calling for help."

"You mean Cohen?" Renzo asked in a rush, panicking. "Or Phaira?"

"No, no," Sydel said, waving her hand impatiently. "The woman from Kings."

"Keep your voice down," Renzo hissed, checking for eavesdroppers. Two weeks ago, he, Phaira, Cohen and Sydel had barely escaped from Kings Canyon in the West, where a bloodhunt was underway to root out and destroy what was known as the NINE, an organized group of powerful psychics from twenty-five years ago. Now, everyone in Kings was dead: members of the powerful Sava crime syndicate, the hired mercenaries, the woman who kidnapped Sydel and the youth she recruited to follow, and an old friend of the family's, Aeden Nox. Most had been killed in a sudden, unexplainable shoot-out, while others, including Nox, had been crushed in the canyon's collapse.

Thirty-two corpses was the last count that Renzo heard. Everywhere he went, the words Kings Canyon seemed to hover at the edge of every conversation: theories about alien attacks, mass suicide, gang warfare, government coverups. It was the biggest scandal to hit the country of Osha in years, but so far, no one seemed to know that Renzo and the other members of the *Arazura* were some of the only survivors. Not yet, anyways.

"The woman who came to see me," Sydel said, more quietly. "She's calling my name. She's east, near the coast, in darkness. I think she's hurt. We need to find her."

"The one with the green hair?" Renzo recalled the girl's hushed confession, days after the incident when they finally felt secure enough to land. When held in Kings, a mysterious woman had emerged at Sydel's frantic call for help: she was an Eko, the same as Sydel, skilled in the art of mental projection and telepathy. She claimed to know Sydel's parents. She was one of the original NINE.

But then everything descended into chaos. Remembering, Renzo's stomach turned: Cohen taken hostage, Sydel bruised and battered by Keller Sava, Phaira shot in the abdomen and dropping off the nose of the *Arazura*...

"We're not going," Renzo stated. "No offense to your kind, but I want nothing more to do with those people. They've done enough damage."

Sydel bit her lip. Then she reached over and took his arm. Surprised, Renzo stiffened at the touch, but she drew even closer.

"This is different, Renzo Byrne," she said firmly. "The longer I have been away from Jala Communia, the more my mind has cleared. And I realize there are holes in my memory. Lost time. You know what that feels like."

Renzo swallowed. She had him by the throat with that. Several months ago, he'd been viciously assaulted. In addition to losing his right leg, his long-term memory was still impacted, huge swathes of childhood now gone. He was fortunate to have regained his genius capacity for mathematics, though he hadn't told anyone in his life just yet.

"What will this woman tell you?" he questioned.

"Everything, I hope."

* * *

Cohen Byrne's right hand remained underneath his jacket as he surveyed the swarm of people in the Daro lab: talking to loved ones, making money transfers, working on travel permits, walking and talking and typing. He glanced at his sister, Phaira. As she retrieved her Lissome, Phaira expanded the screen with a small flick of her fingertip and studied the image, her nose an inch from the pixels.

"You need glasses," Cohen told her.

"I do not." Phaira made a face as she pocketed the Lissome. Then she looked over the railing, searching the swaying crowd below. "You stay here."

"But -"

"For now," she corrected. "Just let me go first."

Cohen harrumphed. The whole point of this is to learn how to work together, he wanted to point out to her, but the look in her eyes made him lose his nerve.

Phaira descended to the first floor, the platform letting out a steady hiss of air on the way down. Cohen focused on the top of her blue head as she wove through the hordes. Despite his protesting, sweat broke along his hairline when he saw Phaira slide her hand under her jacket. She was feeling the handle of her Calis, he knew. Would she draw it in public? Should he draw his own? He hated her finicky pistols with the heavy recoil, but his sharpshooting skills made him a natural for the Vaccaro, a light, precise rifle that hung from a loop inside his heavy overcoat. He could assemble it in under ten seconds, if needed. He let his fingers graze the barrel as he stared at Phaira. She was slowing down. His gaze travelled further up, to where she was looking.

There he was, out in the open like an idiot, sitting in a corner, staring moodily into the crowd. Just like the photo: light hair, deep brown skin, visible scar across the side of his throat. Bounty issued for skipping bail and leaving jurisdiction. Their first-ever mark: Denn Acelin. Cohen's heart leapt with anticipation.

Acelin's face twisted. Suddenly, he shoved his chair back and grabbed the woman next to him, jerking his human shield in front. As screams echoed throughout the network center, Cohen was already assembling the Vaccaro. Phaira's Calis was primed and aimed; her dark mouth was moving, but Cohen couldn't hear what she was yelling over the chaos.

The last component clicked into place, and Cohen had the man centered through his scope. Acelin was walking backwards, the hostage clawing at his grip. Then the bounty caught sight of Cohen on the second floor.

His finger steady on the trigger, Cohen extended his other hand in greeting.

Acelin ducked back behind the hostage, yanking her along as he headed for the exit. Following, Phaira's head turned to the side, in Cohen's direction. He understood.

When Acelin suddenly threw the woman into Phaira, and crashed through the back exit, Cohen was already on his way outside, holstering the Vaccaro inside his jacket. Their rented Subito speeders were still outside, covered with a light layer of snow. Cohen swung his leg over his, starting the thrusters. The engines groaned, but they finally turned over and fired to life. Rounding the corner, he saw Acelin sliding onto his own Subito, the man racing off into the traffic.

Phaira appeared from the shadows. Cohen slid back on the hovering speeder. "Come on!" he yelled.

Phaira hopped onto the seat in front of Cohen and gunned the engine. Cohen grabbed the side rails as the Subito jolted forward.

As they trailed Acelin through the heavy traffic, Cohen shifted his weight and prayed for balance as he withdrew the assembled Vacarro, bracing it against his shoulder.

"Hit the ground underneath him!" Phaira yelled. In the distance, Acelin wove in and out of traffic, trying to lose his pursuers. "Don't try for a direct hit!"

The Subito went over a bump, and Cohen's finger slipped. A blast fired over Phaira's shoulder. A market-stand on the sidestreet burst into flame, violent enough to almost knock them off the speeder.

"What are you doing?" Phaira hollered, her hand pressed to her ear, the other hand swerving the Subito to avoid retaliatory gunshots from pedestrians. "Hit just below his rider!!" She increased the speed and veered to the right, forming an angle with Acelin.

Flushed with embarrassment, Cohen braced the Vaccaro against his shoulder again, squinted through the cold wind, and took his time.

The underbelly of Acelin's Subito burst into sparks. The speeder twisted, out of control.

Suddenly, their own Subito lurched, hit by an angry pedestrian's bullet. Cohen launched off, hitting the ground and rolling into a parked transport, though not hard enough to hurt. Ahead of him, Phaira landed in a stack of boxes left by the curb. The Subito skidded across the pavement in a shower of flashes and snow, slamming into a lightpost with a loud clang.

Up ahead, Acelin had crashed too, the Subito rolling over his leg. His howl of pain echoed down the street. Limping, the man stumbled into an alleyway.

They splintered off. A dripping-wet Phaira pursued Acelin into the alleyway, while Cohen moved around the perimeter of the building to cut the man off.

He was almost at the alley's exit when he heard the echo of a gunshot.

* * *

Flying over grasslands, Renzo was doing his best to remain calm. Still, manning the controls of the *Arazura*, he couldn't help but glance nervously at the girl every five seconds, looking for some kind of signal.

Sydel sat in the co-pilot chair, her eyes closed. Every few minutes, she would open them and tell him that he was going in the right direction, to just keep going east. He wondered what she was picking up on, what it felt like to have someone else's voice in your head. To Renzo, it sounded horrible. He wouldn't wish it for anything.

To distract him from his thoughts, Renzo punched in a string of letters and numbers: a connection code, or cc, that he had called at least three times in the last two weeks.

"I need an update," he said when the line crackled. "Any news on Kings?"

The voice on the other end was snide. "I have other work to do, Renzo. I can't keep accessing patrol data on your whims."

"Did you forget about the deal that you made with my sister, Lander?" Renzo snapped. "You do as you're told. Unless you want another visit."

A huff of breath, but there was tension in it, Renzo could hear. No, the man didn't want to deal with Phaira again, not after last time, when she threatened to sever all the nerves in his arm unless he provided protection for them. Lander was another witness in Kings, one of the hackers kidnapped to aid the cause. He was also a part of the Hitodama, a hacktivist group known for their gothic appearance and ability to find information. And he was an utter pain in Renzo's side.

"What do you want to know?" Lander finally spoke.

"Any changes to the reports," Renzo said. "Any new evidence submitted, new people assigned to the case, any travel or warrants -"

"Okay, okay," Lander huffed.

Listening to the faint sounds of beeps and clicks, Renzo watched the landscape through the *Arazura's* windshield turn to rock. They were nearing the coast, he realized, and the city of Towns. He glanced over at Sydel. She was fidgeting in her seat, but her eyes were still closed.

"New patrol case leader," Lander read off. "Detective Daryn Ozias. No reports filed since three days ago, no submitted evidence. The clean-up crew signed off days ago, and haven't been back to Kings, either." His voice turned smug. "It's as I told you, Renzo, no one cares. Kings was just a bunch of criminals, runaways and mafia men. Patrol has bigger problems to deal with. They're just going through the motions."

Someone should care about Nox, Renzo thought, but he kept it to himself. "I'll call you in two days," he instructed. "Be ready with a report."

As he signed off, Sydel slammed her hands on the *Arazura's* console.

Renzo jumped, causing the *Arazura* to jerk to the left. "What are you doing!" he hollered.

"She's here," Sydel said. "She's on the mountain. Can we land? Quickly?"

Renzo scanned the landscape. Yes, there was a mountain overlooking the city, though not much of one, outfitted with metal towers and wires, no trails or flat areas for landing. "Are you sure?"

Sydel didn't say anything. But when Renzo finally found a landing site for the *Arazura*, she was already out of the cockpit and heading to the exit. Muttering to himself, Renzo tucked a Compact firearm into his waistband and made sure his prosthetic leg was clicked into place. Should he keep the engines running? Standby couldn't hurt.

The sun was just starting to set. Cold, damp air billowed into the *Arazura*. Bracing against the chill, Renzo leaned out of the hatch. The stairs had descended, and Sydel was already on the rocky ground, wandering as if in a dream.

"Will you wait for me, please?" Renzo called after her, stumbling down the stairs. He pushed his glasses closer to his eyes to try and protect them from the wind.

Sydel didn't seem to hear him. She stood on the edge of a gaping crack in the earth, ten feet across, looking down into the depths. When he finally reached Sydel's side, Renzo peered down into the crevice. Only a few feet of grey rock were visible; he couldn't see the bottom.

But something moved in the dark. Renzo's breath caught in his throat.

"She's down there?" he managed.

Dammit, why hadn't she warned him? If this person fell in there, she probably had broken bones. Maybe a fractured skull or back. What was he supposed to do about it? They should call for medical rescue.

"I'm going to go down to her," Sydel said abruptly. "See how bad her injuries truly are. She is conscious, for now, but she needs our help." Renzo couldn't hear what she said after that; her voice dropped to a low mumble, self-talk as she tucked her braids into a knot and knelt down, looking for a foothold.

Renzo caught her arm. "Sydel," he said firmly. "We need to call for medical transport. The city is right down there, it'll be quick -"

"No, I can do this."

"Are you thinking straight? I'm not qualified to help someone who's fallen and cracked open their head, and I'm not sure you are either."

A new, more frightening thought occurred to him. "And what if she tries to attack your mind or something?"

"She might," she admitted. "But I can protect myself, if need be."

"If you call the city for help, you've done your part," he pushed back. "We don't -"

"Renzo." Her voice was firm. "I need to see her. And you know you can't stop me."

Renzo didn't have a response for that. It was true. So he let her arm go.

"Let me get the cable," he muttered with a sigh. "If you break your neck, Cohen will kill me."

* * *

There was no source of light in the alley: only moving shadows, and the sounds of panicked breathing. Whose breath? Phaira's, or Acelin's? Cohen squinted hard, his heart hammering.

Then Acelin's face loomed into view. Cohen reacted, launching himself at Acelin. He pinned the man to the ground and took shot after shot at the man's nose, his throat, whatever he could make contact with. The crunch of bone echoed off the brick walls.

"Cohen! Enough!"

At the sound of his sister's order, Cohen snapped out of his trance and shoved Acelin away. He was boiling hot; he stripped off his gloves and unzipped his overcoat. The cold air hit him in the sternum.

Phaira was in front of him, her brown skin tinged pink from exertion. "A bit much, Cohen," she said curtly, glancing at his bloody knuckles.

"You've done worse," he retorted, doing his best not to pant. "What now?"

Phaira looked like she had more to say, but instead she shrugged one shoulder. "We call it in. Designate a pick-up point. Tell them to have the reward ready for transfer." She glanced at Acelin; he had curled into a ball on the ground. Then she drew out her Lissome and punched in the cc to connect to the *Arazura*. "Ren? Where are you? We're done."

"Okay," came Renzo's voice. "Sure. Got it. But it's going to be a while."

Phaira frowned, catching Cohen's eye. "Did something happen?"

"Not what you think." Renzo hedged. "I can get back to Daro in five hours."

"Tonight! What are you - ?"

"Just stay there. I'll be there before midnight."

"But -"

The line disconnected before Phaira could finish her sentence.

"It's nothing," Cohen said automatically. "Don't read into it."

Phaira didn't respond. When the Lissome clicked back into its neat small square, she slipped it back into her pocket. Then Phaira turned slowly, surveying the alley, the rooftops, the skylines. Her edginess hung on

Cohen like a heavy blanket. Phaira was paranoid, sure, but often right about it. And although she never talked about it, even with no active bounty on her name, Cohen knew his big sister never stopped looking for the next threat.

* * *

Renzo paced in a tight circle, waiting. Sydel had been down in the crevice for several minutes now, with no sign of coming back up. He'd already sent down a medical kit, a portable light, and a stability plank via the *Arazura's* cable, which was still taut, and vibrated every few seconds. He had also taken the time to calculate the distance to the nearest medical facility. He had his argument fully prepared, should Sydel push back. There was still so much to finish regarding his father's death and final preparations...

"Now, Renzo Byrne. Slowly." Sydel's voice bounced up the rocks and into the open air.

Renzo searched for any sign of her, or of anything, down at the bottom of the crevice. Then he activated the pulley on its slowest setting. Gradually, the cable coiled on itself, underneath the *Arazura*. The pressure grooved into the rocky edge, tiny mounds of shaved dust on either side. Then came the silhouette of a body, climbing up. Renzo touched his Compact pistol, still at the back of his waistband. But it was Sydel, one hand holding onto the cable as she stepped from ledge to ledge, the other hand on the stability plank and the patient.

Strapped to the board, secured with the harness, the woman's body was clad in a brown sleeveless dress, with shades of red and rust splattered across it. Her skin was bluish and pale, head lolled to one side, her hair dark brown with green streaks, in several braids. He had expected a much more alien-looking creature, from Sydel and Cohen's accounts.

Renzo dropped to the ground, reaching down to grab Sydel's wrist, helping her over the edge. Drenched in sweat, she almost slipped from his grip. Then he took hold of the plank's handles on either side and heaved. The board slid onto the surface with a soft rush. The woman never moved.

Sydel remained on her hands and knees, catching her breath. Renzo ran his hands through his hair a few times, before he realized his hands, and now his hair, were caked with sand.

He turned to the green-haired woman. She was covered with bruises, mottled and purple, and her right leg was bent in an unnatural angle, with deep gouges in her skin. Her arms were badly scratched, one bicep wrapped in gauze and already showing red. Was she dead? It would make the transfer process easier if she were.

Renzo reached out with his free hand, two fingers extended to check for a pulse in her neck.

Just before he touched her, though, her eyes snapped open. Inky black. Irises too large for a normal human. Bloodshot and consuming him.

"What's wrong?" came Sydel's hoarse voice.

When he looked back to the green-haired one, she was still unconscious. Just as before. Had he imagined it all?

* * *

Acelin was taken into custody, brought into the back of Daro Collections. Hands were shaken. Money transferred. Posting deactivated.

Now Phaira and Cohen were in a bar near the skerries, waiting out the night, drinks in hand, blues music playing in their individual booth. Running his finger around the edge of his glass, Cohen surveyed the bar, wondering how many mercenaries were in this place. Who was still on the clock, and who was merely looking for a good time. It wasn't crowded, but there was a certain vibe in the atmosphere. Serious. Wary and watching.

His mind turned to their father. Renzo, the way he huffed and glared at them when they left. How Phaira insisted on going after the bounty to make some easy rana, leaving Renzo to take care of their father's final arrangements. Cohen lifted his glass, filled to the brim with dark ale. "Maybe we should have gone to the funeral," he said to his sister.

"We were busy," Phaira mumbled over the rim of her SunFlare.

"Come on, Phair."

"What? We needed the rana. Now we can buy some food and these drinks and fuel for the *Arazura*..."

"You're not curious at all where he's been all this time? If he ever thought about...?"

"Co, I'm not curious, and I don't care," Phaira interrupted. Her blue hair swung back over the leather seat as she swallowed the last of her SunFlare, a swirling orange cocktail rimmed with cayenne pepper. She coughed from the afterburn. "You'd do better to forget he ever existed," she added with a slight wheeze. "Renzo's dealing with it. Then we can move on."

Cohen didn't quite know what to say. The door to the pub swung open, and a blast of cold, damp air shot through the bar, mixed with a second smell, one that Cohen recognized immediately: mekaline. A street drug, and the hallucinogenic to which Phaira was once addicted. Someone was smoking it, just outside.

He glanced at her, curious if she had caught the scent. But Phaira didn't react; she was staring down at the table, one finger pushing through a droplet of liquor and streaking it outwards, like a fading star. He watched her design, and wondered if he should bring it up. But what if he just made things worse? She never listened to him anyways, and she was already so short with him over their father.

"I'll buy you another drink," he offered. "If you tell me a story about him. A good one," he added.

With a quick sweep of her palm, the liquid design was eradicated, smeared into nothing.

"I'll buy my own, if that's the deal."

II.

Renzo and Sydel managed to heave the stretcher onto the gurney in the medical lab, the left half of Sydel's quarters. Sydel's hands hovered over the prone body as Renzo waited, his eyes darting back and forth.

"Well?" he prodded. "What are you going to do?"

There were beads of sweat on her brow, and her fingers trembled.

"Don't you have everything you need?" Renzo tried, gesturing at all the closed metal drawers, all the cabinets containing medicines, gauze, tools, everything that he'd bought to supply her with, so they would never have to worry about seeking outside medical attention.

"Yes," Sydel admitted. Her voice shook. "I think so, anyways."

"So, what, then?"

"I can't do this alone."

"You healed Cohen's burns. And when Phaira was shot, you -"

"This is different," Sydel interrupted. She balled her hands into fists and brought them to her chest. "Cohen's wounds were superficial. And Phaira's wounds were lucky, they never hit any major organs."

She gestured helplessly at the body. "Her wounds are into the muscle, layers deep. Her legs are broken. Maybe her spine, too. I am no expert. I'm not a doctor. I have no confidence in my knowledge, it was never a focus in my studies, other than the basic. What if I make her worse?" Her voice grew more and more rushed with every excuse.

"Then she goes to a medlab," Renzo said firmly. "We just say we found her and -"

Sydel shook her head.

"Someone will cover the cost, if they think she's a transient."

"No."

"Why not?" he exploded. "You just said you can't help her!"

"She's terrified, and alone, and she begged me to keep her hidden," Sydel interrupted.

"She was conscious down there?" Those black eyes flashed in his mind again. Maybe he hadn't imagined it after all.

"What about Anandi?" Sydel ignored the question. "Could she suggest someone here who specializes in trauma, someone I can consult with? Who can be discrete?"

"Maybe," Renzo muttered. He pulled out his Lissome, punched in his friend's cc and waited for the connection. "If she dies in here," he told Sydel, "that's on you."

Sydel nodded.

"Renzo." Anandi's musical voice rippled through the soundsystem. "What now?"

"Hello to you too, Ani."

"Oh, come on, I know you're calling because you need something."

"Sorry," Renzo said, embarrassed. "You're right. Sorry. We have an emergency. I need a doctor, someone who can give advice on broken bones. Maybe a broken back," he added, glancing over at Sydel for confirmation.

"What? Is Phaira okay?"

"No, no, it's not Phaira or any of us. It's some woman we found -"

"CaLarca." Sydel's voice rang across the room. "That's the name she gave me. Her name is CaLarca."

"CaLarca," Renzo relayed. "And the damage is bad enough that Sydel doesn't feel confident in her abilities. Do you know anyone in Towns who could help?"

The sounds of rustling and hushed conversation. Then a new voice came through. "Renzo?"

"Sir?" Renzo said automatically at Emir Ajyo's voice. Then he chastised himself for acting like a nervous teenager around Anandi's father.

"Go south to Plainfield. The public garage. I'll be there with supplies. Tell Sydel to prepare a full evaluation in the meantime."

"You'll - wait, what?"

But Emir was already gone.

Then Anandi was back on the line. "Just make sure he gets back to me within forty-eight hours. He's due." Her voice went quiet. "It's been a few years, but he was a pretty great doctor once upon a time, Ren. Don't worry."

The line disconnected. Renzo leaned against the wall, stunned. Emir was a doctor? They'd never told him that before. There was a strange irony in the fact that

Emir was a medical professional, but chose to live as a hacktivist in the slums with his daughter. Part of that, Renzo knew, was due to his blood disorder, controlled only through transfusions from said daughter. But what about his practice?

"That was Anandi's father?" Sydel was asking him. "Where is Plainfield? Is he coming on board?" She looked terrified at the idea. He wondered why.

"Towns and Plainfield are twin cities on the coast. It's an hour south," Renzo said, heading for the cockpit. "Do what he asked in the meantime. You can do that at least, right?"

* * *

When the *Arazura* descended into Plainfield and locked onto the great parking hanger, stretching twenty stories high, the man with the snow-white hair was waiting for them, weighed down with bags and equipment.

Renzo watched from afar as Sydel and Emir conversed. They conducted a number of tests, little flashes of metal, peering into screens, prodding of all the deep, flayed gouges, unwrapping the bandages to peer at the ripped-off chunk from the woman's arm. Emir unearthed one of the handheld ultrasounds from the medical bay; placing it against his eye, he travelled the length of CaLarca's legs, first the right and then the left. Renzo caught a glimpse of the negative image on the tiny screen: it was some kind of portable x-ray, showing the bones under the skin, how they were bowed and in some places, cracked. When completed, Emir asked Sydel to hold the device in place. Then with quick, practiced hands, he set CaLarca's broken leg. It looked horribly painful to Renzo, each jerk and sickening snap, but CaLarca never stirred as Emir and Sydel tightly bound the limb.

After CaLarca's lower back was braced and bound, and the unconscious woman returned to her prone position, Emir focused on the deep contusions in her arms. Using slim, silver surgical knives, his beard and mouth covered by a mask, Emir began to strip the dead, infected skin. Sydel assisted, keeping one hand on the woman's head, presumably keeping her unconscious.

Then Emir removed a rectangular case from his pack of supplies and unlocked it. Renzo craned his neck to see. The case was full of translucent paper-thin sheets, three inches squared. There was also another instrument in there, something with a bent, flattened attachment.

"This is going to hurt her," Emir warned. "The pain will be excruciating. And it may be difficult to watch."

Renzo saw Sydel swallow. "I can manage."

A tiny blue flame flickered at the edge of the attachment. Emir laid one strip of translucent film over the hole in Ca'Larca's left bicep. Then, like a welder holding a blowtorch, he pushed the head of the burner along the film, again and again.

The smell of burning flesh filled the room. Renzo gagged and clapped his hand over his mouth.

Three beeps sounded through the room. Oh, his beautiful ship; he thanked the *Arazura* profusely for the distraction.

"That's Phaira and Cohen," he called through his fingers. "I have to get back to Daro by midnight."

Neither Emir nor Sydel turned away, absorbed. Renzo retreated, walking quickly to the cockpit, hungry at the prospect of recirculated air and the distraction of flying. The beeps sounded again. Sliding into the pilot's chair, Renzo flicked the connection.

"On my way," he reported. "But there's something you should know."

* * *

"Why is she wearing my clothes?" Phaira's indignant voice echoed through the *Arazura*.

Standing in the threshold of Sydel's room, Renzo rolled his eyes. Instant drama, as soon as his sister was back onboard. He looked over at Cohen, wondering if he felt the same. But his brother stood in the corner, his arms crossed, his face unreadable.

"Please be calm," Sydel was saying to Phaira. "You've got a cut on your arm, let me - "

But Phaira brushed her aside, and stormed over to Renzo; she was only an inch taller, but she was lording that inch with all her might. "Why would you bring that woman onto my ship?" she snapped. "What are you thinking?"

"Our ship," Renzo corrected hotly, consciously lifting onto the balls of his feet. "Actually, my ship. I'm the one who built it, paid for it...."

Oh. I shouldn't have said that, he realized, snapping his mouth shut. Had she picked up on what he just said? He hadn't quite figured out how to tell Phaira where the money came from to build the *Arazura*.

But his sister didn't seem to register, continuing to talk: "This is the favor that kept us waiting until midnight? And you dragged Emir into all of this?"

"For me, yes," Sydel interrupted. "I asked him to. For them both to help me."

"And I'm happy to do so, Phaira," came Emir's protest. "It wasn't an imposition."

"This is the one you met in Kings Canyon. You said she was an Eko. Powerful," Phaira told Sydel, as if daring her to contradict it.

Sydel's thin lips pressed together. "You don't trust me."

Phaira regarded the girl for a few moments. Then she spoke: "You know I don't."

"Phair!" Cohen exclaimed.

"No," Phaira interrupted, lifting a finger to stop his outburst. "Don't. I know what Sydel is capable of, and so do you."

Renzo looked from his sister to his brother. He had his suspicions before, and the bristling tension was now confirmation: something happened in Kings. Irritation rose in him; they were always keeping secrets from him, even as children, it drove him crazy.

"She came to me in Kings," Sydel said. "She sought me out. Now she has asked for my help. I can't just leave her in the hands of strangers."

"We're strangers too, Sydel," Phaira pointed out. "And we also need to stay hidden. Taking on some strange woman isn't condusive to that."

"Neither is going on a bounty hunt," Renzo couldn't help but point out.

He received one of his sister's familiar glares in return.

"When the base collapsed," Phaira continued. "All those mercenaries went crazy on each other. It must have been triggered by something. What if it was her?"

"That's not possible," Sydel said. "I've never heard of such a thing."

Which means nothing, Renzo thought, with a queer twist in his stomach.

"I only want answers, Phaira," Sydel continued. "So I can move on. I hope you can support me in this."

"And if she is here to hurt us?" Phaira accused. "Does that mean anything to you?"

Sydel's gaze wavered. "If she attempts to harm anyone, I will not stand in the way of retribution."

Not words you expect to hear out of Sydel's mouth. It made Renzo even more curious about what she was thinking. Still, no one said anything.

After several long seconds, Phaira turned her attention to Sydel's bed, the beeping mechanics next to it, and the heavily bandaged woman on it. "Can she be woken?"

"Her given name is CaLarca," Sydel said pointedly. "And yes. But it would be very painful."

"So keep it under control. We need to talk."

Sydel opened her mouth to protest, but went silent when Renzo shot her a look. His sister was hot-tempered and abrasive, but she was rightly cautious, given the events of the past month. And he was just as anxious to see who this CaLarca was.

Renzo, Cohen, Phaira and Emir stood in a semi-circle. Sydel glided to the head of the bed. Then she raised her hand.

The woman stirred. In the corner of his eye, Renzo saw Phaira's fingers graze the handle of a blade holstered at her thigh. Even Emir was shifting from foot to foot.

Then CaLarca's eyes snapped open.

A blast of pain shot through Renzo's head. White light. High voices.

Just as quickly, it was gone. But in that second, Phaira's blade was in her hand, reversed, her arm drawn back to throw.

Renzo grabbed her forearm: not to lower it, just to hold it in place. "Wait," he hissed.

"You're safe," Emir spoke up from the foot of the bed "I'm a doctor. Emir Ajyo. You were badly injured from a fall. Can you understand me?"

A low hiss came from the woman's mouth. Emir lifted both hands and backed away.

Phaira wrenched her arm from Renzo, and sheathed her knife. "That's it," she announced. "She's out of here."

"No." The green-haired woman croaked. "You will not. You cannot."

Renzo quickly moved in front of his sister. "This is not the place for you," he told the woman. "Emir and Sydel did their best, but we can contact...."

Something shifted in CaLarca. "Please," she rasped. "I'm alone. I have no one. Don't...."

Her chest rose and fell, struggling for breath, her forehead densely wrinkled with pain. Still at her bedside, Sydel turned over her palm. The woman's body sank back into the mattress. She was unconscious again.

"We weren't finished," Phaira said to Sydel curtly.

"Leave her alone," Renzo shot back. "Come outside," he directed the group. "We need to make a decision."

In the corridor, a vote was cast. Phaira railed against CaLarca: it was too dangerous, too unpredictable, they had to get rid of her. Cohen was visibly reluctant, but he stood by Sydel, who pleaded again for mercy.

Renzo was cross with Sydel for bringing this mess into the *Arazura*, but at the same time, he recalled the way she'd taken his arm, pleaded with him for answers to the void in her brain. And he was curious just who this CaLarca was, and what she was really capable of.

Phaira was right in that taking on an outsider was dangerous, given their precarious future. He couldn't secure their future without more information, and no matter how many times Lander hacked into the law patrol, there were some questions that could only be answered by this woman, he knew it. She was badly injured, she wasn't going anywhere, and he'd make sure she had no means to communicate with anyone on the outside.

So for now, he stated, CaLarca could stay.

Three-to-one. So Phaira went silent. It wasn't over, not by far, Renzo knew, but for now the decision was respected.

Emir offered to catch public transport back to Plainfield, and save them the trip. When the *Arazura* landed, adjacent to the Daro train station, Phaira, Renzo and Cohen walked Emir to the exit.

"Sorry to drag you out here, Emir," Phaira apologized, still sullen. "It was very considerate of you to help."

"Truthfully, Phaira, I had an ulterior motive for seeing you, anyways," Emir said, one hand on the doorframe. "A favor to ask." He struggled with his next words. "You all know about my blood disorder, I presume."

Phaira didn't respond. Cohen was very intent on not looking at Emir's arms. Admittedly, Renzo found it hard to keep his gaze from jumping over; the older man's sleeves were rolled up, his skin scarred from so many blood transfusions. But he held firm, and nodded in response to Emir's question.

"There's a treatment further south, in Liera," Emir continued. "Experimental, but encouraging results. I've decided to undergo the process. It will take some time, so Anandi wishes to come along."

"Well, now's the time to disappear," Renzo began.

"Anandi has asked if you will accompany us, Phaira," Emir interrupted gently.

"Me?" Phaira said, surprised. "Why?"

"Protection," Emir said. "Plus, I will be rendered unconscious during the procedure, for days, possibly. I think she could use a friend in the silence."

"For how long?"

"Ideally, no more than three weeks," Emir said. "Will you consider it?"

Phaira had a look on her face that Renzo couldn't quite interpret. When she looked to each of her brothers, Renzo nodded at her, impatient. Why was she hesitating? Emir and Anandi would keep her concealed, and they owed the father and daughter team for so much already.

"Yes. Of course," she finally said. "I'll go with you. When?"

"We hoped to leave tomorrow, via rail," Emir said. "There is one stop to make, in Honorwell, before we head down the coast to Liera."

Emir ducked through the exit. His snow-white head stopped, then bobbed back into the *Arazura*.

"What will you do about that woman in there?" he asked. "She has a long road to recovery. I can't imagine the three of you are interested in handling that."

"She's going to a medlab, eventually. But before that, we talk to her," Renzo said grimly. "Get more information about what happened and where she's from."

"And what she is," Cohen reminded him.

"And who she works for," Phaira finished the thought.

III.

Only a couple of hours had passed since Emir's de-
parture, but Phaira was already packing her leather
satchel. Sitting on her unmade bed, she pulled on black
lace-up boots. Renzo leaned against her doorway, watching the back of her blue head and her fingers, as they
expertly tied knots.

"Staying here in Daro?" his sister's voice floated back.

"Yes. For Father's final arrangements." There was
clear annoyance in his voice, and he let it ring.

"I didn't ask to go with Emir and Anandi," Phaira
said over her shoulder. "I would have preferred to stay.
Keep watch over what's happening with that woman.
And Sydel -"

"Let's lay it out, Phair," Renzo said, pushing off
the doorframe. "What's with you and Sydel? You went
through all that effort to find her. Then when we get her
back, you can barely look at her. Why?"

Phaira said nothing. Her jagged hair swept over her
profile, hiding her expression.

"I understand Cohen, being in love with her and all,"
Renzo said. "But why are you hiding things from me?
You don't trust me with whatever you're holding onto?"

Phaira's boot hit the floor with a loud BANG. "If
we're being straight with each other, Ren," she hissed
back, lifting her gaze, "building this ship must have cost,

what? Ten million rana? More? I assumed that Anandi had connections to finance it, but I guess not. So, where did the money come from?"

Staring at his sister, Renzo chewed the inside of his mouth. Instinctively, he ran the back of his hand up the smooth cool metal of the doorframe. This day had been coming, he knew it would come at some point. He knew how it looked to the outside eye. He knew it was going to make things bad again, when they had just made peace with each other. But in a way, it seemed like Phaira already knew what he was going to say; she was watching him, her hand gripping the strap of her satchel, almost flinching with anticipation.

It felt so strange to open back up this chapter in their life. But once again, the focus was back to Renzo's assault, his hospitalization, his accusation of local playboy Nican Macatia as his attacker, and Phaira's pursuit of Nican in the name of justice. When the boy accidentally fell off a bridge, his wealthy family issued a bounty for his sister's head. It was the start of everything.

"It just showed up in my accounts," Renzo finally said. After ducking several attempts on her life, Phaira disappeared, and the money showed up in Renzo's account the next day. Blood money, his conscience reminded him. Simpering, apologetic money.

"And those odd jobs you worked?" Phaira interrupted his thoughts. "At the Vendor Mills?"

"Some were real," Renzo admitted. "Most were not. I've been drawing from the account as needed, and moving it constantly."

"How much is left?"

"Most of it I invested in the *Arazura*. For all of us, not just me," he reminded her, though his voice sounded strangled.

Phaira just gazed at him. He couldn't read the expression on her face.

"It was just money, and it was in my grasp," Renzo pressed on. "You can't blame me for taking it. How many years did we barely scrape by?"

"You don't have to explain."

Phaira stood up. She pulled a wrinkled black overcoat from the floor, slipping her two Calis pistols into holsters. Once again, her blue hair masked her face. If they had a different relationship, he might have embraced her, insisted that she stop with the pretenses. Told her that the money from the Macatias was used for good, not for selfish reasons, the way it should have been. How he never meant to hurt her, but tried to protect her and Cohen.

But Renzo didn't have the words. And Phaira was shifting into that self-contained, all-business persona, where she heard nothing and saw nothing but her objective. She was already out the door and far away, even before she even lifted one black boot from the floor.

So, after several moments of silence, he left.

And within the quarter-hour, Phaira set off for the railway.

* * *

Infection. When Sydel changed the woman's bandages, Renzo caught a glimpse of red skin underneath. Maybe Emir's tools were not sterilized properly. Or it was just too late by the time they reached her in the bottom of the crevice.

CaLarca moaned in her sleep. Sydel washed the wounds and let them dry in the open air. The smell of antiseptic and flesh made Renzo feel woozy. And every now and again, he felt a jolt, saw the quickest flash of light, heard someone laughing. It had to be CaLarca. She was shorting out, so to speak. An Eko like Sydel, with fantastic psychic abilities. He wondered if they should all be wearing HALOs, the half-circle devices he'd invented to interrupt psychic transmission.

Someone was behind him. Renzo looked over, and then up at his younger brother. Cohen was scowling. It surprised Renzo to see it; usually Cohen was the most jovial one in the family. "What's your problem?" Renzo asked, nudging him in the side.

"I don't trust her," Cohen muttered.

"You voted to keep her here."

"For Syd."

"Just for her?"

Cohen's mouth twisted. "She and Syd had some weird exchange in Kings," he said curtly. "Then she disappears, and Syd gets dragged off and beaten up. That lady didn't even try to help her. Or me. And now she's back. There's a reason."

"You sound like Phaira. Paranoid."

"Whatever. I don't trust her. And I sure don't trust her alone with Sydel."

"Well, get over it, because we have things to resolve," Renzo shot back, irritated at Cohen's dramatics. "You're coming with me. She can handle herself."

As if to confirm Renzo's statement, Cohen peered into the room. They watched Sydel, methodically passing her hands over CaLarca's broken body. Her mouth moved in silent whispers.

"Are you sure you don't want to come and get some air?" Cohen called over to Sydel.

"No, I should stay," Sydel said. She didn't look at him. "In case she wakes up in pain."

Renzo knew his brother, he could tell what Cohen was feeling: frustration, guilt, uncertainty about the right thing to say, whether it was fair, or not to be jealous. *Oh, Cohen,* he thought with a sigh. *It's temporary, kid. She still likes you.* Sometimes Cohen struck him as a grown man; other times, like a wounded puppy. Maybe that's what it was like, when there was such an age difference between them? He could see the child or the man, depending on the angle.

"Come on," he told his younger brother, nudging him again. "Let's get this over with."

* * *

When their father was confirmed dead, all medical and state records were released into Renzo's custody, including the address of Dasean's most recent residence. The apartment was on the other side of Daro, perhaps twenty kilometers from their old building.

Twenty kilometers. They hadn't seen Dasean in years. And he was only minutes away? Renzo couldn't believe it.

The apartment was on the third floor. Insects scurried into cracks in the walls. Renzo held his breath as he trudged up the stairs, careful to test the strength of every rotting wood plank. The door was jammed. Cohen threw his shoulder into it to force it open.

A blast of freezing air shot through the opening, mixing with the odor of rotten food and urine. Renzo shuddered as he slipped inside. Cohen followed, closing the door with a grunt and leaning against it. "Now what?" he asked.

"We figure out if there's anything we want to keep. Or sell. And junk the rest, I guess."

It took several minutes to forge a path through the clutter: years of piled-up garbage, boxes and discarded clothes. The walls were rippled with spidery cracks, dark spots and water stains. By the window, a thin mattress held one threadbare sheet. Shivering, Renzo kicked at the fabric. It was practically frozen into folds.

"Ren?" Cohen's voice filtered in from the other side of the space.

Renzo made his way back through the forged path. Some papers tipped over, spilling dust into the air and making him sneeze. Even with the cold air, Renzo's back was already damp with sweat, his glasses fogging up.

There was one small clearing in the back corner, where Cohen stood, with a small table, and a single weathered photograph pasted to the wall above it. A woman with long, wavy brown hair, holding a blanket-wrapped bundle in her arms.

Renzo swallowed hard. He couldn't pinpoint any particular memory, but emotions rushed into him just the same. Which one of them was in that blanket?

"That's her, isn't it?"

His brother was just looking for confirmation. He knew what their mother looked like.

So, Renzo only nodded, trying to grasp onto the wisps of memory, just out of reach. There had to be more, buried somewhere in his bruised mind. But the doctors had warned Renzo about his long-term memory, how he may never regain the recollections of childhood.

For the most part, that was true. He could barely remember a time when his parents were together, both alive and healthy. There were other memories, instead, from after their mother got sick: how quickly their father disintegrated, becoming so controlling, paranoid and erratic. Sometimes violent. He would disappear for days on end. He would threaten to drown them for their own good. Several nights, Renzo and Phaira kept guard over Cohen, just a toddler then, huddled in a bedroom, a crowbar within arm's length. Until one day, their mother died, and he was gone, and they realized they were alone, truly alone to fend for themselves. He remembered that shift in the world, like the planet moving on its axis.

Renzo nudged Cohen with his elbow. "Take it with you. Cut it off the wall if you have to."

Cohen hesitated.

"It doesn't matter anymore," Renzo told his brother. "He's gone. Take whatever you want." He took one long look around the room, quiet anger flickering in his chest at the sight of his father's filth, hoarded remnants of a life that he never felt the need to share with his children.

Cohen flicked open a switchblade, and began to peel the photograph from the wall, stuck so long that little trails of paper and glue were buried into the drywall. Renzo watched, his skin crawling with disgust. He didn't want to touch anything. He didn't want a single item in this dump. It was a mistake to come here. He'd call a service, have them clean out the apartment, dispose of everything. He'd been the head of this family for long enough; he didn't need any more bitter reminders of what might have been.

There was the sound of static. Renzo glanced out the window. Through the grease-smeared glass, he could see across the street, where one of the building-top billboards was flickering - a public notice was about to be broadcast.

"Co," Renzo said, drawing his brother's attention over. Then, with a grunt, he forced one of the crusted windows open. Cohen squeezed next to him, peering across the street at the screen coming to life.

An image emerged: a solid woman in grey and blue police uniform. Perhaps forty, her face was somber, yet angular, with close-cropped hair and deep brown skin. Authority rang throughher voice as she spoke, her words echoing through the street.

"My name is Detective Daryn Ozias, and I need your help."

His guts twisted with fear.

"Isn't that - ?" Cohen began.

Renzo held up a hand to quiet him, trying to hear the muffled words coming from the loudspeaker. The officer's picture distorted every few seconds; the wiring in this Daro neighborhood wasn't up to code, of course, it was a miracle that the broadcast even lit up.

"Many of you read about the incident that occurred in Kings Canyon two weeks ago," Ozias was saying. "After initial investigation, our department is still looking for answers."

That's some measure of relief, Renzo thought. He doubted it would last.

"You might question why we are continuing the search," Ozias continued. "Thirty-two dead individuals, many of whom had criminal records, with no clear connection to each other. These are just facts to many of you, but with permission from the head of agency, I want to show you why I need answers."

The screen shifted to a panoramic image of red rocky desert and cliffs. Kings Canyon, Renzo recognized it. On one side of the picture, the mass of red rock, the great base collapse. On the other, twisted, bloody corpses were strewn across the canyon floor. The camera focused on the long shot, and then close-ups of faces: white, strangled eyes, dark red throats, claw marks in the sand, tear tracks down dust-crusted cheeks.

"Regardless of their background," Ozias's voice was heard over the image. "Everyone deserves answers, and justice. This cannot happen again. We need the public's help in identifying these individuals, and any potential witnesses to this horrific crime. I call on the people to put aside their fears and step forward. Monetary compensation is a possibility, for leads that go somewhere. I have faith in the goodness of people, and the inherent respect for the parents, families, children, and friends of these fallen individuals, who deserve to know what really happened in Kings. If you have any information, contact your local law enforcement. Thank you for your time."

The screen went dead. Ozias's voice still seemed to echo through the apartment.

Cohen was the first one to speak. "We need to disappear."

"Yeah," Renzo concurred, hardly able to think with his heart hammering in his chest. "Yeah, we do. For good."

IV

The *Arazura* was still where they left it, locked away in the one decent public garage in Daro. Numb with exhaustion, Cohen slammed his fist into the panel, unlocking the door. When the stairs unfolded, Cohen was surprised to see Sydel at the top. "You're filthy," she called down.

Cohen sighed, rubbing his face. "It was a mess. But it's done. Everything cleared away and destroyed." He started up the stairs, each foot dragging.

"Destroyed?" Her voice was surprised. "I thought this was your father's place of residence, and his belongings."

"Everything had to go," Cohen said. "Ren is just making his last rounds, and then we're taking off. I don't know if you saw that bulletin."

"I saw it." When he cleared the landing, and they were on equal footing, she spoke again. "I'm just glad you're back."

Cohen frowned. He could hear her tight breath through her nostils. "What's the matter?"

She didn't say anything, and she was staring at the floor; nearly a foot shorter than him, all he could see was her braided hair and brown shoulders.

Impulsively, he reached over and took her hand. "Come on," he said, beckoning for her to follow.

When they were in his cabin, the door closed to the world, Cohen slouched to peer into Sydel's face. Her skin was ashy, her face long with fatigue, he realized with a jolt. "Are you upset about the bulletin?" he asked. "It'll be okay, we just have to lie low again."

Sydel shook her head, avoiding his eyes.

"Did something else happen?"

Her words came out in a rush. "I know I pushed to keep CaLarca in our care. But what if I'm wrong? What if she's here to hurt me, or all of you? I can't stop questioning my judgment, why I sought her out, after everything that's happened. If something's really wrong with me."

Cohen didn't know how to respond. He'd wondered the same thing.

"You were trying to do the right thing," he finally said.

"For who, Cohen?"

"She was hurt, and you wanted to help her. You're a good person."

"Not a very smart person, though," Sydel mumbled.

She's always so hard on herself, Cohen mused. He never understood why, especially after her big power surge in Kings. "Well, you can sit next to me," he said, knocking her elbow gently with his. "Be brainless together."

"Cohen," Sydel warned, though a smile played at the corners of her mouth.

"Look," Cohen said, more serious this time. "You've got me here. And Ren. And Phair when she gets back.

Plus, you're so strong now! Even if she's trouble, we can handle her. Right? We know how Ekos work."

"She's not just an Eko," Sydel said. "That's what concerns me. She's an Eko, and a Nadi."

"A Nadi? What's that?"

"Another NINE trait." Her hands undulated, as if to conjure the answers. "Her body can generate huge amounts of energy, and it has to be expelled in some way, or her organs will fail.... or worse."

"Is that what happened in Kings when you - you know?" Cohen winced at the memory of that white blinding light, sweeping through the floor, killing Huma's minions. Nadi. Nadi. The word repeated in his brain.

Sydel nodded. "But only that one time," she added in a hurry. "CaLarca's energy output is constant. I can't imagine the pain."

"Wait, you said that it has to be expelled," Cohen interrupted. "Has it already happened?"

Sydel's mouth pinched with guilt. Cohen looked at her hands, hidden in the folds of her skirt. He grasped her wrists and brought them to the light.

"Syd!" he cried. "What'd you do?"

Her palms were red and blistered, the worst damage in the center, radiating out.

"I served as conduit. Drew the Nadi out," Sydel confessed. "She would have died otherwise."

"How'd you even know how to do that?"

Sydel shrugged one shoulder.

"Well, you're not doing that anymore," Cohen said, staring at her hands, his nausea turning to anger. "Wake her up and figure out another way. I don't care about her energy - whatever, this isn't right, you can't do this to yourself. "

Her hands slipped from his. Then her thin fingers were on his shoulders, and she was kissing him lightly on each cheek.

When she broke away, Cohen was frozen. Pride bloomed in his chest. He fought the urge to grin. "What was that for?" he asked casually.

"For being my friend. And always thinking the best of me."

His heart dropped into his guts. But Cohen forced a smile. "Of course," he managed. "Always there when you need me."

* * *

The sun was beginning to set in Daro. Exhausted from walking, Renzo sat down in a rusty bus shelter, just outside of the university. His mind was still spinning from the law broadcast. Their existence was almost wiped clean from the city; Dasean's apartment was barren, no trace of fingerprints or any identifying features. He'd already deleted his father's memorial service records, just in case. The university was the last place to clean out. But first, a moment to breathe.

His thoughts turned to Aeden Nox's memorial service. They'd signed the guestbook, in lieu of attending. They couldn't attend it, even though Phaira was openly guilt-ridden, citing Nox's elderly parents, and how they would be wondering why she wasn't paying her last respects after being his friend for so long. It's no good, Renzo told her. Bad timing. It's not safe.

So, they remained in the *Arazura*, huddled underground, and the funeral went on as scheduled. They hadn't even had the opportunity to vist his gravesite yet. Now it might never happen. And he had to remove any trace of their presence.

Unearthing his personal Lissome, Renzo found Nox's official service page online; in the picture, he was smartly dressed in grey uniform with several decals, looking straight into the lens with his short-cropped red hair and beard. It still made him angry to look at Nox, even though the man was dead, and killed in a pretty unpleasant manner. It wasn't the kindest sentiment, but it was honest. And Renzo was tired of niceties. No one was a saint. Nox was a good friend in a lot of ways, but he also made a lot of stupid decisions.

Renzo expanded the Lissome, bypassed the security measures, and scrolled through the information, looking for any mention of him or his siblings.

Deepest sympathy, so sorry, loss, passing, rest, peace....

Funny how those words never changed. That vocabulary was the same when their mother finally died from a bone disease, fifteen years ago. There weren't many people outside of their family unit. But of the few that showed up, every one went through the motions of respectable grief. They chose the proper words, the strategic pats on the hand or shoulder, and then they retreated as far away from the death-place as possible. A sick routine that meant nothing, Renzo knew. It only drew out the devastation.

That was when Dasean first disappeared. There was no memorial service, just an inexpensive burial for their mother, over in an hour. But during that hour, no one knew where their father was.

Nor for the hours that followed. Renzo was thirteen, Phaira was almost twelve, and Cohen was only four. They came home to a barely-functioning apartment that reeked of antiseptic and old skin. Their father was gone, no note, no trace, no indication of when he might come back.

Renzo cooked and sorted out what money remained for living expenses. Phaira cleaned out their mother's room. Cohen cried and cried, clinging to Phaira's legs.

A few distant cousins called Renzo, clucking with sympathy. He listened without emotion to their regrets, their reasons for staying away, how they wanted to help but couldn't possibly take in a child, let alone three.

As the year passed, though, those occasional calls changed to warnings. Dasean wove in and out of their lives, each time more erratic, stealing their saved money, making threats. He was too far gone, the whispers came through the line. Too many hospitalizations, too many arrests. Sooner or later, he would be dead. Renzo was the oldest. He should do the right thing and place Cohen and Phaira in foster care. Then he would be free to accept early entrance into the local university, take the full scholarship that came in the mail, unexpectedly, when he turned fifteen.

"You have so much potential," they all told him, "but you must take the opportunity when it strikes, while you are young, while you are wanted."

* * *

CaLarca's cracked lips parted, and a long, low moan came out. Cohen didn't react, his arms crossed over his chest. Sydel was on the other side of the bed, her hand hovering above CaLarca's temple, her fingers moving as if playing a piano.

"Slowly," Sydel warned the woman. "Move slowly, and breathe deeply. Your muscles are atrophied. It will hurt."

Sweat broke across the woman's brow, her face pinched with pain. Then CaLarca tilted her head back, gazing up at Sydel's palm and frowning. "What did you do?" she rasped.

Flushing, Sydel hid her hand behind her back. "You were burning up."

"You did that for me?"

"She's done a lot of things for you," Cohen broke in. "But not anymore. You need to take care of your own Nadi energy, or whatever it is."

"Cohen," Sydel hissed. She probably thought he was being rude. But he was furious at her wounds, and at this stranger hurting her.

"He is right," CaLarca coughed.

I am? Cohen blinked, surprised.

The woman took in a few deep breaths. Then she continued. "Being a conduit - for another's Nadi output - that can stop your heart."

"I can manage it," Sydel insisted.

The woman's voice had an edge of anger to it. "You will not. It's dangerous. And you should only experiment - on the willing."

Sydel's mouth dropped open, a deep flush filling her face. At the sight, Cohen was torn between satisfaction and utter disgust.

CaLarca's head turned, her eyes fixed on Cohen. "Who are you?"

"He is Cohen," Sydel said. "He's my companion."

"From the canyon," CaLarca breathed. "With that old woman - and that black-haired lunatic - part of the kill squad." The last words were spoken through clenched teeth.

"No," Cohen said shortly. "I was there to protect Sydel. What were you doing there?" he added pointedly.

CaLarca's black eyes fixed on him. Then one hand lifted from the bed, the fingers slightly curled into each other. Something began to glow in the center of her palm. Then a wisp of white emerged, swirling like a vortex, building and thickening, twisting tighter and tighter.

Then the smoke dissipated, and in CaLarca's hand lay a small knife with a silver handle.

"Manifestation," Sydel gasped. "You can do that?"

The woman's hand dropped over the edge of the bed. She released the knife. As it fell, it dissolved, puffs of smoke spreading across the metal floor.

"I can teach you," was her raspy response. "I can show you."

* * *

Daro University was mostly empty, as school was not in session for another two weeks. Renzo wandered the halls of the mathematics department. That front desk was where Dasean threatened to strip down naked unless he was allowed access to his oldest son. That north stairwell was where Renzo found his father, filthy, mumbling and drunk, people gingerly stepping around him. Both times, security had taken him outside. Renzo wondered, both then and now, if they had beaten him. Renzo came to expect the sight of dirty, folded paper shoved into his university mailbox. The nonsensical ranting. Pleas for forgiveness. Threats in exchange for money. Sometimes, Renzo sent a portion of his stipend to the return address, just to gain some peace for a few months.

"Are you looking for someone, sir?" a voice inquired from behind him.

He looked over his shoulder. Graduate student, official university name badge, her left eyebrow quirked high. No wonder she was following him; he was wandering around the first floor, mumbling to himself.

"Actually, no," Renzo replied, clearing his throat and pushing up his glasses. In doing so, he suddenly noted the oil streaks on his sleeve.

"I'm a former apprentice," he said weakly. "I thought there might be some mail in storage for me. I didn't provide a forwarding address when I left."

The student didn't seem to believe him. That same dark eyebrow lifted another millimeter and held steady. "What's your name?"

"Renzo Byrne."

Was he mad, or was there was a flicker of recognition in the student's eyes? At least that eyebrow went down. Renzo had a fleeting image of being carried out, kicking, by security, in the same fashion as his father. He preferred to avoid that embarrassment for as long as possible.

"Wait here, sir," the student said, shuffling into the office suites.

Renzo quickly wiped his hands on his pants, and then took the cleaner part of his sleeve and gave his face a wipe. At least school wasn't in session, and his former colleagues weren't around to see how useless he'd become, in comparison to their paychecks and awards.

Once upon a time, Renzo was the foremost apprentice in the experimental mathematics department. Now he refused to even look at complex equations; not because he might fail, but because he knew he wouldn't. Even with all the head trauma, his brain had miraculously healed. He could go back to the university at any time: his reputation restored, his path to acclaim reestablished, his world consumed by grant funding and medals. He should want that.

"Here you go." A bundle of papers dropped into Renzo's hands, with their tattered edges, and multicolored paper.

"Thanks. Now go deactivate the mailbox," Renzo said.

At the student's surprised expression, he added, "It's a confidentiality issue. I'm sure it's not the first time that someone has asked you."

The student nodded, and left. Renzo riffled through the stack, half-heartedly looking for that familiar handwriting, something from his father in that pile, some indication of what was going on in his father's head before some unknown thug killed him.

But there was nothing.

Was he disappointed?

Renzo riffled through the stack again. Junk, solicitation, sympathy card, and a small white envelope from a place called Toomba. Far, far south. In the Cyan Mountains? He couldn't remember. Inside, the letter was brief, but to the point. It was from some mystery woman claiming to be his maternal grandmother. Vyoma Meklos. Weird name. He'd never heard of it. Though, what was their mother's maiden name? She had gone by Lora Byrne, and she never talked about her past, even when Renzo and Phaira pressed her for details. He'd forgotten that part about their mother, how stubborn and silent she could be when pushed.

Renzo flipped the letter back and forth, searching for more clues. There were none. It was a fluke, some kind of scheme. There were never any grandparents in his life, and he wasn't about to believe otherwise. He tucked the stack of papers under one arm and shuffled outside.

When he finally made his way back to the public garage, he stepped back into the *Arazura* with relief, noting that the exterior was still pristine. Leaving extra money with the attendants was always the trick. He wandered into the corridors, searching for his brother. The door to Sydel's room was ajar. Inside, Sydel and Cohen were hunched over the bed.

"What's going on in there?" Renzo called through.

Startled, Sydel and Cohen stood upright. The green-haired woman was revealed behind them: pale, red-eyed, but awake.

"Oh," Renzo said awkwardly. "You're awake. Great."

"You're Renzo?" Her scratchy voice wafted over the threshold. "The builder?"

"Maybe... what am I building?" Renzo asked warily, stepping into the room. Despite his growing irritation, Renzo's gaze wandered to CaLarca's legs; one was still bound tightly from ankle to thigh, the other scratched and exposed, but strangely thin. She'd removed Phaira's socks, and her toes had a hint of blue to them. Was it lack of oxygen, or some mutation?

"She has a great deal of muscle weakness," Sydel spoke up. "I believe that she will need some kind of brace, or support structure, as she regains her strength and re-learns to walk. I thought perhaps you might be able to do something?"

"Wait," Cohen said. "Wait a second. How long is she staying with us? I thought this was a temporary thing. And we're set to disappear, you know."

Sydel glanced at Renzo. He lifted his eyebrows back at her, questioning.

Please, she mouthed.

Renzo sighed. "It's fine for now, I guess."

"We don't do a thing until she starts talking," Cohen said darkly.

"I have nothing to say to you," CaLarca shot back.

"Look, when I was in Kings," Cohen began, glaring down at the green-haired woman, "Keller and Xanto and the rest of those people, they were organizing revenge for some mass murder from twenty-five years ago, by what they called the NINE. Some group of people with powers, who killed people and messed up the minds of kids. Were you a part of it?"

CaLarca said nothing. In the corner of his eye, Renzo saw his brother's hand dip behind him; he was reaching for a concealed weapon, just in case.

"Well?" Renzo added. "You'd better say something before Cohen tosses you off the ship."

Surprisingly, the woman's shoulders dropped. Her head fell.

"Yes," she admitted. "I'm one of the NINE."

Sydel gasped. Cohen looked like he was about to knock CaLarca out. But Renzo felt nothing. Maybe because she was being honest? He didn't know.

But he addressed CaLarca directly. "You keep talking. And I'll build braces for you. Deal?"

CaLarca blinked. "You can do that? You would do that?"

Renzo lifted his right pant leg, revealing the sleek, silver prosthetic underneath, his own custom design. "I can do anything. As long as you hold up your end of the bargain. Sydel has a lot of questions."

Cohen's eyes darted between Sydel and Renzo, like he couldn't believe what just transpired.

"Come on out," Renzo told his younger brother. "She's right, you don't need to hear about it. We need to get ready to go."

Blood rushed into Cohen's round face. Then he stalked past Renzo, into the hallway and the adjoining room. A succession of loud bangs on metal followed.

Renzo rubbed the bridge of his nose. *Nineteen*, he reminded himself. *He's nineteen.*

"Thank you." CaLarca's voice was naked with gratitude. It made him uncomfortable.

"I'll draw up plans," he said brusquely, and turned on his heel, heading for the door.

His private quarters never looked so good.

In the safety of solitude, Renzo sketched out ideas for the leg braces, to keep his hands busy as his mind wandered. Where would they go from here? Should they go to Liera, where Phaira, Emir and Anandi were headed? Or was that too obvious? He'd tried to send a message to them, warning them about the public broadcast, but the connections were fuzzy, and Renzo felt paranoid about saying anything more over the airwaves, not with so many new ears straining for secrets.

Sounds echoed through the wall of the cabin, coming from Cohen's adjoining one. He thought about knocking on Cohen's door, trying to talk to his little brother. But Cohen was so raw, particularly when it came to Sydel. It was better to keep away. In this situation, Renzo could be the impartial one, the mediator if need be. Sometimes there were advantages to missing an emotional chip, as he thought of it. He wasn't caught up in sentiment or expectation.

He closed his eyes and visualized the braces in his mind: every dimension, numbers calculating and taking shape. The last time he'd visualized an invention, he had a partner to bounce off his ideas, Theron Sava, though he didn't know who the man was at the time. Theron was one of the volunteer mechanics who worked on the *Arazura*. One day, they'd struck up a conversation, and Theron suggested working on a new prosthetic for Renzo's leg. Who would have guessed that some mobster was good with delicate mechanics? But the man was quiet, sharp and just as exacting as Renzo. Working side by

side over days, they laid out the schematics for the prosthetic, then they brainstormed on what turned out to be
HALOs. It was a wholly new experience for Renzo; he
didn't work well with anyone, even before his assault and
head trauma. Trying to synchronize minds was a lesson
in impatience: in school, in life, even with his colleagues
at the university. But he'd worked well with that man.
Now Renzo was back to being frustrated with the world.

"So it was true, then?"

Renzo's ears perked up at the sound of Sydel's voice.
Half of his Lissome sat at his side, he'd hidden the other
half in Sydel's room after the incident in Kings. Just in
case he needed to listen. Now he could hear Sydel's faint,
nervous voice. "What they said about you, about your
kind, attacking and killing those people years ago?"

A long pause. The the green-haired woman spoke: "I
always wondered, did Marette raise you?"

Renzo could hear the hunger in Sydel's voice. "I don't
know who that is. Was Marette - ?"

"You don't know her." The woman sounded surprised.
"So, Yann took you? Interesting. Has he claimed to be
your father? Because he isn't."

Renzo made a face, remembering the Jala Communia
and the balding, watery-eyed man who was its leader.
Yann healed Phaira's wounds, sure, but then he cast
Sydel out, and Renzo and his siblings had to deal with
everything that followed. But this was different - Yann
was part of that NINE group, too?

"No," Sydel replied to the woman's question. "He's never claimed to be my father."

"One point for Yann, then. And your mother?"

"You tell me."

Silently, Renzo applauded Sydel for pushing.

"Tehmi," Ca'Larca finally said. "Her name was Tehmi Shovann. And your father was Joran Asanto."

"Are they both dead?"

"Yes."

Using one hand, Renzo brought up an infoscreen, searching for records of those names. They came up immediately, their blurry pictures and sparse demographics. Tehmi Shovann, twenty-five years old, her burned body uncovered by hikers in the Kings Canyon. Copious amounts of blood was found at the site that belonged to her husband, Joran Asanto, a wealthy businessman; he was presumed to be buried somewhere in the desert.

The Asanto Foundation, Renzo remembered, *that's right. I've heard of them before. That must have been established in his memory....*

Then Sydel spoke again, much quieter this time:

"The term NINE - what does the second N stand for?"

CaLarca was silent.

But Sydel pressed on. "I was brought up as an Eko. I only learned about the Nadi trait from Huma. And Cohen says that the Savas spoke of something called Insynn: precognition of some kind, which I presume is the 'I.' But what about the second N in NINE? What else is there to learn?"

Renzo heard a sharp inhalation. Was the green-haired woman in pain? There were no voices, just the sound of shuffling, and fabric brushing.

Finally, a whisper echoed through the Lissome: "I'm sorry. It's all too much. Rest now."

A few minutes later, there was a knock on Renzo's door.

"What," Renzo said, just loud enough to carry.

The door slid open. Sydel stood outside his doorway.

The other half of his Lissome rolled between her thumb and forefinger.

His eyes on his designwork, Renzo extended his right hand, beckoning.

Her fingers brushed his, burning hot.

"Hear everything you wanted?" came her low voice.

"It's for everyone's safety," he retorted. "Don't be so offended."

Her voice trailed behind her as she left. "Too late for that, Renzo Byrne."

V.

M ay I come in?"
　　Cohen let his head flop back down on his pillow. He didn't trust himself to speak. Instead, he focused on breathing evenlly, in and out, and watched as Sydel sat on his mattress, twisting a piece of hair between her fingers.

"You're upset with me, too," she sighed. "I haven't done anything to warrant it, so can we please -"

"You haven't done anything?" Cohen interrupted. "You're keeping that woman here."

Sydel looked stricken. "She has nowhere else to go."

"Who cares?" Cohen burst out. "Syd, really, who cares? It doesn't matter if she's alone, she's one of those NINE killers. Keller and Xanto and all of them were telling the truth. Their brains were scrambled, their parents were killed, and she was a part of it. Doesn't that mean anything to you?"

"I killed people too," she whispered. "I'm no better."

"You didn't know what you were doing," Cohen countered. Exasperated, he rolled onto his stomach. "You were getting beat up and - it's not the same thing."

"What makes you so sure?" Sydel's voice was sharper now too, her face growing pink. "You just assume that it was a mistake? Or better yet, that it never happened? That seems to be a familiar response in this family. It's just another life snuffed out, who cares, nothing to think about."

"Hey, that's not fair," Cohen protested angrily. "Of course it means something. You think I don't remember in the canyon, how it felt to pick off those mercenaries? How that felt to see them bleed out? I think about it; it means something to me. But we did it all for you, remember?"

"Well I don't want it!" Sydel shouted. "I don't want it from you, or anyone!"

Then she ran out of the room.

Cohen pounded his fists on the bed. Why did everything have to be so complicated? Why couldn't Sydel see the danger in all of this?

It was CaLarca's fault.

Cohen slid his hand under the mattress, feeling for the piece of paper stowed beneath. It was crumpled, the pencil marks smudged, but still legible. The name of Aeden Nox's friends from Daro. He hadn't spoken to them much, but he remembered their introductions, when Nox dragged Cohen into bars post-training. In between teasing him for being so quiet, they suggested he call them if he ever wanted to get into law enforcement. After Kings, he'd written the names down and hidden the paper, just in case. Now he stared at the letters. He could put in an anonymous call and describe the green-haired woman. Her involvement in unsolved murders. Her possible involvement in the Kings Canyon massacre. He was convinced that she had something to do with all those mercenaries turning on each other; it was all too weird, too convenient. It was too dangerous to keep her on the *Arazura*. He should arrange a drop-off. Give Sydel a chance to breathe and see the world for what it was.

Wouldn't it be helping them all?

* * *

There was no way around it. Renzo needed fuel, and he needed measurements for CaLarca's legs. He hated the idea of breaking from his thought process. But the *Arazura's* fuel gauge was flashing red, warning of low levels. He had no choice.

Renzo eased the *Arazura* into the closest Vendor Mill and ordered the fuel cell exchange. The mill was mostly empty, thanks to the late hour. The attendant was barely awake as he went through the motions, sliding under the *Arazura* with his trolley. It wouldn't take long to get back in the air.

Back inside, she was waiting for him, propped up on Sydel's bed, her legs before her, freshly bandaged. She wore one of Phaira's long-sleeved grey tunics with the hood up. Curly tendrils framed her face, brown and green. He hadn't noticed before, but she had freckles across her nose, like a child. How old was she, anyways?

"Older than you think," was her quiet response. "One of the benefits of Nadi is our ability to slow aging. Something to do with the constant regeneration of cells."

"I've told Sydel and I tell you now - don't nose into my mind," Renzo said curtly. "Isn't that against your kind's rules?"

"There are no rules," CaLarca said.

Renzo waited for more, but the woman said nothing.

"I need measurements," Renzo said, pulling out his tape measure. "For the braces. Just takes a minute."

"Fine," she muttered, turning her head from him.

"So you were one of the original NINE. You were, what? A kid? A teenager?" Renzo asked, briskly measuring the length of CaLarca's bandaged legs.

"I don't have emotional attachment to the question," he added. "I guess I'm just curious if you were of age when you chose to kill people. And what you'll do when you can get out of this bed. You're not staying here, you know. One passenger with superpowers is plenty."

"You're funny." It was said flatly, with no indication that she saw any humor at all.

"You're probably the only one ever to think so," he replied, mimicking her tone of voice.

She was studying him. For the first time, he looked directly into her eyes. They weren't all black, like he thought, but a deep, deep brown. The irises were enlarged, but not as much as he initially thought.

As he peered at her, she batted her eyelashes slowly.

Renzo grimaced. "Don't bother," he told her, the measuring tape snapping back into its tiny case. "I'm not interested."

"I'm not available," she replied, in a lofty tone.

"Lucky you. And yet you don't call him, or her," Renzo pointed out. "They the ones who left you for dead?"

CaLarca's jawline tightened.

"You know, I meant what I said about our agreement," Renzo said. "If you talk, you walk."

"I talk to Sydel, not to you."

"It's my ship," he reminded her, ticking off with his fingers. "My bed, in fact. My bandages, my tools, my medication -"

"Fine, fine," she retorted, huffing. Renzo waited.

"I don't know," CaLarca finally said. "I don't know how I ended up on that cliff. Or how I came to Towns. I have no memory of what I've done since Kings." As she spoke, she seemed to deflate. Her voice grew quieter. "I am alone. That is the truth."

"Congratulations," Renzo said, slipping the tape into his pocket. "You've unlocked the next level of leg brace construction."

The woman said nothing.

Trapped. Immobile. He'd been in that exact same position. He remembered how surreal it was, to have the maddening urge to stand, and no ability to do so.

"You'll go upright again," he told her. "You'll walk. I can make it work."

"You have no reason to."

Some true emotion coming out? Renzo studied her bent head for a moment.

"True," he finally replied. "I don't. So, consider it a rare kindness. We are capable of that, you know, as much as you hate us."

CaLarca glanced up, like she was ready to argue. Then her expression hardened. "You hate me too."

"I hate everyone," he corrected. "Don't think yourself special."

Heading for the cockpit, unpacking his thoughts from the encounter, a call came in. Renzo recognized the cc immediately: Lander. The connection was audio-only, not that unusual in previous interactions, but the sound of heavy breathing put Renzo on edge. "Lander?"

A voice came through. "Lander?"

"What?" Renzo asked, confused. Was there an echo?

"I can't see you." It was Lander, but his speech was garbled. "I can't see you. Why can't I see you?"

"Because it's audio-only," Renzo said sharply. "You're not supposed to - what's wrong with you?"

Words tumbled out, strung together in a breath, very unlike the deep, cryptic voice that Renzo was used to. "Disappearing. Gone and gone, far away."

Was the man high? Renzo didn't have time for this.

"I cut a deal and they let me go. They already knew everything..."

Everything in Renzo's vision went white.

Lander had confessed to that detective. Lander knew everything. He knew that Cohen was in Kings, he knew Phaira was the one who got them out, he knew that Emir was involved. Renzo swore under his breath, again and

again, and smashed his fist on the console. It was over.
They were done. They were going to jail. He didn't know
what to do. Was the attendant done yet? Could they fly
yet?

"You have to tell the truth," Lander kept mumbling.
"The whole truth. Especially when they make threats,
offer this or that. What else could I do? Can you tell
Emir that I'm sorry? I like him, I really do."

"Wait, what? You gave up Emir?" Renzo gasped. "You
sacrificed an old man to save yourself?"

"Couldn't argue," Lander muttered. "Why bother?"

"Did you mention others?" Renzo demanded. "What
else did you say?"

A sharp burst of static made Renzo wince. The security measures began to fluctuate, dipping below secure
standards.

Then the call disconnected, and there was nothing
but dead air.

VI

"Have you heard from Phaira?" Renzo said as he yanked open the door. He caught a flash of white, being tucked under Cohen's pillow, before his younger brother rolled to his feet. Renzo didn't have time to be curious. "Well? Have you?"

"No. I didn't think we'd talk until she got back," Cohen said. "Why, what's going on?"

"She's not responding to her Lissome," Renzo said, already turning to run. "And neither is Anandi."

Outside, the attendant was installing the last of the fuel cells. Inside the cockpit, Renzo conducted a rapid search of police bulletins in the East. There, buried under notices of burglaries and embezzling: a freshly-issued warrant for the arrest of Anandi and Emir Ajyo : charged with illegal acquisition of confidential information, wanted for questioning in the Kings massacre. No mention of Phaira, but she could be caught in the middle of it.

Renzo switched servers, delving into any recent arrests or bookings in the area. There were none that matched any of their descriptions.

A call was coming in. He didn't recognize the cc. Renzo shut down every open infoscreen and threw up firewalls on anything still processing through the server.

Then, shooting a warning look at Cohen to stay quiet, he connected. "Yes?"

"This is Detective Daryn Ozias," came a raspy voice. "Shut down your engines and stand by for boarding."

Renzo's throat closed. Frantic, he searched the exterior cameras. There was the officer from the bulletin, standing outside the *Arazura*, looking it up and down. The attendant had his hands up, shaking his head, clearly denying any knowledge of the ship's owners.

Renzo cut out the audio and shot to his feet.

"Ren?" Cohen hissed.

Renzo put a finger to his lips. "Get Sydel," he mouthed. "Go to her room. Now."

As Cohen bolted from the cockpit, Renzo frantically riffled through the overhead storage compartment. Back when the *Arazura* was being built, on a whim, Renzo registered the name of a rental business, and the ship under it. But where was the documentation?

Vyoma Meklos. The name popped into Renzo's head. He grabbed the pile of mail from the university. The letter came from Toomba, from the Cyan Mountains, at least a thousand kilometres south.

His mind turned. They were going to visit their grandmother. Family reunion. Rented a private transport. Meklos. Good cover name too. Sounded good with all their names. It was something to hold onto.

He finally found the rental packet, slid it under his arm and ran for Sydel's room. Everyone was gathered inside, staring as Renzo streaked past and banged his fist on the far wall. The hidden door slid back, revealing the sensory deprivation tank within, a tall metal cylinder wedged into a five-by-five foot space.

Renzo pointed to Cohen, and then CaLarca. "In there," he mouthed. "Now."

"There isn't enough room," Sydel whispered.

"There's no time!" Renzo hissed back. "Cohen, pick her up."

Cohen flushed, and stalked over to the bed. But when he went to slide his arms beneath CaLarca, she slapped him across the face. The sound resonated through the room. Sydel recoiled with a gasp. Renzo lifted his hands, trying to calm his brother. "Easy, Co," he mouthed, even as he pushed down his own fury. There wasn't time for it, for any of this.

His right cheek red, Cohen snatched up CaLarca in his arms. The woman gasped in pain, clawing at his back. As Sydel squeezed herself between the tank and the wall, Cohen climbed up the ladder. As he swung his leg over the edge, Renzo could sense the water rising. He was so much bigger and heavier than Sydel. Renzo prayed for it to remain contained; if the officer came in and saw a water trail....

But Cohen was finally in the tank, straddling the diameter, feet on a ladder on either side, Renzo knew. The brim of the tank came up to his hips. He shifted his grip, and held CaLarca's squirming body high up on his shoulder. His face was red, glaring down at Renzo.

Then the door slid shut, and Renzo ran.

At the exit, he took a moment to breathe, smooth down his hair, and make sure his glasses were clean and straight on his nose. No sounds followed him; by his ears, the *Arazura* sounded empty. Steeling his nerves, he opened the door.

The officer was waiting on ground level, peering up.

"Good morning," Renzo called down. "What's this all about?"

"Drop the stairs, please." The woman's voice was like gravel.

"You're law?" Renzo stalled.

"Detective Ozias," the woman said. "As I already stated."

He couldn't wait any longer. Renzo flicked the switch, and the stairwell unfurled. The edge settled right by the officer's toes. She didn't flinch. "You're the owner of this ship?"

"No, ma'am," Renzo said. "Rental."

Ozias raised her eyebrows. "Really." The word was drawn out.

Taking a step down, but keeping one hand on the railing, Renzo held out the rental packet. Ozias reached up and took it, flipping through the pages. Her eyes were dark blue, and flicked up to Renzo every few seconds. Finally, she snapped the book shut. "Didn't catch your name."

"Ray Meklos," Renzo said.

"That so?"

"What's this about?" Renzo asked, trying to keep his voice normal.

"I'm looking for Cohen Byrne."

It took every ounce of bodily control for Renzo not to react. And even with every cell straining, he wasn't sure that a flicker of fear wasn't visible. "Cohen?"

"Byrne," Ozias said. "About six-foot-two, two hundred and fifty pounds, short brown hair, nineteen years old. He was a friend and student of Aeden Nox, one of the victims in the Kings Canyon. Apparently, they had a business relationship in the weeks before. Byrne was also seen leaving the scene of the crime in a transport of this description. Know him?"

"This is a rental," Renzo reminded her. "I've only had the ship for a couple of days. Picked it up in Daro."

"For what purpose, I wonder?" The snide way that the officer said the words was like a game.

"Going on a road trip. To the south, to see family. Waiting for my friends, now actually," Renzo added quickly. "They're showing up any time."

Ozias nodded. "I'd like to look inside." She took one step up.

"Is that necessary?" Renzo objected, a spasm of panic in his stomach. "Like I said, we're already late and a long way to go."

"And who else is in there?" Ozias questioned. Was that a hint of a smile on the woman's face?

A cold trickle of sweat went down his spine. He didn't know what to do, if he should just give up, if he should make a scene.

The officer's foot remained on the first step. She didn't ascend or step back. In fact, the woman didn't move, or even blink.

Seconds passed. Nothing changed.

Renzo stared down at her, confused.

Go. The voice floated through Renzo's mind.

He jumped, looking over his shoulder. No one was there.

Go. I can't hold her much longer.

It wasn't Sydel's voice, though.

It was CaLarca's.

Ozias's lips twitched. Her eyes bulged. She was frozen in place. Renzo stared. It was very, very wrong. But it was the break they needed.

Renzo slammed his hand into the control panel, recoiling the stairs and locking the exit. At the same time, he activated the *Arazura's* engines through the Lissome in his pocket.

Running into Sydel's quarters, Renzo recoiled as the secret door slid open. Cohen burst out, tossing CaLarca onto the bed with one heave. CaLarca cried out as her legs hit the bedframe.

"Don't ever ask me to touch her again!" Cohen roared, scratch marks across his arm and face.

Sydel wandered after him, drenched from the waist down, fresh marks on her arms, too.

"What the hell happened in there?" Renzo demanded, listening with one ear for the sound of the engines.
Shouldn't be more than thirty seconds total...

"Cohen. Stay back."

Renzo turned at the sound of Sydel's tight voice. The
girl moved in front of Cohen, one damp arm raised as if to
shield him. "CaLarca cannot stay here," she said evenly.

Cohen's mouth dropped open, as did Renzo's.

"No, please," CaLarca sputtered. Her hands roamed
over her legs, again and again, in a nervous motion. "I
did it for your safety."

"Wait, why? What did she do?" Cohen asked, looking
between the green-haired woman and Sydel.

"She restricted that detective's movements," Sydel
said. "I sensed it."

"Like mind control?" Cohen exclaimed. "You people
can do that?"

Slowly, as if turning a crank, Renzo's mind cycled
back to that day in the Kings Canyon, when the mercenaries turned on each other, stabbing, shooting, mur-
dering each other in a blind fury. If CaLarca could freeze
a man in place, could she force him to attack, too?

There wasn't time to think. They had to get out of
there.

Renzo pointed to CaLarca. "Seal her in, don't talk to
her, don't touch her. That goes for both of you."

"Fine by me," Cohen snapped, darting past Renzo.
"You should just toss her to the detective, let her answer
some questions for once."

"I'm not opening that door to anyone," Renzo shot back. "We deal with her later."

CaLarca's face was streaked with tears. Sydel was trembling. But she followed Cohen into the corridor.

Renzo ducked through the threshold, past the two, and ran for the cockpit. When he entered, the engines began their familiar rumble. Renzo slid into the seat and demagnetized the landing gear. At the same time, he checked all the screens for the videofeed surrounding the *Arazura*. The first step was to get as far away from that Vendor Mill and the surrounding area as possible. When that detective snapped out of that trance, or whatever it was, she would come after them. Would she cross jurisdiction, though, into the East?

A call was coming in. Renzo panicked - it had to be that detective. But it was a different cc. He connected, his fingers hovering.

Then his heart leapt at the sound of Phaira's voice: "We're clear. Trouble, but at the end-point now. Keep offline for now. Guards up."

Renzo inhaled sharply, desperate to know about the warrants on Anandi and Emir and what was happening, but she disconnected before he could say anything.

He pushed the throttle forward, giving the thrusters all he could. Clearing the garage exit in a burst, he yanked the *Arazura* into the sky. From behind, he could hear surprised cries, the sounds of thumping in the corridor. He hoped Cohen had the sense to strap Sydel down, and himself too. For a moment, he wondered if

CaLarca had fallen on the floor. If she had, he didn't feel bad about it.

Gripping the controls, Renzo swerved around one skyscraper, and then another, pulling the *Arazura* into a near vertical lift to clear yet another. Ozias wasn't catching the *Arazura*, not with Renzo at the helm. Law transports weren't made for maneuvering, only for speed in a straight line.

* * *

The ship took another violent turn, sending Cohen into the wall. Cursing, Cohen dragged himself to the common room's console and buckled himself in. Instinctually, he checked to see that Sydel's safety belt was holding.

Her hands opened and closed on her lap. Her hair lifted at the edges, like she was filled with static electricity. She was staring straight ahead, unseeing.

"Syd?" Cohen put his hand on her arm.

He jerked back: her skin was scorching, her body's heat like a microwave, pulsing outwards.

Her head dropped back. Her mouth moved. She was whispering something under her breath, that same hissing noise, the same consonants again and again. Just like Kings, he realized, when he and Phaira found her in a melting room, Keller Sava mangled in a pool of blood.

She was going to explode.

"Syd, stop," he pleaded, trying to catch her eye. "You've got to calm down."

She didn't react. Now her hands were in tight fists. And he swore he saw the faintest glow around her body.

Cohen connected to the cockpit. "Help! I need help in here!" he hollered into the microphone.

"Hold tight!" Renzo's voice came through the sound-system. "Just hold on, I'll get us clear as quickly as I can!"

"We don't have time!" Cohen yelled. "Sydel is blowing up!"

"She's WHAT?"

"I can stop it," another voice interrupted. "Cohen, bring her to me. Don't hesitate. Hurry!"

He hated her. But he had to do something.

Bracing for balance, he undid the latch of their security belts. As Cohen hoisted Sydel into his arms, her skin seared into his. Sweat poured off his forehead. He gritted his teeth, and ran for Sydel's room.

Inside, CaLarca was on the floor, her legs splayed and useless, her hands gripping the bedframe with white knuckles. "Against the wall," she commanded.

Cohen slid on his knees and released Sydel, pushing her shoulders to the paneling. His palms screamed with pain.

CaLarca dragged herself to the girl's spasming body. Bracing herself with her right hand, her left fingers balled into a fist, the middle knuckle jutting out.

Then she plunged her fist into Sydel's abdomen.

Sydel drew in in a ghostly, sucking inhale. A white light burned around her body for a split second, blinding Cohen.

Then it faded. He could see the two women again. Sydel was breathing in little shuddering gulps. CaLarca's hair stood on end.

Long seconds passed. Finally, Sydel slumped over with a moan. When she hit the floor, she curled into a fetal position and went still.

She was a conduit, he realized. *CaLarca pulled out the Nadi energy.*

Horrified, Cohen scrambled over and touched Sydel's arm. It was cold. Her hair was stringy with sweat, but she was alive. They all were.

Then the green-haired woman collapsed.

PART TWO

I.

Sand coated the inside of her mouth. It threatened to choke her, but she held firm, ignoring the sweaty flailing of the battalion leader beneath her. She gritted her teeth so hard that they hurt, until his body grew lax.

Through the clouds, Phaira could see the others in her unit: Brande, Machen, Carruthers, yelling, arms reeling back to throw something. They couldn't see her through the sand clouds. Phaira rolled away, but caught the edge of a white-hot explosion, sand raining down. When she hit the ground, Phaira felt something snap in her back. The automatic compression of her nanotube suit around her chest. As she struggled to get to her feet again, gasping for breath, a volley of bullets sprayed the sand in a half-circle. One bullet ricocheted off her helmet, making her reel back as another bullet went into her right shoulder, in between the armor plating and into her flesh. Pain exploded through her side as warm blood started to soak the material of her suit. Immediately, the nanotube material around the wound tightened, but her arm was useless. She couldn't breathe. She couldn't move. This was the end. The sky was burning.

Strong hands slid under her arms, jerking her backwards. Phaira coughed violently, trying to twist away, but looking up into the face of Nox.

"I've got you." Nox said through his clenched teeth. "Come on. Feet up. I've got you."

"Hello again."

The voice startled Phaira from her reverie. The Macni, or "Mac" rail station bustled with travellers, but Emir Ajyo had managed to find her against the wall, near the restrooms. He held out his hand to shake.

"Hello again," she managed, through the fresh waves of guilt, as Nox's face hovered at the edge of her mind.

"Not feeling well?" Emir asked, holding onto her hand with his warm one.

"What? No, I'm fine," Phaira shook her head, embarrassed as she pulled away. "Sorry, I was just caught up in thought."

"Not very good thoughts, by the look of it," the older man said. "You're worried, I'd say. And very anxious about something."

"What, are you an Eko all of a sudden?" Phaira half-joked, hoisting her satchel over her shoulder. She noted his own duffel bag at his feet, neat and compact.

"Well, since you brought it up, and we're alone, I'm curious. What is your issue with Sydel?" Emir said quietly. "Why don't you trust her?"

Phaira was taken aback. In her shock, though, her mind considered the facts. She was far away from the *Arazura*. Emir had nothing at stake in this. It was the perfect moment to expose Sydel's ability to generate an explosion strong enough to kill anyone in close proximity. It was only by the protective HALO headgear they wore that she and Cohen survived the blast in Kings. But the detonation was the catalyst for the base collapse, shredding its foundational structure. The collapse that killed Aeden Nox, Huma, and so many others.

"Where's Anandi?" Phaira said instead.

"Coming. She's finishing up a few matters, transferring her projects over to a friend. I'm trying to convince her to let it go." His eyes crinkled. "She's having some difficulty."

"Well, I know how hard it is to give up control," Phaira replied. She looked Emir up and down. "What is this disorder of yours, anyways?"

"My body doesn't generate platelets," Emir said. "I have a mutation that thins my blood to the point where, without constant infusions, my heart could stop. Or I could begin to bleed internally."

"And what will this treatment do?"

"It's a series of treatments, actually, to clean the blood, remove the mutation and stimulate platelet creation," Emir explained. "It's a lot of stress on the body, though. I'll be placed into a medical coma."

"Dangerous, then." Phaira concluded. Her heart fluttered. What was she going to witness?

"Quite. I'm an old man. We aren't as hardy," Emir said. Then he shrugged. "But I have to try. And you're here, so at least I know Anandi will be protected."

Phaira went to reassure him, but a warm body suddenly flung into hers. Anandi's hair was shorter now, black tendrils curling around her ears, swept across her forehead. She was enormous in a Lissome screen, but tiny in person, just over five feet tall. Despite her size, though, more than once she'd been instrumental in saving Phaira's life.

"I can't believe you're coming!" Anandi was joyfully saying. "This is so great. I feel better already! I'm really nervous, you know. I mean, for my father, of course, but there's a lot of prying going on after Kings, and being out in the open."

"Okay, okay," Phaira said, gently removing Anandi's hands from her neck. "Don't worry. I'm happy to keep watch."

"Not just that," Anandi chimed in. "Didn't you tell her, Father? It's not just doom and gloom. It's my birthday. We have to stop at my grandmother's anyways, before we get to Liera, so there's going to be a tiny party."

Phaira glanced at Emir, who stroked his beard with a far-away look in his eye. "Really?" she asked him, incredulous. "Shouldn't you get to treatment as soon as possible?"

"One day will not make a difference," Emir said. "Besides, I want to see her happy before I go under."

"Under, but not out," Anandi said, her smile fading. Now Phaira could see the worry behind the facade.

"Never," Emir grinned at his daughter. "I've got too much to teach you."

"Oh!" Anandi exclaimed. "Is that so? Well, I - "

"Fine," Phaira interrupted their exchange. "That's fine, I guess. You have your party, I will just stay low and wait until you're ready."

"Don't be silly," Anandi said, looping her arm through Phaira's. "I want you to be my date. It'll be fun. You can be whoever you want. A countess. A faraway cousin."

"A countess!" Phaira exclaimed. "I doubt that. And your grandmother will know I'm not a cousin."

"Oh, it was just an example," Anandi scoffed. "Please? It's just a couple of hours. Then back to business. For me?"

The girl is unreal, Phaira thought, amused at the dramatics. *But entertaining, at least. Why she is so fixated on me, I have no idea.*

"For you, then," Phaira concluded. "You lunatic. Fine. Count me in."

* * *

The town of Honorwell was arranged in careful rows, individual businesses all housed in the same blue and brown architecture. Historical lighthouses blinked every ten seconds, sleepy, hazy and picturesque along the shore. As they drove down the winding one-lane roads, Phaira stared at the waterside mansions peeking through the greenery. The sandwich-board advertisements for a community picnic welcomed residents in for corn, cookouts and games at an outrageous price. *Rustic resort living, playing at being a small town,* Phaira thought, already uncomfortable; beautiful, to be sure, but warped in some way that she couldn't place.

Emir turned the transport into one of the driveways. The road was lined with trees, the land even and manicured. A break in the landscape, and the estate loomed before them, with its stone and marble, cool grays and whites, and a thousand windows reflecting the sun.

Emir went inside to announce their arrival. Stepping onto the stone path, Phaira surveyed the house. Cameras everywhere, alarms, patrolling bodyguards. As the seconds stretched on, Phaira stared at the white pillars and delicate gold etchings, the statues flanked by winding rose bushes. She didn't even know where to look. Or how to look. Phaira resisted the urge to fidget, to scratch her arms, her hands, anything to distract. "You live in squats when you've got this waiting for you?" she asked Anandi.

Anandi shrugged. "Why are you so fidgety?" she accused.

"I'm not sure that I should be here."

"Why, because it's not running around and beating up people?" Anandi teased. "Most would consider this a nice break, you know."

"Maybe for you," Phaira started, but the intricate door to the estate swung open. Emir emerged from within, this time with an elderly, slightly-stooped woman on his arm. Her silver cane flashed before her, and her clothes billowed, lavender, silken and shimmering.

"Nonni," Anandi called. "You look wonderful." She began to walk up the staircase. A few steps behind,

Phaira followed. On closer look, the woman, Emir's mother, did look well, and quite beautiful. Her black and white-streaked hair was coiled into a chignon. Her golden skin held only lines around her mouth. Her cheeks were smooth, the right one anyway - it was offered to Anandi for a light kiss.

Then her blue-green eyes shifted over Anandi's shoulder. "You brought someone?" Her voice was tight around the consonants.

"Not what you think, Nonni," Anandi sighed, flushing a deep pink. "This is Phaira. She's our bodyguard." As she said the word, she quirked an eyebrow at Phaira as if to ask: *is that right?*

Phaira gave a curt nod to the grandmother. The woman's expression remained cool. Phaira shifted her stance. This was not going to be much of a vacation.

Finally, the grandmother tipped her head to the left, addressing the doorman behind her. "We're still short a girl, so there is a spare bed in your wing, correct? Would you make it up?"

"Nonni!" Anandi exclaimed, growing even redder.

"Mother, she's a friend," Emir said brusquely, sharper than Phaira had ever heard before. "She can stay in a proper guest room."

"I'm sure Ms. Phaira understands how things work in estates like this," the grandmother responded. Her gaze rested on Phaira again, flicking up and down. "Don't you?"

The situation was so surreal that Phaira didn't have room in her brain to be offended. In fact, she battled a sly impulse to scream, to storm into the house, to do something to make the old lady keel over with shock. Why were they even here?

Her mind clicked. Of course. Money. This was a quick stop, a quick rana grab to pay for Emir's procedure. Some peace was required, then.

"It's fine," Phaira said. "It doesn't matter where I sleep. A bed is a bed," she added, shooting Anandi a quick look to silence her.

The grandmother nodded. "Very good. Emir, shall we go inside?"

His mouth pursed, Emir offered his elbow to his mother. Anandi cast a thankful look back at Phaira before following her father.

The butler remained where he was. Phaira sized him up. Was she supposed to bow on entry, or something? A light rain started to fall.

"You can wait here," he finally told her.

"Gee, thanks."

* * *

When the rainshower ended, the sun came out with power. Phaira tilted her face back. She forced herself to appreciate the weather. She'd spent most of her life in pollution, living in dark districts and basement apartments. She should love this.

But her mind twitched with inactivity. And a strange, tiny, sick sense of loneliness.

Renzo's confession that blood money built the *Arazura*; it rattled her, far more than she'd dared to show. But, then again, any reminder of Nican or his family made her paranoid. It was their influence that turned the whole city of Daro against her. Their money funded the bounty hunters to chase her when she ran. She never guessed that their money was strong enough to touch Renzo, too.

Now the *Arazura* was a haunted house, ingrained with anger and the smell of death with every step that Sydel took inside its corridors. Every flicker of the girl's eye held an explosion. No one else seemed to notice, or care. Phaira had a plan to neutralize Sydel out if things grew dangerous again, but it was the agony of waiting, always wondering if it would come to that. When it might come to that.

Over the din of the sea, Phaira heard the soft creak of a door. Anandi came onto the lawn, shielding her eyes from the sun as she looked around the veranda. Phaira heard her name, echoing up. She kept silent and still, perched on the edge of the roof, next to the open attic window, her bare toes curled around the stone gutter. She made a map in her head of everything she saw: the bird cages, ten feet tall, twenty-feet wide, and full of feathers; the ravine just behind it, providing the water source; the snaking, private path to the harbor, glimmering in the sunlight.

"Hey, you up there! I can see your shadow," Anandi's voice rang out, bemused. "Come downstairs. It's time to get ready. I have clothes for you."

"I don't need clothes," Phaira called down, annoyed.

"Lots of options. Come on, little crow. Hop on down and see."

* * *

As Anandi sorted through crinoline and satin, Phaira stood in the center of the bedroom and scowled. "I don't want to get dressed up," she protested, feeling like a whiny child. "I'll sit in the corner, but I'm not your doll."

"Stop being so silly," Anandi said, her voice muffled in the fabrics. "I want you there with me as my guest, not just my muscle. It's a compliment."

Phaira looked down at the floor. "I'm warning you now, I look stupid in fancy gear."

"It's not 'gear', Phaira, it's a dress," Anandi corrected, pulling out a voluminous orange and red gown.

Phaira immediately stepped back. "Not a chance."

"For me, not you." Anandi sighed like a lover. "I always wanted to wear this one." She brushed at the silk with her fingertips; the gesture was a practiced one, checking the seaming, the quality of the fabric. The impulse of someone accustomed to a certain standard of quality. Maybe that impulse to always measure was never lost, once learned.

Musing, Phaira walked the circumference of the room, taking stock. Between two gilded chairs sat a cello, propped in the corner, chestnut and gold and black. "You play that?" she called over her shoulder.

"Oh, it's still here," Anandi exclaimed. She left the orange and red monstrosity hanging on the closet door and shuffled over. "It's been a long time, but I used to be good. Did you play music, growing up?"

Phaira shook her head. Then a memory struck her; she didn't, but her father used to play the piano. When she was little, Phaira liked to sit on the floor by the bench and watch his feet on the pedals. From above, he swayed from side to side, as if caught in a wave. Sometimes their mother sang with him. Remembering, a strange numbness spread in her chest.

Phaira pushed down the sensation, focusing on Anandi and her curious preparations: the angled chair; the stem at the bottom of the cello, placed carefully on the floor; the instrument so hulking, balanced against the girl's torso and between her knees. The balls of her feet popped up, as if she were about to dance. Her right hand held the bow with a delicate grip, her little finger apart from the others. Then Anandi took in a breath, and lowered the bow.

For the next two minutes, Phaira was consumed by the sounds that Anandi produced. Her shuddering fingers, the twisting bow sometimes drawing on one string, sometimes on the full hundred, all worked together to pull out beautiful sobs and strangled laments from the cello. Anandi swayed as she played, sometimes draw-ing in sharp breaths, as if creating the notes hurt. The music hit Phaira at the bottom of her lungs, weighing her down, and Phaira couldn't push down the heaviness in her throat and the pain going through every limb, threatening to swallow her in black.

"Stop," Phaira said suddenly.

The last note jerked with a screech.

"I'm sorry," Phaira added in a rush. "You're amazing. I just -"

"She is, isn't she?" came Emir's voice from behind. He leaned against the doorframe, his face full with quiet pride.

Anandi waved the bow at him. "You know I'm just av-erage at best."

"Will you be ready soon?" Emir asked. "Guests will be here shortly, and you know your grandmother."

"That's why I'm trying to get this one in some accept-able clothing," Anandi joked, jerking her chin at Phaira. Despite her light tone, Phaira saw wariness in the girl's eyes. She hadn't forgotten the outburst.

So Phaira strode to the closet, surprising both Anandi and Emir. Surveying the finery, she plucked out the first shimmer of gray. "Will this fit?" she asked loudly, hoping that it was enough of a distraction. At the same time, her mind whispered, and she wondered if, somewhere in the shadows of Honorwell, behind all the beauty and order, there might be someone with an open hand, an offer of mekaline and release....

"That's so boring! Don't you want a color?" Anandi whined.

"Anandi," Emir warned. "Half an hour, girls. Then it's time to perform."

Perform, Phaira thought. Studying the pale-gray ball-gown in both hands, she breathed in and out, again and again, pushing down that one, final, swell of emotion. Soon, her familiar cool returned, her craving calmed.

It's all about performances here, she reminded herself. *One night. It's one night to get through.*

* * *

Rain fell in soft warm drops. Cakes of marigolds sat on tables. Orchestral music echoed through the ballroom, the notes accompanied by dancers, performers and ac-robats, elegant experts in their crafts, performing in the corners. In the center, the guests mingled, exquisitely dressed in every color of the rainbow, jewels shimmering under the chandeliers.

Phaira pulled up her bodice for the third time. The gray gown was an okay choice; it mostly fit, and it wasn't as tacky as some of the other glittering selections in this room, but the neckline was cut far lower than she was comfortable with. Phaira didn't have much to fill it out, but she wanted the bit she had to stay concealed.

As she shifted her weight, there was a brush against her inner thigh: a blade and a forged identification packet, tucked within a concealed holster, always on her person, just in case. Tonight would be no exception, no matter the crowd.

Someone nudged Phaira in her side. Then Anandi's hot forehead slumped against Phaira's arm. Fine pieces of hair stuck to her forehead, and she smelled of lavender and sweet alcohol. She was definitely drunk.

"Having fun?" she asked Phaira.

"It's very nice."

"Kind of strange being together, isn't it?"

"A little."

"I wish you'd picked out an actual color, Phaira, but you look pretty tonight."

"You look nice too," Phaira said. "Like a sparkler in mid-burn." And Anandi did, so flushed and vibrant, engulfed in those swirls of red and orange silk.

"That's so poetic!" Anandi exclaimed, cuddling up to Phaira's arm. "You would have looked good in this, too - wait, come down here."

Phaira bent at the knees, holding up the bodice of the dress. With careful fingers, Anandi removed the bejeweled comb on the left side of Phaira's hair, smoothed the strands back, and secured it again. Then Anandi lightly slapped Phaira's cheek. "There," she cooed. "Now I can see your face."

Phaira couldn't hold back the surprise on her face, and her smile, as she straightened to her full height. "Enough cavorting with the hired help," she told Anandi, mock-sternly. "There are far cuter girls here to lavish with attention."

She glanced around the ballroom, looking for someone to point out. One guest caught her eye, towering
over all the rest. Her smile fell.

Anandi noticed. "What is it?"

The base of Phaira's throat flushed with heat.
Mortified, she covered it with her hand. "Nothing."

But Anandi had already followed Phaira's line of vision. Her mouth twisted. Hoisting up her gown, Anandi
stomped across the ballroom floor.

Phaira started to go after Anandi, but was caught up
by the mingling crowds. Her brain screamed at her to do
something.

"I don't want you here. Get out!"

Anandi's cry rang through the grand ballroom. The
music stopped. People were staring, but Anandi didn't
seem to notice, glaring up into Theron Sava's impassive
face.

"I was invited, Anandi," Phaira heard his response,
wafting over the heads of the crowd. "My grandfather is
here somewhere. Nice to see you again, too."

"I don't want you here!" Anandi roared. "So leave!
Now! You and anyone else you brought."

Phaira crept closer. She was mostly weaponless and
dressed like a fool, but she could manage something, if
necessary. What was he doing here?

Then Emir appeared at Anandi's side, taking his
daughter's arm. He whispered something in her ear. She
began to protest, but Emir gave her arm a slight jerk,

and kept whispering. Every eye was fixed on the three of them, waiting to see what would happen next.

As Emir stepped back, Anandi's hands drew into fists, her mouth tight with anger.

Then Emir moved in front of his daughter. "Enough," he told Theron quietly. "Enough." He took Anandi's hand and led her into an adjoining room.

When the golden door closed, the crowd began to rumble. The band began to play again. Theron shrugged, saying something to the man at his side. Then he wandered to the far end of the ballroom, ducking through a set of silken white curtains.

Staying ten steps behind, Phaira followed.

Through the curtains sat a small terrace with an intricate stone bench, overlooking the grounds. Theron sat down, leaning back on his hands. His long black hair, tied back with red cord, swung between his shoulders in a perfect vertical line. Rain sheared over the edge of the roof. Phaira focused on the droplets as she walked, and turned on her borrowed high heels when she reached the left side of the bench.

They faced opposite directions: Theron looking over the lawn, Phaira watching the shadows inside the ballroom.

"This is her birthday, Theron," Phaira finally spoke. "She's just a kid. Was that necessary?"

Peripherally, she saw Theron shrug. "I'm just an escort tonight. No ill intentions."

Couples waltzed across the open doors. The wind was cold across Phaira's bare shoulders. She refused to shiver.

"It's good to see you," his voice floated up. "That dress is pretty different. Doesn't really suit you."

Phaira barely heard him, so focused on weighing her two impulses: she could smack him across the face, or she could wrap her body around his. Both were equally overpowering. The last time they saw each other was three weeks ago. She confronted him, demanding answers, and she'd kissed him out of spite, but then everything went hot and lopsided before she got away.

Since then, Phaira replayed that moment a hundred times, and every time, she was left with a different wish.

"You made it out of Kings," Theron continued, even quieter. "I wasn't sure - but I was relieved to hear it."

There were so many things she could say, rushing through her head. *Sorry about your cousins; they were evil, but they were your family, and that has to be painful. But when you said that the NINE killed your parents and left you brain-damaged; was that true? Or a story for sympathy? And was that the goal all along, to gain control over the Sava syndicate?*

Her shame, her wounded pride, her fury at being used, it was all swirling into a violent firestorm inside her chest. She wouldn't start a fight with him here, not in Anandi's moment, and not in this estate full of pretenders.

Movement caught her attention. There was a commotion inside. Squinting, Phaira caught sight of Anandi's dress, that vibrant, dramatic orange. And figures in grey uniforms: local law patrol.

Somewhere, far away it seemed, she heard Theron ask what was wrong.

But Phaira couldn't move, nor choke out an answer, so horrified by the scene in the ballroom: Anandi's hands bound with plastic strips. Emir already restrained, the rest of the guests had backed into the walls, save for the grandmother, who spoke in a low, disgusted voice. ".... enough of you indulging her disrespectful behavior, Emir. Family honor and loyalty mean nothing to either of you. If she cannot behave, then she will be treated as any other adult."

Phaira balled her hands into fists. Anandi had a long record of security breaches. She could go to prison for years. Which was a death sentence for Emir, so dependent on her blood transfusions to stay alive. Phaira had a fleeting vision of the future: Anandi's vitality drained away, a husk of a woman, wracked with the guilt over her father's death. Phaira knew that guilt too well. That future was unacceptable.

Phaira glanced in all directions, forming her plan. She already had a good idea of the security systems in place. The main obstacles were the officers inside, any estate security that might have orders to give chase, and getting off this damned estate.

First, she had to get out of the ballgown.

Yanking up her skirt, Phaira removed the knife from the holster around her thigh, and then plunged the blade into the fabric, ripping it around her thighs, pulling out the crinoline and beaded silk so her legs were exposed. Then she kicked off her dress shoes and sheathed the knife again.

"Give me your firearm," she announced to the night, refusing to look at Theron directly. "I know you have something."

At the edge of her vision, Phaira saw him rise to his feet, reach into his inner pocket and remove a Compact model, gunmetal grey, sleek and small. When she stretched out a hand to take it, he held onto the pistol, keeping her in place.

"Don't get involved," he warned her. "Don't expose yourself."

Phaira kept her eyes at his chest level. "I have to. I promised to protect them."

It seemed to resonate. Theron let go of the Compact. Phaira primed it with a quick click.

Then, before Theron could react, she was behind him, the barrel pressed into his back.

"Now move," she commanded.

II.

When Theron walked inside the estate with his hands lifted, the air was thick with the sounds of gasping and guns priming. Then Theron shook his head, his long hair swaying against his back, and everything went silent.

Wary, Phaira slid out from behind, aiming the Compact at the back of Theron's skull; for good measure, she took hold of his ponytail with her other hand. When she gave it a quick yank, he shot a glare in her direction. But he still didn't say anything.

In the center of the ballroom, Anandi and Emir stared with their mouths open, hands bound, clothes mussed, Anandi with tear tracks down her cheeks. Three patrol officers stood behind them, young, and nervous. Did they even have firearms on them? No sign of any backup.

But why would there be? she reasoned. Just two hackers to bring in. Very little drama anticipated, especially in a sleepy, rich town like this one.

"Whoever you are, release my grandson," came a forceful voice. "You don't know what you are doing."

To the right stood a man in his eighties, once tall in his youth, now stooped over a cane. Theron's grandfather, Phaira surmised. Two bodyguards flanked him, their hands in their inner jacket pockets. A fourth man stood behind the grandfather, holding onto his shoulder and whispering into his ear. He was older, balding, port-ly, but his eyes were black and mean.

"I know more than you do, sir," Phaira told the grand-father. "So stand down."

The old man's jaw clenched. The bodyguards lowered their hands to their sides.

"Do you know who that is?" Anandi's grandmother shrieked. "How dare you - ?"

Phaira fired one shot into the chandelier above. Glass rained down. Anandi's grandmother covered her head as the guests screamed.

"I'd dare to," Phaira said. "I want Anandi and Emir, next to me, now."

The officers looked as startled as the guests, their faces fluctuating between disbelief and anger. But they kept their hands at their sides as Anandi and Emir scur-ried behind Phaira.

"Now we leave," Phaira said. "No one follows."

She gave Theron's hair another tug, and he started to walk backwards, hands still raised. Phaira, Emir and Anandi moved as a group, heading back to the curtains, and the veranda with the stone bench. The ballroom was eerily silent. The party guests stared, hands to mouths. The officers and bodyguards watched every step. Phaira could see how they fidgeted, waiting for the signal to run and strike. She had only seconds.

When all four cleared the threshold, Phaira slammed the doors shut. As Anandi, Emir and Theron gaped, Phaira grabbed a strip of her discarded ballgown and wound it in a figure-eight around the handles, finishing with a quick knot.

Theron was the first to speak. "Are you crazy?"

The sound of a gunshot rang out. Gasping, the three dropped to the terrace floor, but Phaira just pulled out her knife again. Inside, the grandmother was screaming; Phaira heard the word 'bulletproof' over and over again. As she thought, when she'd come out the first time with Theron, now confirmed.

Phaira cut the plastic binds on Anandi and Emir, and tossed the Compact to Emir. "Keep the aim on him. If he tries to run, shoot him."

Then she took hold of Theron's hands, a strip of crinoline in her teeth.

"Really?" Theron asked, incredulous.

"Afraid so," Phaira said through the side of her mouth.

And with a few deft twists, Theron's hands were bound in full view of the glass doors and crowd behind them.

"What are you doing, Phaira?" Anandi cried, already half over the balcony. "We're out, we don't need him!"

"We need a way to get out of this town," Phaira corrected. "And he's going to show us his escape route. Now jump!"

Anandi disappeared from view. Tossing Phaira back the weapon, Emir followed. Phaira aimed the Compact at Theron's head, pulling him along as she stepped up onto the ledge.

Behind them, the double doors banged in their frame. Fists pounded on the windows. The officers were no longer visible; other bodies had replaced them, trying to force a knife through the opening and cut the binding.

"Come on," Phaira commanded Theron. "Go."

"You want me to jump with my hands bound?" Theron hissed. His body wavered, unbalanced on the edge.

"You can manage."

She pushed him. He fell from sight.

Then she vaulted into nothingness.

* * *

It was a good production, but it was only eight feet to the ground, and she'd kept the binding loose enough that Theron could slip one hand free and balance his landing. Phaira hit the ground next to him, slipping a little on her bare feet in the grass. A few feet away, the silhouettes of Anandi and Emir were crouched, waiting. "Where do we go now?" Emir whispered. "What's this secret escape route?"

Phaira heard Theron's intake of breath, about to speak, but Phaira shushed him. Instead, she drew them all into the underhang of the balcony, huddling behind the shrubbery.

"They're expecting that," Phaira told them. "They heard me say it, so the officers and bodyguards are heading that way now."

Sure enough, the sound of pounding footsteps echoed across the lawn, along with radio static and grumbling voices.

"Over there," Phaira whispered, pointing in the opposite direction. "That's where you go, by the birdcages. Any motion sensors will be programmed to accommodate the bird's activity. That, plus the rain, should be enough of a cover to get to the ravine."

"The one just past the cages?" Anandi broke in. "If we follow the water, we should hit the harbor - then maybe get a boat? I don't know. I don't know." She was starting to crumble under the weight of her situation. Phaira could hardly blame her.

"Is there anything that you need out of the house?" she asked the girl.

"The transfusion equipment," Anandi immediately listed.

"We can buy it," Emir corrected. "There's always a black market somewhere."

"Then just me," Phaira murmured. She eyed the lights of the estate, plotting her way back inside. Through the attic, by way of the roof?

"You? You can't do that, we all need to get out of here!" Anandi whispered.

"I'm not leaving my Calises behind," Phaira shot back. "You know how long it took me to get them back after - ?"

"Don't be foolish," came Theron's low voice from in the shadows, making all three jump. "You don't go back for a gun. You have one already. Get them out of here."

"It doesn't concern you," Phaira snapped back.

"You involved me when you stuck that gun in my back," Theron pointed out. "You think it's that easy? That I just reappear and everything is okay? They know your face. You threatened me. What do you think - ?"

"How do you two know each other?" Anandi interrupted.

Phaira swallowed her temper. "Never mind. Let's go," she ordered, tucking the Compact firearm into her thigh holster.

Emir, Anandi and Phaira ran to the tall metal enclosures that housed the grandmother's exotic bird collection. Just beyond the cages was a chainlink fence, with pipes running up from the cement ravine below: the water supply for the birds, Phaira surmised.

"There's a ladder on the other side," Anandi whispered. "I used to sneak down here as a kid. Come on."

After tying her soaked dress around her waist, Anandi scaled the fence first. Emir followed his daughter. His balance wavered a few times, but he managed to make it over and drop to the other side.

Lost a Calis again, Phaira cursed herself as she climbed up the chainlink. *I can't believe it.*

As she swung her leg over, strong fingers took hold of her wrist. Phaira twisted, swinging with her free hand.

Her fist smacked into Theron's palm. Before she could react, he slid a Lissome inside.

"What are you going to tell them?" she asked, half-afraid of the answer.

"I have an idea," Theron said. "Just go."

With her perched on top of the fence, they were eye level with each other. Something about the black night, the cold metal under her thighs and the rain pouring down – Phaira had the sudden, fiery urge to grab Theron and kiss him hard.

Instead, she told him: "I'm still mad at you."

Theron's brow furrowed. "For what?"

Phaira gaped. Was he serious?

But there was no time to ask. She swung her other leg over the fence and leapt.

Just as Anandi had said, there was a rusty metal ladder on the other side, glinting in the darkness. She quickly descended, the cold on her bare feet breaking her fervor. Then she jumped, landing in a puddle with a splash.

Anandi and Emir crouched by the concrete wall. Phaira tossed the Lissome to Anandi. "Can you work with this?"

Anandi's face lit up. "I sure can. But let's move. The water will lead us to the sea."

Emir leaned against the wall. Even though Phaira couldn't see his face, she could feel his fatigue. "Can you manage?" she asked.

"With some help, I can," Emir said, wheezing.

"Lead the way," Phaira instructed Anandi. "I've got him." She looped her arm around Emir's waist and walked with him into the concrete valley.

The sound of waves grew louder, ringing with an eerie clarity. At the ravine's end, next to an access ladder, Phaira set down Emir to rest, while Anandi brought out the Lissome. She sat cross-legged, set the small black square on her bare knee, and raised her hands like a conductor.

Then she began to work, screens unfolding, blinking color and lines of code surrounding her. The ravine glowed a faint blue. Then Anandi announced, "There's a shipping freighter scheduled to leave in five minutes, headed south. It would take us off our planned route to Liera, but we could make it work. I can get a friend to meet us."

Phaira glanced at Emir. In the light of her Lissome, the man's skin was grey. "When does he need another transfusion?"

"I can manage for a day," Emir broke in. "If I am careful."

Phaira scaled the access ladder and peered over the edge, looking for the waterfront. Yes, there was the freighter, rusted and red, the dock lit by a bare bulb, workers loading crates onto the surface. Her gaze travelled across the bay, where yachts and hoverboats bobbed.

"Can you disable the security alarm of the gates to the east?" Phaira asked as she slid down the ladder. "We can take a boat and get to the freighter that way. Too many people on dock loading up - we'll never get by."

"Done," Anandi confirmed. "I've also disabled the cameras and lights around the freighter's portside. It'll just look like a simple electrical short, shouldn't be too suspicious. But we need to get on that ship quickly. In Honorwell, there's a security pulse one thousand meters from shore, designed to shut down any stolen transport -"

"Just let me take the lead, and help your father," Phaira instructed. "No talking. Just movement. Okay?"

Anandi collapsed all the screens into the Lissome and tucked it into her bodice. Then she went to her father, who had barely moved since they stopped to rest. "Papa?" she whispered. "Hang on."

Phaira climbed out of the ravine and slid down the hill. When she reached the bottom, she rolled into the shadows, just before the boardwalk. She heard Emir and Anandi's approach, clumsier and slower, but they were coming, so Phaira moved ahead, vaulting over a low stone fence, inching towards the humming gates to the dock. Across the bay, the freighter was beginning to churn its engines.

Then the light in the lamppost shorted out. The buzzing of the security gate ceased. Phaira pushed through, running to the first boat that caught her eye. Its keys were taped under the driver's cushions.

The motor started immediately, and everything lifted; the boat was a hoverboat, lifting them just above the water's surface. Phaira had never driven one before. But how hard could it be?

Anandi appeared, Emir's arm looped around her shoulder; he dragged his feet as they stumbled across the boardwalk. The boat rocked with their weight as they jumped in. Emir collapsed on landing.

"Papa!" Anandi cried. Phaira shushed her angrily.

Using her knife to cut through the anchoring rope, Phaira backed the hoverboat out, and when clear, shoved the throttle forward. The hoverboat leapt at the touch, quickly gaining speed, headed for the freighter's portside.

Peering through the wind, Phaira saw the freighter pulling out of its docking station and cursed to herself. They'd have to jump for it.

She gunned the engine. Emir and Anandi fell back as the bow angled up. Even hovering, the boat still bounced from the rough waves.

"You'll have to jump onto the ladder!" Phaira yelled over her shoulder. "Can you do it?"

"Papa, come on," Anandi pleaded. The older man was ashen under the moonlight. Phaira turned the boat alongside the churning freighter, steeled her arms on the wheel and increased the speed. The curved ladder that led up to the deck was straight ahead.

"Get along the side now!" Phaira instructed. "I'll try to get as close as I can."

Then she saw the blinking red lights in the distance. The security pulse on the horizon, the one Anandi mentioned: instant engine shutdown if no code was entered when the hoverboat passed.

But if Emir and Anandi can get on there, they can keep going, Phaira reasoned. It doesn't matter if I'm along with them or not at this point. I can find them later.

She jammed the wheel to the left. The boat swooped dangerously close to the freighter. Emir grabbed Anandi's wrists and slapped her hands onto the bottom rung of the ladder.

Then the hovercraft dipped away, and Anandi was left hanging. "Papa!" she screamed.

Phaira steered in again, using her foot to push Emir towards the edge. "Go!" she ordered.

"You first!" the older man yelled back, reaching for the wheel. Phaira shook her head and shoved him away. Thirty seconds before they hit the barrier was no time for damned chivalry.

"Speed up, then!" Emir yelled. There was a flush in his face, like renewed life. "I'll catch you when you jump! Come on!"

Then, with surprising agility, Emir leapt for the ladder, catching the bottom rung. Anandi was two rungs above him, her tattered orange dress billowing behind her. The red security lights were growing large. Phaira braced the accelerator to the floor, and the boat sped ahead of the freighter, cast in blood-red shadows.

Three. Two. One.

She let go of the wheel, stepped onto the edge, and leapt.

The breathless rush of wind propelled her backwards. She braced herself for the shock of cold.

But a hand caught her wrist. Another yanked at the back of her preserver. Phaira scrambled for something solid, and found metal under hand, under foot. Below her, behind her, the hoverboat was flipped by the waves.

Phaira pushed her legs to move, to climb up and up, until she managed to roll onto the deck, soaked, and panting. Anandi was kissing her, as soaked tendrils of hair dripped onto Phaira's face. "Thank you," the girl breathed. "Thank you."

Phaira was too exhausted to do anything but lie there. They'd made it. She'd gotten them out. She moved her free hand over her thigh holster. The knife and identification packet was still there.

When she could breathe without panting, Phaira sat up and surveyed the world. Crates, chains, and tarps. No guards on deck. The freighter headed into open water, as Honorwell twinkled on the coastline. She wasn't sorry to see it fade away.

"We need shelter," Phaira said. "Maybe one of the crates? It'll be hard for a day, no food or water, but we'll have to manage."

Anandi and Emir nodded. Huddled against the cold, Phaira led the way, sliding along the row of magnetized crates, knocking on the walls and listening for echoes. Two down, a steel-grey rusted crate sounded hollow.

Phaira jimmied open the lock. Anandi activated a thin beam of light from her Lissome to illuminate the area. The back half was full of boxes, covered by a burlap tarp. Enough room for the three of them. Phaira stripped off the tarp and handed it over to Anandi and Emir. Then she looked through the contents of the crate: farming supplies, tools, engines, nothing dangerous.

On the floor, Emir leaned against another crate, Anandi on his right side, the tarp covering them both. Anandi held onto her father's arm like a child. "How could she do that?" she was murmuring. "How could Nonni do that to us? To you?"

"Your grandmother has a lot of pride in the family name," Emir said grimly. "It affects her judgment. And her priorities. She's always been difficult, even more so since I left the practice and came with you."

"Calling the authorities is pretty extreme," Phaira said, squeezing the water out of her hair. A shiver coursed through her body; she forced herself to will away the cold.

Emir noticed, and reached out with his left arm. "Come under here," he told her.

Phaira hesitated. But she was in the tatters of her silver dress, barefoot, and with the adrenaline decreasing, her body was getting cold fast.

So reluctantly, she slid under the scratchy tarp. Emir's arm went around her bare shoulders, wet but warm, drawing her against his torso. Phaira stiffened and shot him a look, embarrassed by the touch, but he didn't seem to notice.

"I should have known better," Emir was saying quietly. "I'm so sorry, girls."

The word girls – it was said so casually.

Phaira let her temple rest against Emir's shoulder, and for a brief, secret moment, she pretended she was his other daughter. The warmth lingered. She let it.

Then she sat upright and kept watch, waiting for the first sign of the sun.

III.

When the new day broke, and the freighter docked in a small fishing town down the East Coast, the three stowaways didn't bother to hide their presence. Cold, thirsty and aching, Phaira, Emir and Anandi strode past two very surprised dockworkers on their way to the beach. Phaira could only imagine what she looked like, her hair tangled from the seawater, the dress in tatters around her thighs. Anandi fared better, her orange dress dirtied, but mostly intact. Emir looked the worst, gray and clammy, his cheeks sunken in. His hand drifted over to his heart every now and again, Phaira noticed. She wondered if Anandi had.

As the group disembarked, a silver ground transport rolled across the gravel, stopping just a few feet away. The door lifted without sound. From the darkness within, a woman stepped into the morning light, dressed in wool-and-bejeweled tunic and trousers, her black hair wound up in an elegant twist at the nape of her neck.

"Ulene," Emir greeted the woman.

"Hello, Mother," Anandi seconded.

Mother? Surprised, Phaira peered at the woman. Was there a resemblance? Not really, except for the black hair.

"I have everything you need," Ulene said, her voice feminine, light but nervous. "This car is privately owned, no registration, no passports needed to get to Liera.

Destination entered for the automated driver. Hospital scrubs to look the part once you get there. I have a kit inside as well, Emir; if you do a light transfusion, it should keep you in stable condition until you get there."

"Thank you, Mother," Anandi said. Her tone was awkward. "I'm sorry that I had to call."

"Oh no, no. I'm happy to help, of course," Ulene deferred, one shoulder lifted like a little girl.

Phaira stared at the family before her. There were hidden stories among these three. But she was too exhausted to care about family dysfunction. At least Anandi's parents were both there, and willing to help her.

Then Anandi's arm slid through Phaira's. "This is our bodyguard, Phaira. She got us out of Nonni's estate. Phaira, this is my mother, Ulene."

Ulene extended a hand, and Phaira shook it, wincing at the pressure on her scratched palms. Ulene didn't seem to notice, a strange, bashful smile on her face.

"We should go," Emir finally said. "Ulene? Would you care to join us?"

"Oh!" Ulene said, surprised, releasing Phaira's hand. "Oh, thank you, but I should get back to work. You should all rest. I'd like to know how things make out later, though, if you don't mind."

"Of course," Emir confirmed.

Anandi and Ulene hugged. Then a second gleaming transport pulled up, and the woman slipped inside, the motor soundless as it backed away from the group.

Inside the borrowed vehicle, Emir set up the transfusion tubes. Anandi extended her elbow for the hookup. Phaira flopped onto the white cushions as the door hissed shut. A faint rumble started beneath her feet. They were on their way, safe for the moment.

"Your mother is a bit odd," Phaira said to Anandi, careful with her words.

"Oh, I know," Anandi sighed. "She's brilliant in business, and very nice, and I love her. But..." She made a gesture around her head. "She's not always 'present', so to speak. Works a lot. Kind of whirls in and out of my life."

Phaira watched as blood ran through the tube between father and daughter. What drew Emir and Ulene together in the first place? she wondered. They seemed so different, with such a strange mix of warm knowing and cool regard for each other.

Another question, though, hovered in her mind. And finally, she asked Anandi, feigning casualness: "What's with you and Theron?"

Anandi huffed. "Oh, that. Our families have history. People in my family have historically been healers for Savas, 'on the side,' if you know what I mean. It's why Papa quit the practice. That, and his condition, of course. They wanted more and more of his time. Too much interference and arm-pulling. It was making him even sicker."

Phaira glanced at Emir. The man said nothing, gazing out the window.

"Nonni sure wasn't happy, I know that," Anandi rambled on. "You should have seen the fit she threw when Papa requested his inheritance to pursue this treatment."

Then she frowned. "And how do you know Theron, anyways? I think that's the most I've ever heard him talk. We were forced to socialize when we were really young, you know, always pushed together, and told: 'oh, why don't you two go play?'"

"We've met before," Phaira said.

"Well, he's turned out to be decent-looking, I guess, but he's seriously weird," Anandi warned. "I can't imagine him as the syndicate head, how it's possibly going to be successful -"

"Anandi," came Emir's warning voice.

Anandi closed her mouth. Phaira sank into the soft interior of the transport, mulling over Anandi's words. Then fatigue wiped out her thoughts.

* * *

Liera Medical Center was located at the edge of the city, the office tucked into the eleventh floor of a dull gray building. From the sidewalk, Phaira counted each window, up and up. No alarms or cameras. Narrow ledges between windows. Service ladder access, but tucked away from public sight, only visible if someone knew where to look. She turned in a circle, observing the surroundings. Slow, lumbering traffic. Barely a trace of a sound of anything in the air. A good place to tuck away, and risk a life.

Access to the eleventh floor was accessible by pass-
code only, entered by Emir. On the other side of the door,
Dr. Sabik was there to greet them. He was an older man
with coffee-brown skin, a neat mustache and round chin,
his grey hair in a short, frizzy ponytail. He and Emir embraced, Sabik giving the other man a thump on the back.
A sign of encouragement? Anandi didn't look reassured
at all.

The long corridor held doors on either side: doors
to facilities, exam rooms, and one with showers. Phaira
begged off the rest of the tour, and within minutes, she
was in the hot water, rinsing off the salt and muck of
the night, revealing scratches and bruises underneath.
Her feet were a mess, but it was tolerable. Scrubs sat in
a folded pile outside the shower when she stepped out.
Burgundy and scatchy, but far better than the tattered
mess of a dress she dropped into the trash.

When everyone had cleaned themselves off and dressed
in fresh clothing, the threesome met in Dr. Sabik's office. Phaira surveyed the room. Certificates, books, the
usual design. Eerily quiet, though. Did this doctor have
no staff to assist him?

"Phaira, is it?" Dr. Sabik was asking, sitting on the
edge of his desk. His eyebrows knitted together in a
thoughtful stare. "Emir, I thought you only had one
daughter."

"I do," Emir clarified. "She's a friend, here for moral
support. But she could use some clarification on what's
going to happen in the next few days."

Anandi's fingers slipped into Phaira's hand. Her palm was still damp from the shower.

"We're attempting a permanent solution to Emir's blood disorder. The treatment is a literal 'reboot' of his system. Certain points are stimulated, chemicals pumped in, complete flush of the system, infused with fresh donor blood. The process should take about a week. Ideally, by then, his body will be stimulated enough to produce the enzymes needed for blood clotting. There is significant risk to Emir in doing this. Brain damage, cardiac arrest. But I will watch him very carefully."

Phaira wasn't quite sure what the doctor was talking about, but she nodded just the same. "When do you start?"

"I wasn't sure when you would be arriving," Dr. Sabik mused. "So I need some time to set up the equipment. Tomorrow morning? You can all stay here. There's space for overnight guests, rooms on the right, nearest to the elevator."

I *need to check security in the meantime,* Phaira thought. *Even with all the cover, we're all wanted now by the law...*

"Sabik," Emir interrupted her thoughts. "Will you take Anandi to those suites? I need to speak to Phaira privately."

Dr. Sabik nodded, but Anandi recoiled. "Why?"

"Please," Emir told his daughter. "Do as I ask."

Anandi looked at Phaira, stricken.

I don't know what he wants, Phaira told the girl with her facial expression, shrugging and widening her eyes.

Anandi's shoulders slumped. She dropped Phaira's hand and shuffled out of the office. Sabik shut the door softly behind them. Then it was just Emir and Phaira in the room.

"Do you understand what will be happening, Phaira?"

"Enough of it. Why?"

"Because there's a good chance I might not wake up."

Phaira's stomach clenched. So, he was making his final arrangements. Before she could stop, the words spilled out: "Are you sure you want to do this?"

"Anandi shouldn't be bound to an old, sick father. She deserves to be free."

"She may not have that choice," Phaira warned him. "Sooner or later the law's going to catch up with us. I can't hold them back forever. If she's not careful..."

"If this is successful," Emir said quietly. "If I come out of this alive, I'll take her place. Turn myself in for the crimes."

"You can't do that," Phaira hissed. "You can't. It would kill her to know that you sacrificed -"

"Send in the doctor," Emir politely cut her off. "Perhaps you could check on Anandi. Make sure she's handling all of this well."

Phaira's impulse was to argue with the man. But discomfort grew between them instead. He wasn't her father. She had no power to change his mind.

So Phaira did what she was told.

At the end of the hallway, one door was ajar. Inside was a small suite with two twin beds, two dressers, and one cracked window overlooking the city. Anandi sat on the bed closest to the door, looking at her feet. The weight of Emir's decision bore down on Phaira's back. Trying to set it aside, she asked the girl: "Can we call Renzo and check in? Before we shut off all contacts?"

The question woke Anandi from her stupor. She took the encrypted Lissome from the bedside table. "Quickly," she reminded Phaira. "The network is hot right now. No more than five seconds." Then she left the room: to wander, to eavesdrop, Phaira couldn't guess at her inner life right now, nor did she want to. Intead, she punched in the cc to connect to the *Arazura*.

"We're clear," she said when she heard the familiar click. "Trouble, but at the end-point now. Keep offline for now. Guards up."

An intake of breath on the other end; Renzo was about to speak. But Anandi said no more than five seconds. No choice but to disconnect, and only hope he wasn't about to tell her something awful had happened.

The Lissome began to buzz again. Did Renzo call her back? Quickly, Phaira broke the connection.

Ten seconds later, the Lissome came to life again, buzzing patiently. Phaira stared at it. Then she felt it: that familiar flutter and sink in her chest.

Who else could it be?

* * *

Wearing dark trousers, wool overcoat and leather gloves, Phaira's satchel slung over his shoulder, Theron had his back to the building, head tilted back to look at the grey sky. Phaira stared at him through the lobby window. What was he looking for? Why was he here?

Wary, Phaira finally pushed open the glass door. Theron turned at the sound. He held a box in his arms. One side of his mouth turned up in a smile. "Delivery."

Seriously weird. The most he's ever spoken to anyone. Anandi's words floated through Phaira's mind as she tentatively took the box from him. Yes, her two Calis pistols were inside, hidden under a swatch of cloth. Then Theron laid her satchel at her feet, like an offering. She tapped it with her toe. "What did you tell your grandfather?"

Theron's smirk faded. "That you were auditioning to be my bodyguard. And the party was a test on current security measures. Which everyone failed, miserably."

Phaira couldn't help it. She laughed like something burst inside of her, laughed until tears formed. "That is the worst story I've ever heard," she gasped. "Then why did I take Emir and Anandi along?"

"Because you were their current bodyguard. I said that we arranged it all on the balcony. They believed it," Theron said, a satisfied ring to his voice. "They believed it even more when I convinced the officers they were in error.

"Hence the reason I'm here, besides as delivery boy," he added, averting his eyes. "To work out the terms of the contract."

Phaira's laughter died. She wasn't available for hire, not for the kind of work that the Sava Syndicate did. She'd made that clear, again and again. How could he make that kind of claim to his grandfather?

"Well, that, and to find out why you're angry with me," Theron said, interrupting her thoughts. "I thought we were – well - friends, at least."

Phaira exhaled through her nose, set down the box and straightened to her fullest height. He still had at least six inches on her. Dammit.

"You lied to me," she told him shortly. "And you threatened my family."

Theron frowned. "I never threatened your brothers."

"No, but you snuck around to spend time with them," Phaira said pointedly. "That's what you said, remember? You were 'assessing me at all angles?' And it just so happens that Cohen gets kidnapped by your cousins, I get involved and shot - again, I might add - and by the end of it all, your cousins are dead and you're the king of the world. It's very convienient."

"That's what you think this was all about?" He sounded genuinely puzzled. "Some big master plan to get you to kill my cousins, so I could take over the syndicate?"

Wasn't it?

"You do think that," Theron muttered. "Well, you're not the first to throw that theory at me. I know how it looks." He sounded oddly disappointed.

"What's the truth, then?"

"I told you, I knew what Keller was planning. And I knew he had recruited Huma for protection. But I wasn't involved. And I wasn't trying to get you involved, either. But then I saw – I mean, when you told me about Huma, what she did to you and your family, I could figure out what might happen. You were going to confront her, kill her, even. That's why I worked with Renzo on HALOs; that's why I tried to warn Cohen away from Keller. To try and ensure you had the means to get out alive."

As he spoke, Phaira studied the sharp angles of his face, searching for clues that he was lying. But questions still swam around in Phaira's mind. She looked away and leaned to the right, balancing the box in one hand as she bent down to pick up the satchel with the other. In the motion, she caught sight of his boot, scuffing the ground.

Then he spoke again: "Do you ever think about that week on the cliffs?"

Phaira froze. The beach town in the north; his strange house of windows. She'd spent a week there, recovering from trauma, hiding from the world, only a month ago (was it really only a month?) He served as her unexpected host; they trained together, shared a few odd, poignant moments. One of the better weeks of her life, if she were honest with herself. But she couldn't say that out loud. What if it was just thrown back at her?

She straighted back to standing, avoiding his gaze.

"I just thought – I might stay in Liera," she heard him say. "And maybe I could see you again. For longer than five minutes."

Her upper arms prickled, and her face grew hot. Mortified, Phaira ducked her head. "I have to go."

And she spun on her heel and hurried back into the building. The lobby door closed and latched behind her.

Behind the cover of mailboxes, the heat in her face receded. Then a wave of shame followed.

But Theron was already gone.

IV.

The next morning, Emir was officially admitted for treatment. Anandi remained with her father and Dr. Sabik as the process began. Phaira walked down the long hallway, dragging her fingertips against the rippled wall, back and forth, the hundred foot stretch again and again, a hypnotic, distracting loop as she waited for news.

Finally, Anandi emerged. The girl walked as if through water, wandering in the direction of their shared room. Phaira couldn't think of what to say to her. So, she offered her arm.

Anandi leaned into Phaira with a surprising heaviness. "I don't know what to do," she finally said. "I'm not ready to see him like this."

"I know, but he has a chance at a full life," Phaira told her. "Not only for him, but for you."

"I'd rather he be with me than take the risk and die."

"Well, he's doing all this for you," Phaira said shortly. "I don't even know what that feels like."

Stopping her trek, Anandi peered up into Phaira's face. "I don't think I ever asked you about your parents. Or any of you. You three always seem so self-contained."

"Because there isn't anything good to say about it," Phaira deferred, opening the door for Anandi. "You should go and lie down."

"Are they alive?"

"No."

Anandi waited. Phaira shook her head, one tight swing.

Disappointment on her face, Anandi brushed past. Standing in the threshold, Phaira pressed her mouth together. She never talked about her parents at all, not to anyone. But the girl needed some kind of comfort. She probably wouldn't even hear half of it, so consumed with her father's health.

So Phaira tried to be brief. "Our mother died when we were young," she announced in a rush. "And our father was mentally ill. They found him about a week ago. Stabbed."

Anandi whirled around, shocked. "You never said! Phaira, I'm so sorry -"

"It's fine," Phaira interrupted. "We weren't close, not like you and Emir."

Anandi gave a tiny smile. "We weren't always. Only in the past year."

"Really?"

"Really. It was – "

Then Anandi stopped at the sound of beeping, echoing, erratic and high-pitched, followed by urgent clicking.

Phaira ducked back her head to look down the hall. The door to Emir's room was open. It was the source of the sound.

Inside the treatment room, Dr. Sabik pumped on Emir's chest. Anandi gave a horrible, shuddering inhale, and ran to her father's head. "Papa!" she shrieked, slapping his face. "Papa!"

"Get her out of here!" Dr. Sabik barked over his shoulder at Phaira.

But she was frozen in the doorway. She couldn't stop staring at Emir, how his face drifted to the side, sunken in and waxy like a rubber mask. It didn't even look like him. Was that the life going out of him?

"Ms. Phaira!"

It took all Phaira's willpower to take hold of Anandi and pull her away. Anandi fought the whole time, trying to claw Phaira's hands off her.

Then the girl collapsed, heaving with sobs, her hands in her hair, pressed against Phaira's legs and pinning her to the spot.

* * *

Hours later, Phaira held Anandi's hand as the girl finally succumbed to exhaustion. When Anandi's breathing slowed, and the grip on her hand loosened enough to slip away, Phaira made her escape.

Outside, the cold thin air made her lightheaded. Phaira flattened her back against the wall, staring across the city landscape, at the buzzing lights of transports and trains. She looked down, past the ledge she stood on, trying to find a streetlight. Some indication of how far down the fall would be. Or where a mekaline dealer might be found, somewhere in the shadows of Liera.

No, I can't. She gripped the corner so tightly that pain stabbed her palm. *I can't. It'll ruin everything.* One relapse was bad enough, she was lucky that she pulled herself out of the spiral after Kings Canyon.

But the images wouldn't stop in her head. Anandi screaming, begging for her father to come back to life. The way Emir's face grew sunken and waxen as the heartbeat stopped, and how long it seemed until the rhythm started again. How Anandi couldn't stop crying. How Phaira couldn't help but think of Nox, his own heart slowing, choking with pain and red dust.

She couldn't stay sober with all those thoughts in her head. She needed to forget, somehow.

Maybe with someone.

Phaira activated her Lissome. With a flick of her opposite finger, she searched for the pingback for the last call. The location appeared, right on top of her position. Surprised, she craned her neck to look up; there were no lights on in the floors above. But there was the service ladder, on the side of the building.

And on the fourteenth floor, the window was ajar.

Slipping through, Phaira stepped down onto the lush carpet, kneading her toes into the fibers to muffle her movement. Her body was covered in goosebumps. She willed them to go away.

Despite her efforts at silence, he still heard her. Phaira heard the click of a safety being shut off, followed by an exclamation: "What are you doing? I could have shot you. And -"

Before he could finish his sentence, Phaira was across the room, snatching the Compact firearm away. One snap, and the gunclip fell to the floor. The pistol followed, making a soft thunk on the carpet. Then Phaira climbed on top of Theron, searched for his face with her fingers, and cut off his startled inhale with her mouth.

Finally. Finally. The culmination of a thousand fantasies she'd held on to for weeks, the crushing intensity she remembered, the icy flush over her skin, his solid body underneath his shirt, his incredibly sensual mouth, his unbound hair in her hands, smelling like cedar...

Then his hands were on her shoulders. Pushing gently. Pushing her off.

He was rejecting her.

Horrified, she scrambled off Theron. But his hand found her upper arm and held fast. "Don't do that," came his voice. "Just wait."

Trying to twist out of his grip, she realized she couldn't breathe. To her horror, her eyes filled with tears. *Don't do it, don't!* she scolded herself. *It's bad enough that you threw yourself at him like a damn fool, don't cry on top of it.*

Blinking furiously, she perched on the edge of the bed, but kept her back to him, willing for her control to return, for her lungs to unclench.

"Phaira, what's going on?"

She stared at the glimmer of the window across the room, wishing she could leap through it.

"Phaira, come on."

"Emir flatlined," she finally said, brushing her sleeve over her cheek to absorb any last trace of evidence. "He's in a coma. They don't know if he'll wake up."

"What about you?"

"Me? I'm fine," Phaira muttered, fiddling with the neckline of her shirt. "I got overwhelmed, that's all. It's nothing." The last thing she wanted was to talk about her stupid ongoing grief about Nox, her hopeless father, her sickly mother. It was all too humiliating. "It doesn't matter. I'm leaving. Sorry for..."

She couldn't finish the sentence. "Sorry," she repeated, moving to stand up, burning for just one little hit of meka, just one hit, to forget any of this ever happened.

But his hand remained around her arm. "Turn around."

She shook her head. Her hair brushed her shoulders, the only sound in the room.

"It's been a really long time since... you just surprised me, is all."

Phaira didn't move.

"But that doesn't mean that I don't... that I haven't thought about..."

Listening to him stammer, she wondered how deeply he blushed. They were both grateful for the dead of night, she suspected, the great equalizer. Even as the blackness swirled, and all she could feel were sparks, and all she could hear was breath, running in and out.

Phaira twisted at the waist, seeking him out. The room was so dark that she could only make out his silhouette, two feet behind her on the bed. Outside, she could hear the wind blowing through construction pipes across the alley, a strange, soothing backdrop. The mattress shifted underneath her. His shadow grew. She could make out his shoulders, the planes of his face. The edges of his warmth hit her skin. She moved into it, closed her eyes, and made a wish.

Don't ask me questions. Don't make me talk. I just want to forget.

* * *

A horn blared three times. Startled, Phaira lifted her head. In the dim light, she could see her surroundings for the first time: the pearl-colored sheets and steel gray comforter, the snow-white carpet, the paintings on the immaculate walls, a walnut desk with a keycard. A proper bedroom, and an expensive one at that.

Dammit. She hadn't meant to fall asleep.

Theron lay on his back next to her, one arm over his head, the other stretched towards her. She stared at his fingers, half-curled on the mattress.

It all came back to her, the swimming darkness, the heightened sensations. Hands under shirts, over faces. A few uncomfortable moments when his long hair got caught underneath her body. But for the most part, their clothes stayed on, until they were overcome with heat and exhaustion. Then they had lain next to each other on the bed, not speaking or touching. Staring in the direction of the ceiling, wrestling with her desire to run and her strange longing to stay, the darkness made Phaira's eyes heavy. All this slowness, it unnerved her. But there was something delicate about these moments, she sensed.

Now a few hours had passed, and it was daybreak. She had to get back to the eleventh floor before he woke up, and things got even more awkward.

It was bizarre to see Theron so clearly. Despite the early hour, he was still striking. She could only imagine how puffy-eyed and messy she must look. It's not fair, she wanted to yell at the universe.

Then he opened his eyes. "You're leaving?"

"I'm going back downstairs."

He nodded. "I should head back North, too. Things to do. People waiting."

A strange weight pushed on her sternum. "You don't have to go yet."

Did I really say that out loud?

"Or at all," she added in a hurry. "You're already so far away. Just disappear. Run away."

Theron smirked, stretching his arms overhead. "I'm a little difficult to hide."

More than anything, she wanted to shut the curtains and press against him. Instead, Phaira curled her body into a tight ball. "You said you wanted to build your own life," she said, a little louder than she meant to. "That you weren't like them."

"You remember that?"

"Yes," Phaira said pointedly. "So why go back?"

"Are you asking me to run? Or to stay in town?"

Flustered, Phaira turned to lie on her stomach, her arms folded underneath her torso, and let her hair swing in front of her face. "I have to take care of Anandi," she told the mattress. "And Emir."

"I'll stay if you ask me to."

His directness made Phaira even more nervous. "Well... do you want me to come back tonight?" she challenged.

"Only if you use the door next time."

Phaira's mouth dropped open. Then she let out a laugh, pushing her hair behind her ears and peering over her shoulder. "Don't kid yourself. You loved it."

"Like I said." She couldn't quite place the expression on his face as he gazed at her. "Long time."

V

Within the hour, Phaira was back on the eleventh floor. When Anandi stirred, and opened her swollen eyes, Phaira was lying next to her, propped on pillows, waiting.

They changed their clothes, and went to check on Emir's condition. No change. Sabik wasn't there; some unknown nurse was monitoring Emir's machines. The old man's face was still rubbery. Phaira stayed in the doorway as Anandi crawled into bed with her father and pressed her face into his shoulder.

Phaira patrolled the floor, took note of any changes in staff, ensured that Anandi ate something, and committed to a full fourteen hours of support, from seven to nine. Then she brought Anandi back to their borrowed bed, locked the door from the inside, and waited for the girl to fall asleep. Sabik had offered sedatives, so it didn't take long.

Though, when the girl finally succumbed, her clenched jaw growing slack, Phaira was overwhelmed with uncertainty. She stared out the window, feeling the pull of that access ladder on the side of the building; she could imagine its rungs, the rusty feel of them under her palms, the cold air on her face.

He might not be there, she reasoned, as she stepped onto the ledge. He could have left.

Or, even worse, the window could be bolted, and the curtain drawn.

No, she determined. *He's there. He's waiting by the window for me. I know it.*

And when she finally made the climb to the fourteen floor, he was holding it open for her.

"Hello," she said, a little shy.

"Hello." His low voice made her skin prickle. She kept her head down as she climbed over the windowsill. Inside, the room wasn't quite as dark as the previous night, some faint light now, more shadows this time.

Her nerves rippled. Instead of stepping down onto the carpet, Phaira settled on the windowsill, her back in the cold air, neither here nor there, just in case. Theron didn't object; he leaned against the wall, next to her.

"You're still here, I see," she said lightly.

"Still here."

"What did you do all day?"

"Slept a bit. Not much else."

Phaira swung her feet, her heels lightly tapping the wall. Then she glanced into the room again. "What is this place, anyways?"

"Safehouse," Theron said. Then he shrugged. "I broke in," he added, a little sheepishly.

"Will you get in trouble?"

Theron shrugged again. "Doubt it. Don't care."

He pushed off the wall and stood in front of her. His fingertips touched her knees, and his hands began to lightly slide up her thighs. "Is this okay?"

Tiny, pleasant ripples coursed through her body. "Are you asking for permission?"

"I keep thinking you're going to put me in an armbar or something."

That made her smile. "Maybe I should," Phaira quipped, running her hands down his arms. "Have you been practicing?"

"No." There was a smirk in his voice.

"Bastard," she accused, holding his right wrist, like she might twist it at any moment. "You're asking for it."

The challenge hung in the air. Phaira stared up at the angles of his cheekbones, the light in his eyes, the curve of his ear, drawn in shadows and dark lines. The whole situation was so surreal, and wicked, that Phaira couldn't help but grin.

"I'm so glad you stayed."

The sound of her voice surprised her.

Him, too, by the look on his face.

So Phaira kissed him before he could make any comment.

* * *

Over the next week, a routine was established. Phaira roamed the hallways of the eleventh floor during the day. Emir had finally stabilized, enough for the procedure to resume. Anandi spent her days at her father's bedside, her fear and paranoia spilling over to Phaira when they met for meals. Even Dr. Sabik pulled Phaira aside, warning her of all the possible outcomes, doom in every word, as if she were Emir's daughter and needed to prepare for the worst.

When the night came, and Anandi slept, it was a relief to scale the ladder to the fourteenth floor. The window was always open a crack, and Theron was always there, waiting on the other side for her.

And any prior hesitation was long gone. On the third night, Theron picked a surprised Phaira up from the windowsill, drew her legs around his waist and pressed her to the wall, pulling at her scrubs. He kept saying her name between breaths. It made her feel powerful. She loved having such an impact on him; she loved how lean he was, strong shoulders and hard arms; how they both preferred the window open, so the rush of cold air mixed with hot skin.

On the fourth night, when they lay entwined on the floor, burned up and drifting, Phaira's eyes suddenly filled with tears. *What are you doing? Stop crying!* she scolded herself, mortified. *What is the matter with you? Why are you thinking about all that now?*

"Are you okay?"

She could tell him to mind his own business. She could stroke his ego and say that the tears were happy ones.

"My father died," she finally muttered. "Two weeks ago."

Theron said nothing. Phaira was temped to lift her head, to try and make out the expression on his face in the night. Instead she closed her eyes, pushing down the emotion in her chest.

"What happened?"

"He had a lot of problems. I don't know why I'm even thinking about it right now. Way too old to get emotional about your parents, right?"

"No. I still think about my parents. I still feel...untethered... with them not in the world. You know?"

Of course, she remembered. His parents were killed when he was a child. At least she had Renzo and Cohen to cling to. He had no one but his awful cousins.

Still, the darkness, his confession, it made her want to keep talking. "The last time I saw him was about five years ago. He showed up at my apartment, angry about something. Kept trying to hit me. Called me a hundred horrible names. It was almost worse than being hit. That probably sounds strange."

"No, I get that," came his quiet reply. "I've been on the receiving end, too."

She waited for him to continue. But he said nothing more, and she was relieved to sink into him, to take comfort from being held, to feel his chest rise and fall under her cheek. Maybe he drew comfort from her presence, too. She could never quite tell what he was thinking. But that was fine.

I don't really want to know, she reasoned. *I want only moments, for as long as the moons are up.*

* * *

As Phaira slipped her shirt back on, the dawn just breaking over the horizon, her mind turned to the eleventh floor, where Anandi slept. The girl was suspicious. Phaira had caught her staring, her mouth tight and worried. A few times, she went to ask Phaira something, but lost her nerve.

She thinks I'm sneaking out at night to get high.

Oddly, she hadn't thought about mekaline once since that first night. It was too bad that Anandi was worried, but Phaira wasn't about to confess anything.

She looked over her shoulder, seeking out Theron's shape in the darkness. How she loved flustering him, instigating him. And he was changing, little by little, letting go more and more, surprising her at every turn. No, she wasn't stopping her nights, not as long as they were in Liera. She didn't care what anyone thought.

Theron slid towards the edge of the bed, unfolding his long legs to the floor. Phaira gestured at her medical scrubs. "I'm almost getting used to these," she quipped. "Maybe I should go into medicine."

Theron gave her a faint half-smile.

He's sad to see me go, she realized.

So Phaira came between his knees, ran her thumbs along his jawline and slid her fingertips into his cool, silky hair. She'd never been with a man with long hair before; it was oddly appealing, the feel and weight of it. She did it again, taking in the sensations: the sound of his exhale; the pressure of his palms stacked on the small of her back; his chest pressed against her stomach.

She was oddly sad too, leaving him alone. Maybe he wasn't alone, though. Maybe he conducted business deals, or arranged crimes, or solicited other women's attentions. Anything was possible.

"What do you do all day?" Phaira asked him. "Not here," she quickly corrected. "Back home. What's your job in the syndicate?"

"Caretaker," Theron said. "I stay with my grandfather. He's been ill a lot. I take him to meetings, and appointments, mostly."

"Do you like him?" She remembered back to the party on Honorwell, how the grandfather reacted when she took Theron hostage.

"I respect him."

Phaira made a face. "That means nothing."

"It means a lot," Theron said. "He raised me. He was lousy at it, but I had a home, at least."

"He was tough on you?"

Theron smirked. "Compared to my cousins, I'm a pretty big disappointment." Then he shrugged. "I was a small kid: sickly, sensitive, pretty ugly. He preferred Keller and the others. Much better fit for the family name."

"I can't imagine growing up with those three," Phaira said. She didn't know much about Kadise, Xanto and Keller Sava, but she'd heard enough stories. And of course, Phaira recalled with a pinch, she was the reason that Kadise Sava was dead, throwing a knife into the woman's chest while rescuing Emir.

"Can't say I'm sad that they're gone." Theron went quiet for a few moments. "Might have been better for the future, though, if they were still alive."

She had to ask him. "Are you really going to take over the syndicate?"

Theron shrugged again. "I don't know what's going to happen when my grandfather dies."

Phaira stared at the crown of his head. *Then run,* her thoughts insisted. *Why don't you just run? So what if your grandfather raised you? You don't owe him your life. You don't owe any of them. Leave the country. Start over somewhere else.*

But I don't want him to go away.

Phaira pushed down the tiny complaint at the back of her mind. *It doesn't matter what I want,* she told herself. *This is a fling. It'll be done any day now, when Emir has recovered. Or when Theron is called back. Stop acting like a stupid schoolgirl.*

"I bet you were cute." An awkward thing to announce, but it was the only thing she could think to say that was light enough to break the mood. "When you were a kid. And even if you weren't, look at you now. Not bad at all."

That seemed to work. Theron chuckled. "Still pretty rough to look at."

"Yes, it's been a real hardship to sleep with you."

His arms tightened around her back. His warmth grew hot, pressed through her shirt. She was flipped sideways with longing, deep in her gut, as his mouth drifted across her collarbones, just above the neckline of her scrubs.

Stay light, she told herself. *Stay on the surface. This is coming to an end.*

* * *

On the seventh night, Phaira was in bed, curled next to Theron, drifting to sleep when she felt the mattress jump.

Theron was shuddering next to her, quick little jerks, his body alive with electricity.

"Theron?" Phaira whispered, tapping his face.

The seizure continued. Frightened, she pulled the bed sheet off and forced herself to focus on his breathing. If it lasted longer than three minutes, she would go back to the eleventh floor medlab and find Dr. Sabik.

Thirty seconds.

She clenched her fists and released them, again and again. The urge to hold him down was agonizing.

Sixty seconds.

Then the motions began to slow. Theron took in big gulps of air, his forehead slick with sweat. It took several minutes for the man to regain his senses. When his blinking slowed, and his pupils focused, he turned away from her.

"Stop," Phaira said over his shoulder. "It's okay. Sixty-five seconds."

"You counted?" He sounded mortified.

"Yes. I read about what to do."

"Why would you do that?"

"Because it was scary last time," Phaira admitted. Theron suffered a seizure in front of her, after bounty hunters broke in and destroyed his estate. "I'd never seen one before. I wanted to understand it."

He mumbled something inaudible, one hand covering his face. His shame made Phaira fidgety; her impulse was to make up some excuse and get out of that room. She forced herself to be still and wait, curling her toes under the sheet.

"Will you do something for me?" The strain in his voice was gone, replaced by fatigue. "Tell me what happened in Kings?"

Images swam through Phaira's head: options, threats, possible outcomes. "Is it for your grandfather?"

Theron let out a low huff through his fingers. "He's forbidden any mention of Keller, Xanto and Kadise. I don't think he much cares for the details." His hand fell away. "I just want to know what happened in there."

Now Phaira really wished she had left. "I don't know if I should," she finally admitted.

"Why?" The word was clipped.

I don't know what you'll do with the information.

But she didn't need to say it. "You don't trust me?" he accused.

"I wasn't the only one there, remember?" Phaira retorted. "It's not just about me. You've got to understand - I don't know what to say yet. To anyone."

Theron said nothing.

"How much do you know?" she finally asked, when the quiet grew too awkward.

"Just the death toll. Did you see what happened with all those mercenaries? Why they all died in the canyon?"

"I saw a bit," Phaira admitted. "From a distance. I blacked out after I was shot. I don't know why they turned on each other like that."

"I was sorry to hear that Nox didn't make it."

Phaira held her deafening guilt in check.

"Did you see Keller?" he asked her.

"Only briefly, running around the base. And then at the very end, when he was already dead."

"He wasn't crushed by the collapse, then?"

"No," Phaira said. "I don't know what happened to him." That was true enough. She didn't understand one iota of what happened in Kings, when the bright white light engulfed the world. But despite her fear of Sydel's power, she wasn't willing to expose the girl yet.

"What about Huma?"

That part, Phaira was glad to share. "Oh, you should have seen it," she whispered. "I stopped her without the HALO on, if you can believe it."

"I believe it."

Thrilled, she shifted closer to him, eager to tell him more.

The sharp rapping at the door made them both jump.

Phaira rolled onto her hands and knees. Theron was already on his feet.

Then the sound of a drill made the walls shake.

Phaira was already half out of the window. When she turned to make sure he was behind her, Theron's arms were around her.

"What are you doing?" she hissed, struggling to pull away. "Come on!"

But then his hands were on either side of her face, his forehead pressed to hers, amid the rattling of the door.

Run, her mind screamed. *He made his choice. Run.*

Phaira broke away and vaulted over the windowsill into the early morning wind.

There was a crash behind her. As she hung onto the building's ledge, shouts filled the room inside. She held her breath, waiting for the rattle of gunfire.

Instead, she heard Theron's angry voice. "Who the hell gave you this location? You disrespectful -"

"We apologize, sir," came a man's meek response. "But your medical alert went off, and if there is no response at the door, we are required to ensure your wellbeing."

Theron's seizure. He had some kind of sensor on him that alerted his grandfather when he had an incident. How humiliating, to be tracked like that.

"Don't touch me." Theron's sharp voice came through the window.

"Sir, the patrol is incoming," came a second man's voice, apologetic. "They're headed to this location on some arrest warrant. Please, down the back steps. We have a transport waiting to take you home."

Arrest warrant.

Phaira's heart dropped, fourteen floors to street level.

She pulled herself up, sliding over to the service ladder. The local patrol was coming for Anandi, Emir, and very likely her. They had minutes, if they were lucky.

Phaira slid down the ladder, the metal squeaking under her bare hands and feet. The window to Anandi's suite was still open, but the room was empty. She quickly dressed in the pair of scrubs left balled on the floor. There was a small drawstring back of toiletries in the bathroom; she dumped out all the bottles and slid her Calises inside, slinging it over her back.

The corridor was empty, and silent. Hopefully, both Anandi and Sabik were in the room with Emir. The elevator had an access panel to the right of the doors. Phaira popped it open and short-circuited the wiring. Several floors above, she heard the elevator stop with a loud shudder and bang. Then she laid her Lissome two feet in front of the doors, projected a sensor from wall to wall, and set an alarm to go off if the stream was interrupted.

Next, she ducked into one of the storage closets. Nothing conventional for conflict, but options at least, and her second line of defense. The drawstring bag was filled with rubber tubing, suture kits, and syringes filled with sedatives. A stack of x-ray aprons were on a shelf. Would they stop a bullet? No, they were lead-based, if she remembered correctly, but it could provide a decent layer of protection. So she took a scalpel, and cut until the bulky square became a slim rectangle. Then she bound her torso with it, underneath her scrubs.

Sabik and Anandi both jumped as Phaira burst into the room. "Patrol incoming," she told them, first pointing at Sabik. "Destroy any documents you have on these two. Then back here. No calls outside."

Sabik shrank back. For a moment, she wondered if she would have to knock him out, but he finally darted out of the room. She heard shredders whirring within moments.

Anandi was gripping Emir's unconscious hand. She dropped it when Phaira tossed a CHROMA at her. It was already set to dark blue, 12-hours, the maximum time for the temporary hair color application. "Do it," Phaira told her. "And then use this if anyone stops you." She pushed her forged identification packet into Anandi's hands. "Memorize it. You can't hesitate if they ask you questions."

"You're coming with us," Anandi gasped "Don't leave us behind, Phaira, please."

"I'm not leaving. But you have to be ready to go without me."

Sabik re-entered the room, his coat and hat in hand, like he was about to go home for dinner.

"Is Emir stable enough to be moved?" Phaira asked. A swishing sound filled the room, and she glanced back at Anandi. The CHROMA worked, the girl's hair was the same deep blue as Phaira's. The photo in the ID packet was just blurry enough to mask distinguishing features, so she could pass.

"It's very risky," Sabik said. "But if Anandi helps -"

"Her name is Ikani Mala now, got that?"

"She's - what?" the doctor sputtered.

Phaira took the CHROMA and strode out of the room. As she headed back down the corridor, she changed the setting to a deep auburn, 12-hour period. When she slid it over her hair, the strands swung back a deep chestnut. Then she slipped a medical mask over the lower part of her face. The black make-up around her eyes was a give-away, but on first glance, someone might just chalk it up to exhaustion.

An alarm went off. But the Lissome's stream in front of the elevaror was unbroken. No, this was building-wide: lockdown. But if the Savas had an exit, even with the lockdown, there had to be a bypass, and she had a feeling Sabik knew about it.

Anandi and Sabik wheeled Emir out in a wheelchair. The older man was slumped into his chest. Sabik held an intravenous bag, sweating visibly. Anandi's hair was up in a weird facsimile of Phaira's.

"I know there's a secret exit out of this building," Phaira barked at Sabik. "Where is it?"

"Through my office," the doctor said after a long, shocked pause. "There's a concealed stairwell. Years ago, it was used by mobsters to smuggle...."

"It's still being used," Phaira corrected. "And I doubt it's in the building schematics. So, that's our best option."

"How do you know that?" Anandi exclaimed.

"No time. Let's move."

Sabik locked his office door. Then he fumbled for something under the edge of his desk, finally emerging with a key. Underneath the wallpaper in the corner, along the seam, there was a series of metallic rings, some kind of antique design feature. On closer look, however, one of the loops contained a keyhole.

The door swung open with a creak. On the other side, the wood and dust and stone made Phaira close to sneezing. She peered down, blinking to adjust her vision. A coiling suspension stairwell, buoyed by random beams and wires. Rickety, and she couldn't see the bottom. And they'd have to carry the wheelchair. Her brain flashed with a prophecy: something snapping, that sickening dip and all four of them plunging to blackness.

"Go ahead of us," Phaira ordered Anandi. "The building's in lockdown, and the exit here might be too. If it is, you'll have to bypass it."

To Sabik, she gestured to the wheelchair handles. "I can lift most of it, if you can keep me balanced up top."

As Anandi ran down the stairs, Phaira and Sabik began the task of carrying Emir in the wheelchair, descending one careful step at a time. The stairs creaked and shimmied with their weight. The slow process made Phaira feel close to crazy. Emir wasn't a light man, and in a wheelchair he was even heavier. Sabik wasn't much help, twisting to look at every sound.

When they reached the tenth-floor landing, an alarm sounded above. Someone had stepped into her Lissome's stream.

"Quicker," Phaira whispered, heaving the wheelchair base onto her shoulder, wincing with pain as she went to step down from the platform.

"Phaira." The counter-whisper shocked her.

It was Emir: awake, blinking with confusion. When she went to shush him, he shook his head. With trembling fingers, he unbuckled his safety belt. "If you help me," he wheezed. "I can walk."

Sabik went to argue, but Emir was already out of his seat, and slung onto Phaira's back, his arms around her neck. Sabik hooked the intravenous bag to the back of Emir's waistband and left the wheelchair on the landing.

They flew down the staircase, much faster now, even with Emir's dragging feet. The structure now swayed freely side to side. Phaira held onto the older man's wrists and focused on maintaining her balance with each step.

Within minutes, they were on the first floor, Phaira thanking the gods for solid stone foundations. Anandi was already working on the bypass, having popped open the panel by the door. The sound of sirens filtered through the walls, but the patrol was far away, on the other side of the building. If they were lucky, the patrol would stay there just long enough....

A familiar creak echoed down the stairwell.

Anandi let out a strangled cry. With effort, Phaira removed Emir's hands and transferred him to Sabik's waiting shoulder. "Get as far away as possible," she told him. "No calls. If you're stopped, Ikani has identification, let her do the talking."

"Don't leave us, Phaira, please!" Anandi whispered. "I can't do this!"

"And Emir was going to sacrifice himself for you," Phaira interrupted her pleas. "When he recovered, when the law finally caught up to you, he was going to go to jail in your place."

"What?" Anandi gasped.

Phaira ignored her and handed her one of the Calis pistols. The other one went to Sabik. "Do not lose these," she ordered the two. "And don't try to fire them, the recoil will dislocate your shoulder. Just for effect, got it? And only if it's necessary."

And back to Anandi: "No more sniveling. Take the lead and save your father."

Mouth trembling, Anandi made the final electric link. The door popped open. Sabik pushed through, hoisting Emir into the sunlight. Anandi followed.

Phaira slammed the door shut. The sound of footsteps, clomping down the stairwell, grew louder.

Ren, Co, she thought. *I'm sorry.*

"You down there! Hands on your head and turn around!"

Phaira shut off the breaker. The stairwell was plunged into blackness.

As shouts echoed off the walls, beams of flashlight broke through the dark, a mad flurry of movement. Using her senses, Phaira began to climb up the underside of the staircase, the wires cutting into her palms, moving up one flight, and then another. When she hit the third-floor landing, she held on with one hand, drew out a syringe from the drawstring bag with the other. She used her teeth to remove the rubber cap. Then she waited.

At the first swish of movement by her head, she drove the needle into the officer's calf muscle. The punctured officer cried out and stumbled down the last few steps so he crashed into the door, already weakened from the paralytic. The second officer hollered with surprise, his pistol over the railing, searching for her. His flashlight saw nothing but floating dust.

She was already on the other side of the staircase, swinging up, rubber tubing in hand, snapping the officer in the eye. When his head ricocheted and his hands flew to his face, she drove a fist into his gut. When his hands lowered, she cracked an elbow across his jaw, sending the officer skidding down the steps.

A crackle, a flash of blue, and a sudden hard pinch on her ribs. Phaira stared down at the shockround cables buried in her makeshift armor underneath her scrub top. The officer holding the shockround looked down and back up at Phaira. The crackling stopped, and Phaira yanked on the cables, sending the officer tumbling down the stairs.

She sprinted up the stairs two at a time. This was a game. Could she make it back to Sabik's office?

Two flights left, then one.

The eleventh floor again.

She made it. She won.

The door opened from the other side. Ducking into Sabik's office, Phaira ripped off her medical mask. The air felt fresh against her mouth, cold in her nostrils.

Then the officers tackled her from behind.

VI

Clink, clink, clink. Phaira rapped her handcuffs on the edge of the table in a steady rhythm. She licked the edge of her split lip. Still some blood. Her eye was swelling up too.

Detective Ozias settled into her seat. She was a broad, stern-looking woman, clad in expensive greys and blues. She had come all the way in from Daro, Phaira overheard the clerks whispering.

"You're in a lot of trouble, miss," the detective began.

Phaira made a face. "Don't patronize me."

"I'll do what I like," Ozias shot back. "You assaulted officers of the law."

"If they were officers, they never identified themselves," Phaira pointed out. "All I saw were a bunch of men attacking me in a stairwell. I can legally defend myself from mortal harm."

"Oh, is that so?" Ozias remarked. "You were well-prepared for your attack. Your get-up was interesting. Pretty creative, actually. And the man stated that they had a warrant -"

"Anyone can say that," Phaira countered. "I never heard the words 'law' or 'patrol.'"

Ozias gazed at her. The woman had a way of studying Phaira without blinking. She could practically see the gears in her head turning, notes written and stored in her brain.

Then Ozias leaned back in her chair. "It's a curious incident, this one. None of those officers received life-threatening injuries. Every move you made was to disarm and subdue. I get the sense that you could kill your way out of this precinct if you wanted to."

Phaira kept up the clinking rhythm of her handcuffs.

"Funny," Ozias continued, tapping one finger on the table. "When Anandi and Emir Ajyo were first placed under arrest in Honorwell, there was some talk about a blue-haired woman who helped them to escape. I should say, there was, initially, before everyone involved had a sudden lapse in memory."

Theron wasn't kidding, Phaira thought. *He did buy those officers' silence. That's not helping me now, though.*

"And then we send agents to retrieve the Ajyos in another location, and lo, there's another woman in their vicinity, shielding them from arrest."

Her eyes flicked up to Phaira's hair, still chestnut-colored from the CHROMA application. "Wrong hair color, of course," she added wryly.

Phaira refused to blink.

"Do you know what my main case is right now?" the woman continued. "Kings Canyon massacre. You've heard of what happened there. You might have seen my bulletin, asking for the public's help."

"Everyone knows," Phaira said. "And no, I missed that update."

"Well, more than anyone, I want to know what happened in there to all those people. That's why I reached out to the public. And why I'm talking to you now."

Phaira forced herself to breathe normally. *Cohen. Sydel. So many people who will be exposed if I'm not careful. I can't give a thing away.*

"Within hours, there were rumors about some woman who waged some guerilla operation to extract hostages," Ozias continued. "Considered highly dangerous. The same incident that Emir Ajyo was supposedly involved with -"

"If I'm some professional mercenary, as you seem to think I am," Phaira interrupted. "You know I'll say nothing. You might as well take me back to holding."

"Even in exchange for immunity?" Ozias offered. "Even if it was self-defense, you still did some damage to those officers in Liera. Assault charges carry jail time."

Ozias splayed open her hands on the table. "But if you can provide some information about Kings, I'll drop the charges. And really, a service was done in ridding the world of those Savas and mercenaries."

She sure talked a lot. And she sounded genuine, in a strange way. But it also sounded like she was weaving a very careful web to edge Phaira into compliance.

There was a knock at the door. Ozias called out: "What?"

"Lawyer's here."

Ozias frowned. "Public defender?"

"No, ma'am." The voice was strained.

Ozias shot a look at Phaira as the door opened.

There was a woman on the other side of it: strikingly pretty, with wavy blonde hair and straight brown eyebrows. The scent of white peach and plum filled the room. She wore an expensive leather skirt and crisp purple jacket, and as she entered, she raised a hand that glittered with gold.

"No more questions," the woman announced. "I'm Jetsun, legal counsel. I hope you were smart and stayed quiet, Ms. Phaira."

"Phaira," Ozias exclaimed, both annoyed and jubilant at the revelation. "You are Phaira Lore."

Phaira shot the blonde woman a look. Jetsun ignored it and laid a hand on Phaira's shoulder. "This is a waste of time, and you know it, detective. So, let's work this out so we can all go home."

"You're not doing anything, lady," Phaira retorted, shifting away from those manicured nails. "I don't know you, and I didn't hire you."

"No, a friend sent me," Jetsun said, catching Phaira's eyes with her own.

They were the color of amber.

Phaira was speechless. Ozias seemed to make the same connection, strangely enough. When she spoke, she sounded disappointed. "You're one of them."

It wasn't clear whom the comment was addressed to. But the meaning was clear to Phaira. Theron sent this woman to the precinct, another cousin in the line of

Savas. And now Ozias believed that Phaira was part of the syndicate.

"No." Phaira slid her chair away from the blonde woman. "I don't want her. I don't want her here."

"Don't be ridiculous," Jetsun said pleasantly. "Do you want to be sent to prison?"

"Thanks, but no thanks," Phaira cut her off. "Tell your boss that the concern is appreciated, but respectfully declined."

Ozias turned back to Jetsun, who was working to contain her indignation. "You heard her," she ordered. "Get out."

"She's traumatized. Not in her right mind," Jetsun said with a tight smile. "I'm going to make a call, and then we'll revisit this conversation. Please keep to pleasantries until I return."

The woman swept out of the room, her high-heeled boots clicking on the linoleum floor. Both Phaira and Ozias watched her go. When the door slammed shut, Phaira shifted towards Ozias, her handcuffed wrists clanging on the table.

"I'm not part of the Savas," she announced in a rush. It seemed crucial to say the words outloud.

"They seem to think you are," Ozias said. "They don't send in lawyers to shield just anyone."

"It's complicated. But I don't work for them. Write that down," Phaira instructed, tapping her finger on the table.

"Then you'd better figure out what to say to that woman when she gets back," Ozias warned, like a friend advising another. "Those people don't like to be told no. Or be embarrassed in public."

Like at Anandi's party, Phaira thought, remembering the look on the grandfather's face. *They don't forget.*

Another knock on the door. Phaira braced herself as Ozias leaned back to bark, "What?"

As the door opened, the light highlighted the officer's dark skin.

The same skin, the same build, the same outfit and face as Detective Ozias.

Phaira recoiled. Was she losing her mind from grief and guilt?

Ozias leapt out of her seat with a shout. The other Ozias was quicker though, palming the detective's face and shoving her into the wall. Ozias twitched, her hands slapping against the brick. Then the detective slumped to the floor.

And an icy cold sensation started in the back of Phaira's skull.

No. No!

Phaira stumbled back into the corner of the cell, fumbling with the handcuffs, desperately trying to wrench them off.

Not again. Not again.

But the icy spread cupped the back of her head, like a dead lover's caress.

Feel the fear, she reminded herself. *Feel the fear.*

In response, her heart exploded in a scattered, dangerous rhythm. White spots danced in front of her vision. The adrenaline rush made her lightheaded. But the ice receded.

Then the white spots changed to black.

Her heart began to slow. Her lungs constricted.

Suddenly, her foot lifted, and she was walking with her arms in front of her. She couldn't stop, and she couldn't lower her arms, as yanked by the wrists by a rope.

"How funny," the fake Ozias said as Phaira stumbled closer. Her voice was deep and raspy. "Look who we have here. The blue-haired girl. You're Phaira. You were his friend, even his lover a couple of times. You were inside Kings Canyon with him. He even went back for you, before the collapse."

"What?" Phaira gasped. "Who are you?"

Ozias's face shimmered. The skin lightened, and the features twisted. The hair lightened to red. Freckles appeared. Phaira's throat ballooned from holding all her screams. It was Nox's face, Nox's eyes looking into her. Horrified, Phaira fought the urge to vomit, though the control over her body was so acute, she didn't even know if she could.

The rough voice continued. "You should know, Phaira: he was well on his way to dying when I found him. He wasn't afraid. Would you like to know his final thoughts?"

Nox's hands lay on her upper arms, his thumbs stroking the skin, as if to soothe. Then one hand lifted to touch her right temple. Phaira couldn't move, or even blink. But she could protect herself, just like Sydel taught her. Feel the fear. Feel the fear. The adrenaline was the key. It had to work.

The fake Nox frowned, tapping the center of her forehead. "She's got a nice little Eko barrier," he muttered, seemingly to himself. "How far do I push?"

His grip tightened on her arms. "She knows where they are. Just a little extra effort to bypass, and -"

Phaira made her body quake. She forced choking noises from her throat, like she was suffocating, throwing her head back.

Nox stopped talking. Some of the black spots in Phaira's vision cleared. Her muscles stopped spasming; they were still hardened, but working. Just enough to grant her some mobility.

Her arms shot out to smash the fake Nox in the nose with the heel of her hands. Even using all her strength, she only managed a moderate blow. But it was enough to make Nox reel, drop his focus, and release her body from his control.

Roaring, Phaira swung her bound arms in an arc, catching Nox across the cheekbone. When he stumbled, she smashed him again in the temple, and then again as he dropped to the ground, adding a stomp to his ribs for good measure. The replica's eyes bugged out as he drew in a sharp, startled breath. She didn't stay to hear the exhale, bolting for the door.

An angry shout behind her. Ozias had woken up. The sounds of struggling followed Phaira down the corridor as she sprinted, searching for a door, a window, anything that might lead her to the outside. She could hardly run straight, knocking into the wall a few times in the process as she lost her balance. Someone tried to stop her, a blur of grey and blue, but the blur was on the floor in two seconds, and she was leaping over him.

Another blur in front her: yellow and purple, hissing a stream of words: "What are you doing? Get back in there!"

Phaira grabbed Jetsun Sava by the lapels of her plum jacket. "Get me out of here," she begged, her teeth chattering. "Now. Please."

Jetsun glanced over Phaira's shoulder. As every second passed, Phaira fought the urge to knock this woman over and sprint for any sign of a door.

"I'm assuming there's a mortal threat in there, which is why I had to take you into my legal custody," Jetsun finally said. "Correct?"

"Whatever you say," Phaira shot back. It was the lesser of two evils. She could explain it later. Every cell in her body was on fire, waiting for that rope, that sickening pull. "Please. Take me out of here."

"Fine," Jetsun finally muttered, taking hold of Phaira's handcuffs. "Head down. No more talking. Just run."

PART THREE

I.

CaLarca lay awake, staring at the ceiling. Specks of dust fell from the rafters, highlighted by the two moons. Following her cardiac arrest on the *Arazura*, she couldn't stay awake for more than an hour, her only view through the tiny attic window, slate-grey sky, and the rocks of Toomba.

She was in the Cyan Mountain range, several hundred kilometers south from where she was first found by Sydel and Renzo. But Toomba was far above ground level, CaLarca could tell. The thin air made her woozy, and she dreamed constantly of her husband and son, screaming for her, running away, and the world engulfed in fire.

When she first awoke on the *Arazura*, disoriented, terrified, and in violent pain, she managed to get her hands on a Lissome, and punched in the cc for home. But there was nothing. And when CaLarca punched in her farm's coordinates, there were only rubble and scorch marks in the satellite images. An all-consuming fire. Her husband, Ganasan, reported dead. Her tiny, shining son, Bennet, swallowed into the abyss. They haunted her sleep, disappeared from every room she entered, hovered in the rafters of the attic.

The Nadi was building in her again. The energy scorched her palms, twisted up her insides. For years, she'd relied on her physicality to keep it in check. Now, in the brief moments she was awake, everything was on fire. She spent every agonizing moment trying to manifest the rolling Nadi into something, anything. So many times, she was on the brink of just letting the Nadi consume her. It would be painful, but it would all be over. What reason did she have to stay alive?

No. I have to get back there. I have to walk again. I have to find them. I have to know for certain.

So, in the darkness of the attic, CaLarca made knives, over and over again: blackened, malformed switchlades, melted down one side.

And every manifestation built another layer for revenge.

* * *

The stench of alcohol made her nose hurt. CaLarca opened her eyes, and swallowed her gasp.

Sydel stood by the window. Her fingers trailed the exposed wooden frame of the wall. The hyperwhite moon lit her profile. Underneath her hood, the girl's cheeks were bright pink.

Blinking, CaLarca struggled to sit up on her elbows. When the thick quilt fell from her shoulders, she shivered. This place was so cold and damp, she never felt warm, even in the daytime. "Come over here," she croaked.

Sydel sat on the edge of the mattress, plucking at the fabric of the heavy wool jacket she wore, weaving back and forth. "We should just leave. Shouldn't we." It was a flat statement, mumbled in her soft, girlish voice. "It's wrong of me to stay with them. Dangerous. And confusing. They can't really understand."

Was she serious, or dead drunk? She had to be careful with her words. CaLarca always felt like someone was listening in this place; everything echoed here, surrounded by rocks and reverberations.

Then she caught sight of the girl's head. Sydel had taken a pair of scissors to her hair. Great, violent chunks had been taken out, her beautiful, looping braids, gone.

CaLarca checked for any other exposed wounds. Nothing visible.

But was the girl self-destructing?

"If you leave, where will you go?" CaLarca tried.

"Wherever I might belong. Back to Jala Communia, maybe, if Yann will take me back?"

If he's still there, CaLarca thought. *Or alive.* "You don't wish to stay with this family?" she asked lightly. "I thought that you cared very much for them."

"I do. Of course, I do. And Cohen..."

Does she love him? CaLarca wondered, not for the first time. He was certainly infatuated with Sydel. But whether that was love or just male posturing, she wasn't sure.

Sydel's words came out in a fevered rush. "I killed people in Kings. That is why Phaira won't speak to me. Renzo doesn't even know, and Cohen doesn't realize how dangerous I am. I almost killed everyone on the *Arazura* because I couldn't control -"

Her head dropped again. "I'm a monster."

Shame, CaLarca thought, staring at the top of Sydel's head. *I didn't expect that.*

But between her constricted life and the trauma of Kings Canyon, she's vulnerable and open to suggestion. She can help me.

"You need to learn how to control your Nadi," she told the girl. "I can teach you, but there's something more to this." She wet her lips before asking. "Would you allow me to look into your memory?"

Sydel pulled the hood away. Her scraggly, half-shorn hair was exposed as she lowered her head.

CaLarca listened for the sound of footsteps in the night.

Then she dove into Sydel's mind.

Blackness. Then the picture grew clearer: a dome of shadows, and scorch marks, gossamer threads of memory, flickering with light. One hard cluster stood, rigid and thickened, memories that had been worked over too many times, CaLarca realized, abused and severed. *Serious damage has been done, very methodical damage. Was Yann really capable of that kind of manipulation?*

Sydel's voice floated across the landscape. "What did you see?"

CaLarca withdrew, back to the darkness, finally returning to the pale white of the twin moons outside the attic window. Her heart fluttered. She put a hand to her chest, willing it to calm.

"Who has done this to you before?" she demanded. "Who has gone into your mind?"

"No one." Sydel said nervously. "Why? What did you see?"

"Damage," CaLarca said. "Significant damage. Erasure. Memory manipulation."

Sydel grew even paler. "That can't be true," she sputtered. "Who would - why would anyone do that to me?"

"You know who did it, Sydel. Don't be so naïve."

"But he would never -"

"How old are you?"

"Eighteen."

"You know that's not true," CaLarca told her. "I knew you as a babe, twenty-five years ago."

"I know, but -"

"Yann wanted you to regress," CaLarca concluded, leaning back into her pillow, disgusted. "To forget every step of your natural evolvement. And he damaged your brain to do so, instead of seeking out a proper teacher to help you to control your gifts."

Tears dropped onto the girl's thin fingers. CaLarca watched them fall, a strange twist in her stomach. Not sympathy, exactly. Pity. And a little irritation. She didn't have patience for silly sentiment, not anymore. But she did know the mannerisms of motherhood, and now was the time to use them to her advantage.

"It's okay. I'm here now," she soothed. "I will teach you. I can help you grow stronger and more confident of your gifts."

She took hold of Sydel's chin, forcing the girl to look up. "But you must begin to separate yourself from this family. For their own protection. We both must."

Sydel's brown eyes shone. "It will break his heart," she whispered.

She's talking about Cohen, CaLarca realized. *That's disappointing.*

"Yes, it might," CaLarca whispered back. "But we must sacrifice for those we love. To keep them safe."

CaLarca caught the silhouette of the girl's head, nodding.

And when Sydel hugged her, hope sparked, somewhere deep within CaLarca's burning core.

II.

Outside, the sun was setting. The great overhang of the mountain loomed over the village;. Toomba residents lived inside its shelter, protected from the harsh elements by the great rocky walls, with a river running past every door, and gushing over a waterfall, dropping into nothing but fog. To some, perhaps it was beautiful. To CaLarca, it looked bleak and destitute. She shivered, even with her legs covered by a heavy quilt.

Sydel took a seat next to her on a rock, glancing at CaLarca like an anxious child. A hood covered her head, though CaLarca could see short tufts of hair by her hairline.

Twenty feet before them, the brothers sat around a bonfire. They wore the clothes of the townspeople here: heavy wools and knits, patched together, animal furs over their shoulders. Better to blend in, Renzo suggested, and the grandmother, Vyoma, had responded, taking donations from the townspeople to clothe them all. It all smelled of sweat and mothballs.

Now Vyoma was telling a story. As she spoke, the brothers leaned forward. CaLarca watched the grandmother. Steel-gray hair cut in a chin-length bob, the woman was square and sturdy, like she had been in existence for centuries, unmoving from her house in the mountains. Her mind was also stone, her thoughts impossible for CaLarca to catch onto.

"I ran away when I was sixteen to join the armed forces. Served twice now." She spoke pleasantly enough, with a marked edge to her voice. "I'd hoped my daughter might continue the tradition, but it was not to be."

"So that's where Phaira gets it from," Cohen murmured to Renzo, just loud enough for CaLarca to hear. She resisted the urge to snort, huddling deeper into her chair.

"When did you stop speaking to her?" Renzo asked the grandmother.

Vyoma let out a steady stream of breath through pursed lips. "Your father was a good man, but deeply troubled. And they were so young. I disapproved, and they disappeared. So, I let it be."

"And you never tried to find us?" Cohen asked, looking crestfallen.

"I didn't know you existed," Vyoma said. "I only learned of the three of you when I learned of Lora's death. From the moment of Renzo's birth, there was a no-contact order against me."

"You can't just get those kind of orders," Renzo said warily. "There has to be a justifiable reason for one."

"They cited religious persecution."

"That's ridiculous!" Renzo exclaimed. "Neither of them were the least bit religious."

"Agreed. But the order was enforced."

The fire crackled. Bored, CaLarca turned her head. The edge of the *Arazura* peeked out of a cavern. The means to her way home, so close, so untouchable.

When she returned her attention to the fire, something was different. A haze of anger, billowing from the older brother.

When Renzo finally spoke, his words were clipped. "You know how many years we spent in poverty, trying to avoid eviction? Trying to keep Cohen out of government custody? I was left alone, with nothing. With no one. If I'd known you were around..."

"Your father was alive until recently, Renzo, and your legal guardian until Cohen turned nineteen," Vyoma reminded him. "It didn't matter if he abandoned you. The order was still in place."

"We could have gone to the courts. We could have come here, lived with you. Or at least Cohen and Phaira could have." Renzo's voice grew sharper. "If I'd known there was someone, anyone out there -"

"It was not an option," Vyoma interrupted. "There is no use in arguing with me about it. Besides, poverty builds character. Toughens you up."

Both Renzo and CaLarca let out a bark of scorn.

Renzo swiveled to stare at her. But CaLarca only met the sharp eyes of Vyoma. A thousand retorts coursed through her head. *There is no greatness in poverty, you delusional, disrespectful woman. That is a dream to cling to, when caught up in a hopeless situation. A parent would never wish a day of struggle on a child.*

But it doesn't matter what the old woman thinks, she reminded herself.

So CaLarca conceded, lowering her head and breaking eye contact.

It seemed to work. When she glanced up again, Vyoma appeared satisfied, her attention back to her grandsons. Renzo still looked at her, though. CaLarca let the faintest smile show on her face.

Yes, I stood up for you, she confirmed silently. *We are connected. I am the willing scapegoat, so you can remain in good graces. I am the eternal listener and conceder.*

Listen, collect, and stay silent. It was a technique she'd perfected since she was a child, and realized that people were eager to confess to a waiting ear. She could gather a hundred secrets if she showed attentiveness and made all the right noises. In doing so, she earned affection, and more importantly, loyalty. And no one ever seemed to realize that they knew nothing about CaLarca. It suited her fine. She wanted her privacy, and she liked truths, big and little.

CaLarca felt Sydel's gaze on her. Purposefully, CaLarca let a hard shudder go through her body. Sydel stood up quickly. The conversation stopped by the fire. The wind rushed through the canyons, creating a thousand whispery echoes. Cohen rose from his seat and drew closer. Impatient to get back inside, CaLarca hunched into herself, made her appearance weak and pathetic, adding in a few small coughs.

Cohen ignored her. "Can I talk to you?" Cohen asked Sydel, over CaLarca's shoulder. "Please?"

"I need to see to her," came the girl's nervous response. "I've kept her outside for too long. I'm sorry."

The rolling chair jolted, and Cohen swept out of sight. With Sydel pushing, CaLarca passed the fire, Vyoma watching, Renzo looking at the rock floor, a deep furrow on his brow. Soon, Vyoma's house, with its drafty attic peaks, loomed before them. CaLarca exhaled, thinking about her warm bed, and ignoring the sound of sniffles from behind.

* * *

Another week passed.

Renzo ducked into the attic. He held a crate, covered with a flannel blanket, a pair of crutches under his arm. CaLarca pushed her body into a seated position, watching as he set all his items on the table by the window. Underneath the dirty cloth, she caught a glimpse of metal, intricate and twisted, and some kind of black and gray rubbery fabric. Goosebumps rose on her skin. She crossed her arms over her chest.

Sydel appeared at the doorway. "Ren," she breathed. "How wonderful. You did it."

"Of course I did," Renzo said dryly. "Everyone asked so nicely."

"I'm not ready," CaLarca burst out.

Renzo and Sydel turned to stare at her. CaLarca dropped her gaze to the quilt.

"It's the next step," Sydel soothed. "It'll be okay."

Renzo was blunt. "You'll never be ready. But it's time."

Her throat dry, CaLarca glanced at Renzo's right leg, where she knew his prosthetic stood. "Does it ever stop hurting?"

"It hasn't yet," Renzo said. "But it becomes manageable. Then it becomes a part of the background. But you'll do better than I ever will."

"Trust him," Sydel smiled at her. "Believe in him. He's brilliant."

Renzo waved his hand dismissively. "You don't have to trust me," he countered. "Just trust the science."

Renzo's first component was a backbrace, black tentacles to be wrapped around her lower back and sacrum. CaLarca struggled to the edge of the bed, painfully swinging her legs over the edge. Sydel sat behind her, and clicked the device into place. During the process, Renzo averted his gaze, even though CaLarca was fully clothed. An odd sense of decorum. They were all so odd.

When the last fastener held, the whole brace came alive, lifting and compressing her lower back. It felt strange, but something opened up in her chest, her lungs were better able to expand. She felt steadier, stronger.

"Is this all?" Sydel asked over CaLarca's shoulder.

Still looking away, Renzo held out a set of black leggings, made of thick, ribbed material. Confused, CaLarca craned her neck to look inside the crate. It was empty.

"They're leggings," CaLarca said flatly. "You said you would make me braces. What am I supposed to do with these?"

"Yes, I made you leggings in my spare time," Renzo said impatiently, shaking the clothing with his extended hand. "It's a legitimate SCKAFO: stance control knee-ankle-foot orthosis."

CaLarca reached out to take it, but Renzo jerked the material just out of her reach. "Remember the deal," he told her.

CaLarca's mouth dropped. From the gasp behind her, Sydel was also mortified.

"We made a deal," Renzo reminded them both. "Her heroics don't negate the agreement. Appreciated as they were."

This brother was more ruthless than she imagined. In a way, CaLarca felt more respect for him. "What do you want to know?" she asked him demurely.

"What haven't you asked her yet?" Renzo addressed Sydel.

Silence. The SCKAFO shimmered in the light, tempting CaLarca with every turn.

"You spoke of my parents," came Sydel's voice, lower and more forceful than usual. "Who were the others in the NINE?"

CaLarca thought fast. Names. She could give them names. There was nothing out there for them to find.

"Tehmi and Joran were there, yes," she began, gathering each word and checking over them before she spoke.

"Your father figure, Yann Qin. He was slotted into the Eko group. Me, of course."

CaLarca looked at her fingers, four extended. Then she counted: "Shantou and Marette Lyung. Twins, young girls, close to my age. One designated as Nadi, the other as Eko."

CaLarca licked her lips, remembering. "Marette disappeared after Kings. I think Shantou is alive, though I don't know for certain."

"Ganasan Reed. He was categorized as Insynn. That's a precognitive gift," she added. "But I don't know where he is right now." That was an honest answer.

"And two men, Kuri Nimat and Zarek Voss," she finished in a rush. "That was the NINE. May I have the braces now?"

"Those last two the ones who hurt you?" The brother was relentless.

"I don't know," she admitted.

"What does that mean?"

CaLarca ignored Renzo, and twisted at the waist to look at Sydel. "Kuri found me, and asked me to accompany him to Kings, to see to the Sava threat and to your safety. He remained in the shadows when I came to meet you there. But after that, I have no memory. Until you found me."

She made her shoulders tremble. It wasn't difficult to show fear. Sometimes, the feelings seemed real. Maybe since she bore her son, it was easier to tap into vulnerability.

Renzo sighed. "Fine." He extended his arm with the SCKAFO. "Just put them on already."

Sydel took the material and ran her fingers over it. "There's wires in here," she said with wonder.

"I was inspired by the stealthsuit I picked up, when I was building the *Arazura*," Renzo explaining, quickly turning his back again as Sydel helped CaLarca into the leggings. "How the electrical charge stiffens the material. Why not use that technology to provide all-encompassing support, in addition to the bracing aspects?"

"The actual braces are along the seams and around the knees, though you shouldn't feel them," he added over his shoulder. "When you stand on your feet, the mesh activates. Don't worry, you won't be electrocuted, I know you're thinking that. It'll help to control your motion and stabilize your gait. And around the joints, I installed micro-flexors. They'll activate when the footplate senses weight or movement, and lock and unlock the knee at the proper time. Allows for free swing and full-range of motion, eventually."

CaLarca looked down at her legs, now clothed in the grey and black material. They felt tight, but flexible. Was it possible that they would hold her weight? A vision rushed over her - when she tried to stand, her legs would splinter under her.

She gritted her teeth, pushing down her fear. "Will you help?" she asked the other two.

Sydel shifted to CaLarca's side. Her hood fell from her head. When Renzo came to CaLarca's other side, his eyes took in the girl's short, sloppy haircut. Still, he said nothing, and offered his arm to CaLarca.

It took several breaths for her to work up the nerve. Then CaLarca rocked onto her feet for the first time in weeks.

Every inch of her body prepared to collapse. Her knuckles were white, gripping Sydel and Renzo's hands. But though her legs trembled, they held. Her head lifted, higher and higher, and she became taller than Sydel, and only a few inches shorter than Renzo. The room began to spin, delirious, exhilarating.

"Do you need to sit down?" Sydel asked, worry in her voice.

"No," CaLarca said in a rush. Through the window, the sun streaked into the room, lighting up her face, warm for the first time in days. "No. Not yet."

III.

G o slow," Renzo instructed. "Heel to toe. Good."
CaLarca made her way across the rock platform,
gripping her metal crutches, Renzo next to her in case
she fell. Her body whined at her to stop. It was embarass-
ing. She had grown soft in her weeks of immobility, her
shoulders slumped in, her abdomen slack. No wonder she
was burning up with Nadi.

After a few more minutes, she gritted her teeth and
asked to rest. Renzo conceded. She leaned hard on the
crutches to take the weight off her feet, sighing with
relief. Renzo moved to the mountain's edge, his hands
in his pockets, looking over the landscape. She did the
same. Admittedly, now that she was outside every day, in
the daylight, and could actually move, CaLarca admired
the view. The mountains that surrounded them, awash in
gold and orange, snow peaks barely visible through fog,
forests of white birch trees.

There was movement on the adjacent hill, a number
of men and women, trekking through the wilderness.
She recognized one of their faces, heavily bearded now.
The younger brother. He was always roaming with the
hunters, gone from dawn until dusk. She heard he was
good with a sniper rifle, very good in fact. Surprising,
given his size, she wouldn't have assumed he had a delicate touch.

Still, all the better for it, CaLarca thought, watching
the man follow the crowd, a rifle slung across his back.

Cohen just complicated things. She needed Sydel to focus. She could practically taste freedom, and ground-level air.

"You're not ready to pass out, are you?" she heard Renzo quip. "It's a long drop."

"I'm fine," she replied. "Better and better, thanks to your help."

"And Sydel?" The man's voice was sharper now. "Hacking off her hair like that. Sure she's of her right mind?"

Had he heard of Sydel's odd behavior? Last night, CaLarca discovered her in the back of the attic's closet, behind rows of old fur coats, rocking back and forth. It took nearly an hour to coax the girl to go back to her bed. As an afterthought, CaLarca removed everything sharp from the room, a pair of scissors, and a sewing needle stuck into the hem of a donated dress.

"She's young," CaLarca stated, defensive, though she wasn't quite sure why. "And she's been through a lot."

Her mind turned back in time to memories of herself at fourteen. "It's a difficult gift, being a Nadi. She was never trained to contain and control the energy she generates, like I was."

"Nadi. Eko." Renzo scoffed with each term. "Makes no sense. Sounds like you're making it up. But I'm curious, I'll admit that."

He was curious. He was always curious. And generous, in spite of his demeanor. CaLarca studied his profile: classically handsome, sharp cheekbones half-hidden with glasses, blond hair that flopped over his forehead. A new thought occurred to her. What if she could sway the brothers to her side, too? With a ship like the Arazura, with their combined skills, they could track down her family. Maybe she was being too hasty.

"Hand me a branch?" she asked the brother.

Renzo snapped off a twig from the edge of the precipice. CaLarca lowered onto a stone bench, wincing. Then she put her crutches to the side, and with the twig, drew an outline of a human figure in the sand. Down the center of the body, from the brain to the sacrum, she drew two thin lines. Renzo watched the process with a furrowed brow, deepening the wrinkles that already lay there. "That's what, exactly?"

"That's the Nadi channel," CaLarca explained. "It runs through the center of our bodies, opening in the abdominal region and gathering -"

"Uh, no," Renzo corrected. "I've opened up bodies before, and there's no 'channel', CaLarca."

"Energetic channel, Renzo," CaLarca said with exasperation. "I know more about this than you do." Her mind flashed back to Kings, to the diagrams, the pages of study, given to her to read and marvel at.

"Not everything can be explained by science," she added. "I know you understand that, even as you fear the consequences."

Renzo's chin jerked back.

Smirking, she drew delicate nerves, and the outline of muscles around the channel. "If the structure around the channels is strong, the brain impulsively uses them to maintain bodily control." CaLarca pointed to the muscles along the vertical channel. "Like the brakes of a transport." Then she gestured to the nerves. "Or triggering a response to cool and contain, like a mechanism to prevent overheating in an engine."

As she spoke, her mind focused on planning ahead. The sister would be a problem, but she wasn't even there. Renzo was a worthy partner. Cohen had his uses, and he was loyal to Sydel. Maybe they would say yes. Maybe she could fight back with her own group of followers.

She had trailed off in the middle of speaking. Renzo was peering at her.

"Sorry," she apologized, thinking quickly. "My back hurts in this position."

A beeping sound. Renzo pulled his Lissome from his pocket.

His eyes bulged. He looked around wildly, before him, and then behind him.

CaLarca's heart leapt into her throat. "What's wrong?"

"Cohen," he muttered. "Cohen, where is he?"

"He's down there," CaLarca pointed to the trees below. "He was, anyways. But what's wrong?"

Renzo dropped into a crouch. Then he rocked onto his seat, his knees before him. Dust rose from his heels as they slid through the grit and sand. CaLarca saw a glint of silver at the edge of his trouser hem: his prosthetic. The Lissome hung from the tips of his fingers.

"Will you please tell me what's happening? You're scaring me," CaLarca demanded.

"My sister," Renzo muttered, rubbing his bridge of his nose, under his glasses. "She got my message. She's okay."

A wave of panic crashed over CaLarca. "She's coming here?"

"I hope so," Renzo said, staring out into the surrounding mountains. "I hope she can figure it out. I couldn't put any details into the public. Just a note in the network, I wasn't sure if she would pick it up -"

CaLarca wasn't listening anymore. The sister would ruin everything. Phaira had too much influence. Oh, sure, the siblings jockeyed for power, and they argued, but everyone on the *Arazura* looked to Phaira in the end. That woman would never help CaLarca. She'd kick her out and she'd be left with nothing. No support, no money, no Sydel for protection.

She had to convince Sydel to leave before Phaira's return.

* * *

She waited until the end of the training session to tease out the question.

"I've found one of the original NINE. Do you want to meet her?"

"What?" Sydel jumped, falling out of her position. She'd been wobbling in a push-up posture for two minutes to build up her core strength. Now she swung her legs around, staring at CaLarca, who sat in a chair across the room. "Who?"

"Marette." It was odd to say her name after so many years, even stranger to type out the message and send it into the unknown. "One of the twins. The one classified as Nadi."

"Marette." Sydel sounded out the name, as if probing for a memory to attach it to.

"Yes. She's a public figure now, a performer. She responded immediately to my message, though, and asked us to meet her in Zangari. Only a few hours away."

CaLarca paused, letting the words sink in. This was an enormous risk. But CaLarca and Marette got along well when they were younger. There was no bad blood between them, no knowledge of the other's crimes. She was ideal to serve as distraction. Plus, CaLarca couldn't resist the push of curiosity: what did the skinny blonde twin turn into, twenty-five years later?

Then she continued: "This is an opportune time to leave, Sydel. I'm mobile again. You are growing stronger. We can carry on from there, and find our own destiny."

"Leave," Sydel repeated.

"You knew this day was coming," CaLarca reminded her gently. "I know it is difficult."

"Yes," came the girl's voice, strangely flat. "But I know you have my best interests at heart."

A small stab of guilt hit CaLarca. She pushed it aside. "Tomorrow, then."

"Tomorrow."

"And no word to the brothers about this. You know they will try and convince you to change your mind."

"I know."

* * *

That night, CaLarca couldn't sleep. In the dusty attic, she ran through the scenario again and again, checking maps, checking the structure of Renzo's SCKAFO. Strong enough, simple enough. It was just getting out from the hooks of the brothers, any tether that might hook into them and haul them back....

The knock at the door startled her from her thoughts.

"Sydel?" she called. "You don't have to knock."

The door opened. It wasn't Sydel.

CaLarca gasped at the looming shadow, how the man had to duck to enter the room. Her body flooded with defensive Nadi, before she tightened her nerves and forced it back.

Cohen's eyes glittered in the dark. With his new red beard, and the bulky layers of clothing, he looked older and more intimidating than the first time they met, back on the *Arazura*.

CaLarca swallowed before speaking. "What do you want?"

"Will you come?"

His voice was like a rusty hacksaw on wood. He sounds like the rest of these Toomba residents, she thought. They are affecting him, and not for the better.

"With you?" she spoke out loud. "I think not. You -"

"Stop," he growled, the word pushed through his teeth.

Disrespectful thug, she thought, staring hard at him. *I'll be glad to never see you again.*

"It's Sydel," he finally said.

"What?" CaLarca exclaimed. "What's wrong? Where is she?"

"You need to come," Cohen said, ducking through the doorway. "She's acting like - I don't know. Not like herself."

Then he was gone.

What was going on? Why now? CaLarca's body shrieked as she went upright, scrambling for her crutches. As she swung them down the hallway, and fumbled down the narrow staircase, a thousand scenarios raced through her head. Maybe the girl had another uncontrollable Nadi incident, despite all the training and physical strengthening. Or perhaps the brain damage was impacting her, perhaps turning her towards insanity, or hallucinations.

The night air was crisp, the twin moons shining like spotlights. The wind howled as Cohen and CaLarca headed into the center of Toomba, the main cavern where a dozen wooden buildings were housed, protected from the elements. Their footsteps echoed off the walls.

At the end of the path sat the town tavern, radiating music and raucous laughter. As they drew closer, beams of light streamed through the ajar door and windows.

"There?" CaLarca asked, shivering in the cold. "What is she doing in there?"

"What do you think she's doing?" Cohen snapped.

CaLarca held her tongue. When they reached the steps, CaLarca opened an Eko channel, searching for Sydel, hoping she could avoid going inside.

But Sydel's mind was firmly closed.

CaLarca sighed, and swung her crutches up to the platform, preparing to hoist herself up. Cohen remained on the mountain path.

"Aren't you coming in?" she demanded.

"One rejection is enough," Cohen said. But he didn't move from his position. As much as she and the brother despised each other, for Sydel's sake, he would stand watch, she realized, and intervene if needed.

The tavern held ten empty round tables along its left side, the right side packed with bodies along the bar. The harsh overhead lights picked up the glinting bottles, rifles leaning against chairs, men and women laughing, clinking glasses, talking loudly. Through the bodies, CaLarca caught a glimpse of short brown hair, a birdlike neck. She hobbled in that direction. The patrons caught sight of her and made quiet, whooping noises. "Watch out," CaLarca heard someone joke. "Here comes momma."

Then the crowd parted. Sydel was in the center of the table, her face flushed, her hand around a bottle, her hair standing up in tufts. She burned with heat; CaLarca could feel it from across the room.

"Hello," Sydel murmured, propping her chin up with her hands. "You here to lecture me, too?"

"You know this is dangerous," CaLarca said, casting sharp looks to all the patrons, who watched with interest. "What happens if you lose control?"

"If you don't like it, leave."

CaLarca recoiled. Sydel had never spoken to her like that. "You are acting like a sullen, reckless child," she accused.

Sydel shrugged. Her finger traced the edge of her bottle.

Anger simmered in CaLarca's stomach. "You have responsibilities."

"You have responsibilities!" One of the patrons repeated in a high-pitched tone, followed by titters of laughter.

Insensed, CaLarca grabbed Sydel by the upper arm. "Get up," she ordered. "Enough of this."

"Hey, let go!" one of the men exclaimed. Hands clapped on her shoulders. CaLarca tried to throw them off, still gripping Sydel. The girl wasn't fighting back.

In fact, CaLarca realized, Sydel was shaking, as if being electrocuted, her eyes rolling in her head.

Hands yanked her away from Sydel. CaLarca stumbled, desperately swinging her crutches to catch her balance.

Before her, Sydel stopped shaking. Cognizance returned to the girl's red-rimmed eyes, and she whispered, again and again: "What did you do? What did you do to me?"

"Okay, that's enough!" one of the young men announced. "First the giant, and now you. Sydel, how many handlers do you have?" He glared at CaLarca from across the bar. "Get out of here, go back to whatever hole you crawled out of."

More bodies swarmed in front of CaLarca, forcing her backwards. "Freak," she heard in a chorus of whispers, all around her head.

When CaLarca burst through the tavern doors, laughter sounding behind her, Cohen steadied her before she fell down the front steps. And by the look on his face, he understood what had just happened in there.

"She's acting like a fool. I can't believe she said that," CaLarca muttered, more to herself than the brother. "Why would she talk to me like that? Why would she even want to be in a place like that?"

A seed of doubt was growing. She just assumed the girl was a little unsteady, but maybe things were deeper than she initially thought.

The brother mumbled something, lost in the chill wind. CaLarca snapped him a look. "What was that?"

"She'd listen to Phaira," he repeated.

Violent jealousy gripped her chest. "Why?"

Cohen shrugged. "I don't know. It's just different with those two."

"How so?"

Cohen shrugged again. "In Kings, Syd got all crazy after the blast, like she couldn't hear me, no matter what I did. Then Phaira comes in, says her name, and Syd wakes up."

"Well, your sister isn't here, and isn't here often, by all accounts," CaLarca countered. "Sydel can't rely on her. None of you can. You know that's true."

Cohen looked stung, but he didn't argue. For a moment, CaLarca felt a hard twinge of guilt. Where was that coming from? What did she care if the brother was hurt? It was true. She looked back at the door to the tavern. The sounds hadn't diminished. It was going to be a long night.

"I'll stay," she told the brother. "I'll sit here until she comes out, and try and get her back to the house."

"Don't bother," Cohen said, striding past, presumably heading back to his grandmother's house. "Do whatever you want. That goes for the both of you."

CaLarca watched the brother's silhouette grow smaller, and finally disappear from sight. Permission to leave, in a way.

Just until morning, she reminded herself, as she painfully lowered herself onto the porch of the tavern, wrapping her cloak around her, her crutches between her knees. Only a few hours. Then flight.

* * *

"You lied."

CaLarca started from her sleep, her head pressed against one of the wooden poles. The sun was rising over the mountains, cold and orange and pink. The tavern was silent now.

Sydel stood before her, half in shadow, her back to the rising sun. Her hair had been smoothed back with water. She wore no cloak, her bare arms exposed to the cold. She didn't seem to notice.

"Did I - what?" CaLarca croaked. Had she heard correctly? Maybe it was part of a dream.

"You lied." The statement was flat.

"About what?" CaLarca deferred, wincing as she tried to straighten her back.

"You're not alone in the world. You have a child, and a husband, and a farm in the South. I saw it in my head."

CaLarca's guts twisted. This wasn't happening. She'd been so careful to conceal her thoughts. How was this possible?

An Insynn rush, she realized. Sydel experienced an Insynn rush. When the girl went stiff, as if electrocuted, her brain received a flash of CaLarca's past. She had seen that physical reaction before. CaLarca stared at Sydel with an equal mixture of wonder and horror. She was developing Insynn abilities too? What more was possible? How powerful could this girl become?

The girl's voice was sharp. "When you went into my mind, what did you do to me? What did you alter? Can you change it back?"

"I didn't -" CaLarca rose to her feet, gripping the head of her cane. When Sydel stepped back, CaLarca lifted a hand. "I'm not trying to hurt you. I'm trying to help you to understand what's happening. What you experienced last night is called Insynn."

"Insynn," the girl repeated.

"Yes," CaLarca said. "It's one of the NINE abilities, triggered by skin-to-skin contact. Usually, the flashes are precognitive, visions of the future, but sometimes they can go back in time."

And in theory, she thought. *A master Insynn can scroll forward to see a person's eventual cause of death.*

But she couldn't tell Sydel that. The girl was already so unstable.

"I don't want it," Sydel said shrilly. "I can't hold that kind of power too. I can hardly manage the Nadi."

Then her expression shifted from desperate to determined. "Burn it out," she ordered. "Go inside my head and burn it out."

"You can't," CaLarca said. "Accept the facts. You've evolved again. You have access to three incredible gifts."

Sydel didn't respond. In the silence, CaLarca shivered, but grew hopeful. Maybe Sydel was actually listening. Maybe she would forget what she thought she saw.

Cold, thin fingers wrapped around CaLarca's arm. "Come with me."

"We need to - we need to go back and prepare to leave," CaLarca reminded her. The words came out shaky. "I meant what I said about forging ahead -"

"We will."

They walked in silence, all the way back to the grandmother's house. No lights glowed in any window. Sydel propelled CaLarca up the stairs, through the door of the attic they shared. The door clicked shut behind them. In the darkness, stumbling for the bed, a flicker of fear sparked in CaLarca.

"I'm tired of waiting." Sydel's soft voice carried through the night. "Tired of begging for the truth. You'll show me what really happened with the NINE ."

"But we -"

"Give me access to every strand. Every memory. Now."

IV.

M r. Asanto was perched on the end of the bed, dressed in clean wool and cashmere, steely-grey hair on a craggy, tanned face. When CaLarca hesitated, the man smiled at her like they were the closest of friends. "Close the door, if you wouldn't mind."

CaLarca looked over her shoulder, at the staircase, and the shadow of her mother on the first floor. She'd never spoken to one of her parents' friends by herself. It felt very wrong. "I'm not sure that I should."

"I only have a question, Cyrah," Mr. Asanto said gently. "But it's private, and I don't think you want people to overhear."

Then he tilted his head. "I use Cyrah, but do you prefer your surname? I've always gotten the sense that you do."

It was true. Cyrah was the wrong name for her, too delicate, too much like a sigh. CaLarca felt straight and true, and when she turned fourteen, she asked her teachers and fellow students to use it.

He saw her thought process, and nodded. "You do, I can see it. Well, CaLarca, I think you can also tell when someone is lying. So what do you think? Am I being honest?"

Her cheeks flushed. Then she closed the door quickly, leaning back against the wood.

The man put his hands to his chest, fingers overlapped. "I think you can do other things, CaLarca. Things that make your parents very nervous. Things they wish they could just hide away." His gaze travelled to her hand. "Can I see?"

CaLarca rubbed the fingers of her right hand together, and turned her palm up. She didn't have to look down to see the swirling fire, compressing and growing solid, forming into the shape of a boning knife. When the weight solidified, she closed her hands around the handle, and shut her eyes, expecting to hear a gasp, or a cry, or a desperate plea to stop.

"Remarkable."

CaLarca opened her eyes. Mr. Asanto's face was bright with wonder. It was the first time anyone had reacted that way.

"May I see the knife?" he asked her next.

Feeling bolder, CaLarca walked over to Mr. Asanto and placed the knife in his open hand. He held it at either end, studying the detail, the sheen of the blade.

Then, suddenly, he let go. She watched its trajectory as it fell, and just before it hit the floor, dissipating in a puff of smoke.

"Truly remarkable," he whispered. "Do you know what you're called?"

CaLarca shook her head.

"You're a Nadi. It's a very special gift. You have the ability to generate energy in your body, and harness it.

And look how you've already progressed to fully-formed objects!"

CaLarca beamed at the praise.

Then Mr. Asanto sobered. "Now, please forgive me for what I'm about to say, loudly enough for your parents to hear."

CaLarca took a step back as Mr. Asanto's face darkened. His voice grew deafening, and his body glowed with a gray aura.

"You'll stay in my care for three months," he boomed. "In a secure facility, with three meals a day and comfortable lodgings, with others like you for company. But codes of behavior will be followed, and a strict regimen of treatment. And I promise, by the end of the program, you'll no longer be an outcast. You'll finally fit in, and be a normal human being as we were all meant to be. Like I know you want to be for your family."

CaLarca stared at him. He was lying openly, loudly. She let her mind open, searching for her parents. They sat on the staircase, just outside her bedroom door. She could feel their excited heartbeats. They were looking for a cure, she realized, and Mr. Asanto was offering them one. They set her up. They didn't want her to embarrass them anymore.

Tears welled up, and she turned away from Mr. Asanto, dragging the back of her hand across her eyes. Why did they focus on the little, stupid things she could do? What about all the other parts of CaLarca that were good?

A small rap on the floor drew her attention. When she met Mr. Asanto's eyes, he mouthed a word to her.

Freedom.

And there was no grey deceit around him now.

* * *

It was nothing to leave her life behind. Rumors had circulated for years among her classmates that she was a witch; eventually, she stopped correcting it, and kept to herself in school.

When she was packed and ready, her parents embraced her and told her how they looked forward to her return, how they knew Joran Asanto would take care of their baby. CaLarca took in the unexpected warmth, for the brief moment that it lasted.

The train to the Kings Canyons was the most luxurious thing CaLarca had ever seen. On the day's journey northwest, through mountains and farmlands and cities, she walked the length of the train, trailing her fingers over the seats, the railings, the edges of the metal doors. In between wanderings, she sat with Joran and listened to his stories.

"You're not the only one, you know," he told her. "Not by far. There's so many others with your skills, and even greater abilities. My wife Tehmi, for example, can see the future. You'll like her. She's one of the participants in this experiment. She'll watch out for you during all this."

The word experiment made her nervous. "How many kids – people - are doing this?"

"Nine, including you and me."

"Are there other kids, or - ?"

"Yes, three others. Everyone else is a bit older. But you don't have to be friends with them; you just treat them with courtesy, like they are your co-workers."

She liked the way Joran spoke to her like an adult: frank, without dumbing down the details. It made her feel brave enough to ask, "If we're workers, do we get paid?"

Joran grinned. "You do, actually. It's the least I can do, for your participation."

"How much?"

"250,000 rana."

CaLarca couldn't breathe. He must be lying. But there was no gray aura around him.

"It's true," Joran said. "Everyone equally paid, non-taxed, in a secure account that can never be taken away from you. That's for you, CaLarca, not your parents. They never have to know about it."

"You're really that rich?" was the only thing she could think of to say.

Joran smirked. "I guess I am," he admitted.

CaLarca licked her lips. "I'm not going to do any weird surgeries or take medicines or anything," she announced.

Joran laughed. "Deal."

Inside, CaLarca squealed with glee. 250,000 rana! Hers, all hers, nothing for her parents, the government, no one but her. She could go anywhere she wanted. She could buy a house. She could leave Osha. Her mind swam with ideas of what she could do with all that money...

"There is one non-negotiable rule, however," Joran added. "You cannot leave until the end of the program. You must stay underground, and within the borders of the base."

The noise in her head died down. Locking her up underground with strangers, experimenting with her strange, frightening abilities, what was she doing? How could her parents let her go with someone like that?

It's too late, she reasoned, staring out of the window, as the grasses turned to sand. *I made the deal. I'm doing this.*

I'm doing this, she told herself again, steeling her nerves. *I'm not going to be afraid.*

When they disembarked, CaLarca shielded her eyes, looking for civilization. Besides the dusty trainstop, there were rocks and sand, the sky above a piercing blue. More footprints led into the desert, all headed in the same direction.

Joran jumped down next to her. He drew out a parasol and opened it with a poof, holding it over CaLarca's head. The gesture looked so comical to CaLarca, she bit her lips to hold back her giggles. The wooden handle was smooth, with a floral carving along its curved end. And it did block out the sun. She twirled it a bit between her fingers. She felt almost like a lady.

"It's a bit of a walk," he told her, pointing to the horizon. "But it'll be worth it. Come along."

It was more than a little walk. Four hours later, throats dry, lungs parched, they finally came to the edge of the canyon. Kings Canyons, Joran told her, coughing a little. CaLarca took it in. Gorgeous and isolated, the sands were crimson, the rocky cliff-face streaked with silver. A few huts sat by the precipice, long since abandoned, crumbling. Basic shelter, Joran explained. And an easy entry. Because inside one of the stone huts was a cellar, with a trap door built into its floor.

"It's an old military base," Joran told her, when he hauled open the trapdoor, and she stared down into the dark stairwell. "Long since abandoned, so I made it my own. Three distinct levels, training, sleeping, meals and recreation. It's quite extraordinary. You won't even miss the surface."

At the bottom of the stairs appeared a beam of light. Inside, a woman greeted CaLarca, gesturing for her to come, introducing herself as Joran's wife, Tehmi. Sleek and pretty in a faded way, she was also visibly pregnant, and perpetually flushed. Behind her, a makeshift medical clinic came into view, windowless, but white and clean and glistening, packed with IV stands, boxes and crates. Two gurneys were set up. An armchair was pushed into the corner. There was another door on the other side of the room; as she stood in the clinic, CaLarca couldn't stop staring at it, wondering where it led.

"Medical review," Tehmi told her. "There are two requirements for entry into this study. First, an injection. A specific combination of chemicals, designed to activate if your body houses any **NINE** characteristics. If you do, you'll gain a small burn on your back. It will heal quickly."

CaLarca recoiled. "You're going to burn me?"

"It's technically a burn," Tehmi explained. "And it will scar. But it's minor. And required."

"Do I have to?" CaLarca asked, glancing at Joran.

"You can do this," Joran told her. "I know you're strong enough."

They wouldn't do anything to hurt her. They were adults. CaLarca shut her eyes tight, and gathering up her courage, she nodded and stuck out her arm.

A cool, wet swipe on her skin, and a sharp pinch.

Then the small of her back began to prickle. The skin to the right of her spine grew hot, prickling, burning, then searing. Shifting back and forth, CaLarca gripped the edge of the gurney, biting her lip to hold back her cry of pain.

"Very good," she heard Tehmi murmur from behind, holding up the hem of CaLarca's shirt. "Almost there."

In twenty seconds, the heat started to recede. Quickly, Tehmi applied some kind of cold balm, and a bandage. The burn itched under the gauze. CaLarca did her best to ignore it, blinking back her tears.

"Now I have to put you to sleep to do some tests," Tehmi instructed. "You'll have a headache when you wake up, but it will go away."

Still woozy from the burn, she wanted to object. But her thoughts turned to the 250,000 rana, and Joran's promises. She had to comply. She had to get through this.

"There's nothing to be afraid of," Tehmi said, sliding on gloves and wheeling over an intravenous unit. "I promise, before you know it, you'll wake up and be ready to go downstairs and meet everyone. Doesn't that sound exciting?"

Maybe a little. CaLarca swallowed the sick feeling in her stomach as she climbed up onto the gurney. She extended her arm to Tehmi's waiting hands, and braced herself.

A burning pinch, first in the top of her hand. Then a duller one, at the base of her skull.

And everything went dark.

"CaLarca."

Her head was swimming, throbbing with pain, like a knife plunging into her neck.

"Can you hear me?"

"Yes," CaLarca croaked, surprised at the sound. How long had it been? Through her muddled vision, she saw Joran rise from his seat in the corner. Tehmi was gone. She tried to ask why, but her voice wouldn't work.

Joran helped CaLarca to sit up. "Hold onto me," he instructed. "A quick walk downstairs, and then you can rest."

CaLarca could barely see, gripping his arm, stumbling down a flight of red-walled stairs, the world swirling in her drugged vision, turning sideways and forming vortexes.

Everything went black, then to candlelight softness. Warmth enveloped her. She didn't know where she was, the foreign smell, the rough sheets, the too-soft mattress.

A knocking sound. CaLarca opened her eyes. A metal door slid open, letting light into the tiny bedroom.

CaLarca sat up, wincing at the immediate throb in her head, and looked around. The room was small, and square, and furnished with a twin bed, a dresser and a chair in the corner. Her room, CaLarca realized. How much time had passed?

Tehmi stood at the entryway, one hand on her stomach.

"Come along," the woman said pleasantly. "Everyone is here. Time to work."

* * *

Just as Joran said, there were nine participants in the NINE study.

Two girls close to CaLarca's age, fraternal twins. Shantou was the red-haired one; Marette was the blonde. They were like pale aliens, huddled together and whispering. And there was a boy, Ganasan, the youngest, maybe ten years old, so shy that his face was perpetually pink. He didn't speak a word to anyone, even when addressed. When the twins tittered at him, he grew redder.

Looking around, CaLarca was disappointed. Were they her only option for friends?

She preferred the look of the older group. Kuri was maybe twenty, black and bronze, lean and mysterious. She got a funny feeling in her chest when he looked at her. To cover it up, she stared back at him without blinking. That seemed to amuse him.

There were two other men, too. Yann's complexion was pallid, broken blood vessels along the edge of his nose, his voice a perpetual mumble. Voss was even older, olive-skinned and bearded, heavy around the middle and grinning at everyone like some kindly uncle. Tehmi and Joran rounded out the group. Nine of them, underground, for the next three months.

CaLarca was slotted into the Nadi subgroup, along with the blonde Marette, and Voss the bearded uncle. The handsome Kuri, red-haired Shantou and balding Yann were the Ekos. Tehmi and the boy, Ganasan, were both Insynns. Joran didn't identify as anything, strangely enough. He just wandered between the groups, brought materials or injections, listened, nodded, or made notes on his Lissome.

CaLarca watched everyone, too, in the beginning. For the first few days, she refused to participate, huddled in the corner. Her head still pounded and her back itched like mad. In the privacy of her tiny bedroom, she removed the bandage and angled her body in a mirror to catch sight of the strange, swirling lines, a deep orange brown, on the small of her back. It was almost pretty.

In sessions, CaLarca watched Tehmi and Ganasan interact; she was sweet to the boy, patiently explaining things, even as he refused to respond. But sometimes, she let him touch her arm, and vice versa. When that happened, something passed between them, something that made both their bodies stiffen. But it wasn't her group, so she wasn't allowed to ask questions, as per Joran's instructions. She was to get to know her fellow Nadis, memorize the provided diagrams of the body, read Joran's notes on previous studies of Nadis, trade their own knowledge, and experiment. None of which she was ready to do. Not yet.

When the groups broke for the day, and everyone took their designated meal packs, CaLarca explored her new home. There were three floors to the base. The first with a large open room for training and exploration. The second with two large spaces, one for procuring their meal packs and liquids for the day, the other for recreation. The third and lowest floor with several small bedrooms, one for each of them, save for the twins, who shared a single space. All three floors were strangely designed, unfinished in areas. Doors and panels opened to rock, or small, dark holes in the earth, too small to shimmy into. The ventilation system stopped and started, sometimes blowing ice cold, sometimes hot and rusty-smelling. She thought she found a secret door, once, on the third-floor stairwell; when running her hands over the rocky ridges, she felt a line, and then another, hidden from the naked eye, but something was there. Still, she couldn't wedge her fingers into anything, she couldn't figure out what it was. So, she gave up. She had panic attacks in the dark. She cried and cried under the blanket of her bed. No one came to soothe her.

Eventually, CaLarca's fear wore down into exhaustion. It wasn't the worst setting, she reasoned. At least she had meals, and privacy, and safety. She had no other choice. It would be worth it when it was finished.

So CaLarca joined her teammates, and began to talk and read. Through reading, Calarca learned that manifestation was only one part of Nadi; the other two in her group could manipulate energy that already existed in the world. CaLarca generated Nadi from within, and that was rare, just as Joran said. Voss asked her a thousand questions, utterly fascinated with her, to Marette's visible jealousy.

With all the attention, despite her earlier protests, CaLarca was drawn into the excitement and the experimentations. Joran offered the groups a number of methods: hypnosis, psychotropic drugs, sensory deprivation, meditation, adrenaline infusion, whole brain thinking, working to activate the dual hemispheres, all to see whether their NINE abilities were decreased or magnified. With certain treatments, CaLarca's Nadi energy flared hot and dangerous. One time, she grew so engulfed with Nadi that her heart threatened to explode. It was Voss who plunged his fist into her stomach to draw out the excess energy while the other NINE members held her down. When that happened, CaLarca became a celebrity, as did Voss for stopping it. He deferred all the accolades, but CaLarca drank them in.

Everyone wanted to know what went through her head in that moment, how exactly it felt when she was on the brink of explosion. The boy, Ganasan, even brought her dinner in bed that night, blushing as he handed over the tray to her surprised hands. "Just thought you should eat," she heard him mumble before he bolted from the room.

There were more incredible moments. Ganasan experienced what was called a "full Insynn flash," where he received a flashforward of events to come when he touched Tehmi's hand. The boy convulsed so violently that he went unconscious, sending Yann running with the first aid kit. When he finally woke up, covered in sweat and shivering, Ganasan went to his room and refused to speak to anyone. It unnerved the group. For the rest of the day, everyone paused before using their abilities, found themselves breaking from long trains of thought.

In the evening, CaLarca carried a freshly-heated meal pack into Ganasan's room. The door was ajar. Someone else was already in there, sitting on the boy's bedside, talking in a low whisper. At her entry, Kuri's dark eyes swung over to CaLarca's, his words dying off. She felt that funny pull in her chest again, but this time, there was a weird twist to it, as she caught sight of the hazy gray aura around Kuri. Whatever he was saying to the boy, he was lying.

"Think about it," Kuri told the boy. "Whatever you want in exchange." Then he left.

"What is he asking you to do?" CaLarca asked as she set down his tray.

"Nothing," the boy mumbled.

"You don't have to talk to me about it," CaLarca added. "But I know what it's like to lose control. It's scary, right?"

His cheeks flushed crimson. "You brought me dinner?"

CaLarca smiled at him. "Sure. You did it for me."

"He wants my memory." The boy's voice was barely a whisper.

"Your memory?" CaLarca looked over her shoulder for eavesdroppers. "What do you mean?"

"The Insynn rush. He wants to go inside my head and experience what I felt, what I thought. As research." Ganasan glanced at her. "Do you think I should let him? I don't know anything about Ekos. Would it hurt?"

"I don't know," CaLarca admitted. "It might. But – "

She thought about it for a minute, forming the right words. "He should only experiment on people who are willing to do it," she concluded. "So if you don't want to do it, then don't."

"Okay,' he said, smiling for the first time, his eyes shiny. "You're right."

But Kuri was insistent, not just with Ganasan, but with the group. He was always hinting, whispering, asking for permission to peer inside their minds. He claimed it as his specialty as an Eko, as a means to better understand the human soul. His goal was to gain the trust and respect of everyone in the base, and earn the opportunity to "touch" them. So far, no one was willing, save for the red-haired twin, Shantou. When they sat together, a charge of electricity coursed between them. They started spending more time together, CaLarca noticed. Marette, the blonde twin, was on her own more and more, watching mournfully. Ganasan kept staring at CaLarca from across the room, a strange look on his face. CaLarca chose to ignore it.

One night, there was a knock on CaLarca's door, startling her from near-sleep. A rumpled blonde head peered through.

"What do you want?" CaLarca whispered.

"Could I stay in here for a little while?" Marette whispered back.

"I guess. Why?"

The girl shut the door behind her. She looked pale, and disturbed. "Kuri's in there," she confessed to CaLarca.

"Oh." CaLarca didn't know what to say.

Marette moved to the corner, sinking into the armchair. Her bare feet kicked in the air, rustling her white cotton nightgown. "I think he's gross," she confessed to CaLarca, who remained in her bed. "And Shantou's being dumb."

"Maybe," CaLarca said. "How long - I mean, when do you think you might - ?"

Marette shot a wounded look at CaLarca. Both girls went silent. The night was filled with echoes, pipes, clicking rocks, the hint of voices. CaLarca would have thought being underground would be quieter. But there was always something making a sound.

"Should we tell Tehmi what's going on?" CaLarca finally spoke up. "They might be mad."

"We're only supposed to wake them up if it's an emergency," Marette reminded her.

"Yeah, but it's - I don't know - wrong, isn't it? Kuri's so old."

"So is Joran," Marette said with a sniff. "Tehmi's not much older than we are. So why would they care?"

CaLarca suddenly felt very naïve. "I guess you're right."

"What are you doing to do when you get out of here?" Marette continued. "Me and Shantou are going to use our money to travel and sing. We'll be famous. That's the only thing I can think about. Just two more months and total freedom. Not even our parents can stop us, not with the money. We can do whatever we want. What about you?"

"I don't know yet," CaLarca said. She had been so consumed with the experiments that she barely thought about the outside. In a way, she forgot that they were all supposed to leave at some point and go back to their lives.

"You should think big," Marette told her. "We can do anything. Look how much we're changing. Do you know what we could do on the outside? I could do Nadi demonstrations while I perform. Shantou could read the thoughts around people and sing the songs they want to hear most. It'll be easy to be famous, y'know? We can do anything. We can be higher than everyone else."

Discomfort thickened in CaLarca's chest. "I think we should go to sleep," she said, seeing the look of disappointment on Marette's face. "Stay if you want, but I'm going to sleep."

The girl stayed in the armchair. Soon, Marette's breathing grew heavy, and CaLarca knew she was free, but her mind was racing.

How would her parents react on her return? What if they found out that she was heightening her gifts, instead of learning how to eradicate them? What if they found out about the money? Was she really what Marette said, higher than everyone else? Like a god? Is that what they all were now?

We can't go back, she realized. *We're different now. We can never go back.*

* * *

"I said no!" Ganasan shouted. "And I won't say it again!"

Everyone turned at the sound. The boy stood before Kuri, his fists clenched. Kuri took a step back, surprise on his face. Noting the response from the room, he raised his hands. "We're just talking," he announced.

"You're supposed to focus on your own group's activities," Joran spoke out, his voice booming.

Kuri's eyes narrowed. "I'm trying to help him." He addressed the boy again. "Gani, just go and ask Shantou. She did it, and it didn't hurt."

"Don't call me Gani," the boy snapped. "I don't care. You're not doing it, no matter what you threaten."

Everyone wore the same look of shock. *Ganasan is stronger than he looks,* CaLarca thought.

Though, from the anger on Kuri's face, he wasn't used to being told the word 'no.'

"You realize that I could just do it if I wanted to, and you couldn't stop me," Kuri told the boy.

"Stop it!" came Tehmi's voice as she crossed the room. She stood in front of Ganasan, one hand on her pregnant belly, the other outstretched to shield him. "He said no. Leave him alone. I mean it. He has a choice whether to -"

"Does he?" came Voss's retort, surprising them all. "Does he really?"

Tehmi lowered her hand. For a split second, CaLarca saw a wash of fear come over the woman. "Of course," she finally said. "He's just a child."

"Unfortunate for them to be involved in this," the bearded man said. There was a strange, flat tone to his voice. "But they are, and we are, and we both know that there's no freedom, Tehmi. You and Joran made sure of that."

"You all agreed to a contract," Joran announced, with the slightest shake to his words. "To payment, for three months of service, under the rules given to you on entry. Behave yourself, and step away from each other. Now!"

Tehmi gasped then, her hands dropping to her stomach. Joran darted to her side, ignoring Voss and Kuri, who stood together, watching.

In the midst of all of this, CaLarca saw Yann, the quiet balding man, leaving the room.

* * *

Something was changing. Maybe it was the lack of fresh air. Maybe it was simply the difficulty of nine personalities forced to live with each other. But there were more and more conflicts. No one was willing to stay in their designated groups. Cliques began to form. The schedule grew fluid, and then non-existent. On day, CaLarca caught Shantou, Kuri and Voss. They noticed CaLarca lurking outside, and gestured for her to join them. She was so startled that she ran back to her room and locked the door.

The next time it happened, CaLarca joined them. She couldn't help it. She was growing more and more afraid. Joran and Tehmi refused to talk about anything other than getting back on track with the curriculum, yelling more and more, threatening punishments, storming away, hissing at each other like angry parents.

Voss closed the door behind her. Shantou and Kuri were holding hands on the bed.

"I have a favor to ask of you, CaLarca," Voss began. "You're always wandering. You know every corner of this place, I'd wager."

"I can't break out of here, if that's what you want," CaLarca said haughtily.

Voss let out a bark of laughter. "Perceptive little thing, aren't you."

Then his smile faded. "But powerful. One of the most powerful ones here. What do you think about this experiment, CaLarca?"

"I don't know," CaLarca said sullenly. "It's fine."

"And what do you think about our hosts?"

"They're okay."

"You can sense lies," Voss said. "You told me once, in conference. That's related to Nadi, but you've developed some Eko talents, I believe."

"I - maybe." That was true. Something had shifted in her over the course of the week. Her hearing seemed to sharpen. Whispers of thoughts hovered around her. She had been too scared to tell anyone.

"It's okay. We're the same as you," Voss told her gently. "We're changing too. Growing stronger. It's amazing, isn't it?"

CaLarca couldn't think of what else to do but nod.

"But for what purpose?" His voice was smooth. "Why are we here?"

"To learn from each other," she recited.

"And then what?"

"We... go home."

"Do you really think that's the truth? At the end of this, we just leave? Go our own separate ways, with a bag full of rana and powerful abilities? Is that logical?"

"I - I don't know." She was starting to feel sick.

"Where's Joran right now, CaLarca?"

"I don't know. Somewhere, of course."

"I would wager," Voss corrected. "If you searched all three floors, you wouldn't find a trace of him."

CaLarca shrugged. "Well, that's not possible."

Voss ignored her response. "Were you put to sleep when you first arrived, for medical testing?"

Instinctively, CaLarca's hand went to the back of her head. The headache had dulled after a few days, and she hadn't thought about it since. Voss mirrored her movement. So did Shantou and Kuri, lifting their hands to the napes.

"Something was implanted in us," Voss said. "I've become sure of it."

Stricken, CaLarca rubbed at the base of her skull, searching. There was nothing, not a nub, or an edge, or even a bump. No pain, no swelling, nothing. This couldn't be happening. What did they do to her? What did they do to all of them?

"I - I can't - I don't want to talk about this," she announced, stumbling over her feet, backing away from the group.

"You will," Voss's voice floated after her. "Soon enough, you will."

* * *

Candlelight. The twins gathered around a doorframe, cooing. CaLarca peered inside the room. Tehmi was sitting in bed, propped with pillows, holding a tiny, mewling baby. Yann was next to her, bundling sheets into a ball, putting away medical tools. He was a doctor? She never knew that.

"What's her name?" she asked instead.

"Sydel," Tehmi said with a tired smile. "I think Sydel."

"Congratulations," came Kuri's sneer from behind.

Tehmi's smile dropped. With an effort, she put it back on.

Her face blurred, and then the world shifted back to darkness.

Then Shantou's flushed, haunted face hovered over CaLarca's.

"Get up," the redhaired girl panted. "Get up and come with me."

Tehmi's face looked like she was about to gulp in a breath. But she didn't inhale. She didn't blink. She was sprawled across the bed, one hand hanging limp over the edge. In the thin opening of her eyes, the whites were bloodshot. Kuri was in the corner, wringing his hands, tears on his cheeks. The baby whimpered in its bassinet. CaLarca didn't dare to move, or even breathe.

"Can you take the baby?" Shantou interrupted her horror.

The baby wailed, a long, keening cry. CaLarca ran over and slid her hands underneath the warm swaddling, placing Sydel against her shoulder.

"It was an accident," Kuri said shakily. "If she didn't fight me so hard, and just told me the truth - it wasn't my fault."

"Of course it wasn't," Shantou soothed him.

"You were in her head, weren't you?" CaLarca accused, clutching the baby to her chest. "Like you were trying to do to Ganasan. You pushed into her mind too far. You killed her!"

"If she had just told me where the secret exit is," Kuri rambled. "If she told me what their plans were, what they put in our heads –"

Was this really happening? The darkness that surrounded them, the lone candlelight, it was like some surreal dream.

"It's time to leave." Voss's voice floated through the shadows. He stood by the doorframe, surveying the scene without expression. His beard concealed the features, darkened the shadows of his face. He didn't look kind and fatherly anymore.

His eyes fastened on hers. "Help us, CaLarca. Free us."

CaLarca shook her head violently, clutching the baby to her.

"She doesn't know anything," Shantou said, a nasty edge to her voice. "We need to think about what to say to Joran."

Voss ignored her, focusing on CaLarca. "You don't want to stay," he said quietly. "You want to run away and forget that any of this ever happened. You want to forget about all of us. Start your life over, on your terms, not theirs, or your parents. Yours. Let it go. You know you want to."

A spot of black appeared in the corner of CaLarca's eye. She clung to the baby for warmth, for a tether. Her chest felt like it was in a vice. But she couldn't help the words from spilling out. "The stairwell. Third floor platform. I think there's a secret door."

Tears welled in her eyes. The pressure in her chest ceased.

Voss smiled. "Good girl."

CaLarca ran away, ran down the hallway, vomit high in her throat, the baby's wet face against her neck. She hit two bodies, warm and soft, with an *oof*! The baby wailed.

"What's happened? What's wrong?"

It was Yann's voice, Marette's pale face at his side. CaLarca's thoughts were a mad spiral. They were together. Them too? Was everyone sleeping together in this place?

But they weren't part of that group, at least. The lesser evil.

CaLarca held the baby out. "Take her," she ordered. "Take care of her."

Yann immediately put his hands out for the baby. "What did they do?"

For the first time, CaLarca really looked at Yann: his long face, how his hairline was gently receding, how he was much younger than she initially thought. He cradled Sydel, tightening her swaddle, patting her on the back.

"It's over," CaLarca told them, her teeth chattering. "It's over. They're - "

The stairwell. CaLarca ran past Yann and Marette, peering through the access door. On the bottom floor, where there was once a solid red wall of rock, now there was a gaping, black hole. A secret door. She slumped. She was right. There was a way out of here all along.

"Over?" Marette was hissing behind her. "What's going on?"

CaLarca ignored her and took hold of Yann's sleeve, opposite the baby. "Maybe Tehmi is still alive," she offered. Tears choked her voice. "I couldn't tell. But maybe?"

Yann backed away, the white bundle against his chest.

CaLarca stared at the black hole in the stairwell. The others were already gone, wherever the tunnel went on the other side. Where would she go? Should she try to stop them? Could she? It was over. It was all over. She put her hand on the door to push it open.

A hand grabbed hers from behind, small, hot and sweaty. Yelping, CaLarca tried to wrench away, but it held fast.

Ganasan's face floated before her in the darkness. "It's me!" he whispered. "What are you doing?"

Catching her breath, CaLarca looked past him into the corridor. Yann, Marette and Sydel were gone. "It's over," she told the boy. "We have to get as far away from here as fast as possible."

Ganasan didn't seem fazed. He just nodded, and gripped her hand tighter. "Okay," he said firmly. "I'll take care of you, I promise."

It was the last thing she expected to hear in that moment. "You'll - what?" she finally sputtered.

"I will. I know I'm only eleven, but I can do it. Whatever it takes. You're safe with me."

CaLarca couldn't find the words. Ganasan gazed up at her, six inches shorter, clasping her hand like a romantic hero.

"I can't," she said, removing her hand from his. "When I said we, I meant – you stay with Yann and Marette. I have to go. I'm sorry."

She burst through the door into the stairwell, careening into the pitch black of the tunnel. The walls were rough to her touch, maybe five feet across, six feet tall, and full of dust. Coughing, CaLarca bounced off the rocks, stumbling over ridges. Her breath echoed in the darkness. There was light somewhere. There had to be light, eventually. After several long minutes, her hands scrambled over a wall; no, a door, one that moved when she pushed with all her strength.

CaLarca burst into the sun. Immediately, her eyes streamed with tears. It was so bright, too bright, too much oxygen, and she was going to faint. Groping blindly, she found a sun-hot boulder and pressed her back into it for support, panting for breath, blinking furiously, fighting the urge to sink to the ground.

When her vision finally adjusted, she realized she was on the canyon floor, surrounded by the great cliffs of the Kings Canyon. Three silhouettes stood, fifty feet away. A fourth lay on the ground. Even with blurred vision, CaLarca recognized the shade of blood.

The sound of anxious voices in the wind, coming from above. CaLarca craned her neck, squinting to look up. One hundred feet up, anxious faces peered over the edge of the cliff. A family. Four adults, four children.

"They've seen us," CaLarca heard Shantou's panicked whisper. "They don't know what he tried to do."

"You hold them," Kuri hissed back. "I'll wipe their minds. It'll be fine."

She couldn't breathe. She was going to vomit. CaLarca's knees collapsed.

Then a hand lay on top of her head as she retched, and Voss's voice came from above:

"Run, Cyrah."

CaLarca ran down the rocky incline, across the canyon floor, away from the pleas and screams, into the desert. She ran across plains and through oases, until her muscles collapsed under her body weight, sand pouring down her throat as she fell face-first. Then she crawled until she passed out under the blazing sun.

V.

"Enough!" CaLarca pushed Sydel out of her mind. Then she put her hands over her face.

Sydel was choked with tears, too, by the sound of her mottled voice. "CaLarca, I'm so sorry."

CaLarca shook her head, unable to form words.

"When I first treated you, you said you were involved in the assault of the Sava family. You weren't. You clearly weren't."

"Wasn't I?" CaLarca said through her fingers.

"You were a child."

"I was a coward," CaLarca muttered. "I should have done something. I should have tried to stop them."

"Oh, CaLarca. You saved me, nonetheless." The girl's voice was full of gratitude. "Who knows what might have happened if you hadn't given me to Yann."

"Perhaps."

Sydel brushed her hand over her face and stood up. "Thank you. Thank you for showing me the truth. I'm ready now."

CaLarca peered through her fingers. "You're – ready?"

"I want to meet Marette," Sydel said firmly. "I want to help you, however I can. We'll leave in an hour, if you think you're strong enough."

Despite the pain in CaLarca's chest, her heart still leapt with excitement.

"I am," CaLarca confirmed. "It's just memories."

"And the implant?"

"I don't know," CaLarca admitted. "I've never had the courage to look."

Sydel nodded. "Maybe on the way, you might tell me more about your connection with Ganasan. It seems a positive thing."

CaLarca shot out a hand, palm first. "I need a moment," she barked.

"I understand. I hope I didn't hurt you, Cyrah."

Hearing her first name made her cringe. Sydel noticed, and her tone dropped. "I'm sorry. I won't call you that again."

"Thank you," was all CaLarca could manage. Because, in the wake of Sydel's invasion, all CaLarca was able to do was curl into a ball on her bed and throw the quilt over her head, until there was nothing but suffocating darkness. She had been exposed, so many nerves exposed, like being turned inside out, and it made her murderous and fearful and full of rage.

She had to push it all away again. She had to stick to her plan.

* * *

There was nothing to take along, and very little to say in the hours that followed. The landscape changed every hour: from the ride down the Toomba mountain on a trolley, to the transfer that took them through the pass, and finally flat, grassy plains, on route to Zangari, the place where Marette set to meet them. Sydel pressed her forehead against the glass window, silent and staring at the landscape. She looked grim, and impenetrable.

CaLarca's head cleared as the landscape flattened. But her body seemed heavier with every mile that passed, that took them from Toomba.

Just the atmospheric change, she told herself. Patience.

Zangari came up sooner than she expected. The train slowed. Sydel was already on her feet, heading for the exit. CaLarca panicked, trying to hurry her aching body. Through the windows, she caught sight of the swarms of people, pouring through the station, heading for the exits. What was with the crowd? Was there a protest?

Finally on the ground, caught up the swell of motion, CaLarca could feel the excitement in the air: bodies young and old, both male and female, chattering and laughing, checking Lissomes, comparing pictures.

"Where are we supposed to meet her?" Sydel called to CaLarca.

"In the National Park," CaLarca relayed over the din of the crowds. "Down the street. By the white gazebo, in the center of the flower field, she said."

They were not the only ones headed there. Hundreds of people poured into the park's entrance, creating a grand circle of bodies. Craning her neck to look over shoulders, CaLarca realized what they were surrounding: a flower field, half-crushed by a huge platform, and a white gazebo surrounded by metal scaffolding, lights and sound machines.

A burst of static carried over their heads. The crowd roared in response. Through the spaces in the crowd, CaLarca saw a cluster of black move into the center of the circle. Then the black split off in perfect succession (bodyguards, CaLarca quickly realized) and the person within stepped onto the platform.

"Marette!" she gasped.

A few people looked back at her. CaLarca ignored their stares. "Come on," she demanded, taking hold of Sydel's hand and shoving through the crowds, using her cane as a divider. The teenagers protested, threw them dirty looks, some of them even pushed back, but when they saw CaLarca's face, they backed off.

Finally, Sydel and CaLarca squeezed into the front row by the barricades, just as the music began. There were no visible musicians, but loud, thumping beats pumped through the garden space, making the ground vibrate. Then a woman's voice rose through the sound-system, raspy, sultry, wavering between a low growl and a long, piercing call. The audience was in a frenzy, waving their hands, jumping as flashes burst all around them. The metal scaffolding suddenly exploded, and letters burned over the performer's head, raining down sparks as they spelled out EM LEE.

"Who is this?" Sydel yelled into CaLarca's ear.

The singer appeared. Her white-blonde hair was twisted into a complicated heap of dreadlocks, some piled on her head, the others trailing over her shoulders. Her eyes were ringed with black, winged at the edges, her mouth a sharp scarlet. Em Lee wore layers of glitter and leather and organza, a pale pink, drawstring ruffled blouse, a leather jacket. She strutted, hunched over, flung her head back, stretched her hand to the sky, and everyone seemed to respond in unison, swaying and singing along.

CaLarca tore her eyes from the stage and looked from left to right. Behind the platform, the men and women in black talked into their Lissomes, surveying the raucous crowd. One of them took three long strides towards the singer, holding onto a hose. Then he yanked on the hinge. Water blasted out.

But in the moment before impact, Em Lee lifted her hand.

The water ricocheted off an invisible barrier, just inches from her palms, drops spraying in all directions as she continued to sing. The bodyguard never moved, nor did he stop the flow of water. But another man in black was already set up on the other side, with the same kind of hose, blasting water at the performer. She lifted her other hand, and the water was repelled again. She was encircled in water, as if encased in a glass egg. The spray created faint rainbows above her head, the sheen catching the rays of the sunlight, as her song pleaded for forgiveness.

"How are they doing that?" CaLarca heard the man crow next to her. "It's incredible!"

"It's Nadi."

CaLarca turned at Sydel's voice. The girl was staring at the stage. "That's Marette?" she asked.

"Yes," CaLarca confirmed. "But no more talk."

The show was fifty minutes long, one song after another, more tricks employed with water, so Marette appeared as a delicate sprite, caught up in the loud, often inaudible rhythm. An eye-catching gimmick, CaLarca had to admit. And just as she said in Kings, when they were children, she used her Nadi to become a star.

Em Lee. Her initials. Of course.

After the second encore, when the last note floated from her lips, Em Lee's eyes zeroed in on CaLarca, one hundred feet away. She lifted one finger and one white-blonde eyebrow. Then she swept off her platform and into the folds of the bodyguards, who moved like a swarm of flies, carrying her off.

The applause followed like a fog, dissipating as the minutes passed. When she didn't reappear, the sounds of adoration deflated into disappointment. People drifted away, talking and comparing pictures, heading back in the direction of town, or the train station.

"CaLarca." The sound of her name made her jump. It was one of the bodyguards, appearing like a specter at her left. The man's face was unreadable, but the subtle flick of his finger told her where to look. "Em Lee requests your company."

The singer had reappeared in the shadows of the white gazebo, flagged by the remaining bodyguards.

Some of the audience stragglers cheered at the sight, as CaLarca and Sydel were led past the barricade, through the field of blue flowers, past the platform and to the intricate white gazebo.

Above then, Em Lee leaned against the railing, long legs extended. She turned her head so the setting sun highlighted her bone structure. CaLarca hovered at the base of the steps.

"Come up, please," Em Lee instructed, her voice slightly hoarse. She pushed off the rail and opened her arms. Her bright smile was unnerving, as she bent over to embrace CaLarca. "I can't believe you're here!" she breathed. "What happened to your legs?"

CaLarca didn't return the gesture, or answer the question. "We should go somewhere more private, Marette," she said pointedly.

Marette shook her head, her long white-blond dread-locks swaying. "No," she breathed. "This is perfect." In closer proximity, CaLarca could see the hairs that had come undone from the twisted strands, the dark eye circles concealed with make-up, the powdery finish on the woman's skin. She wasn't as young as she first appeared. A bit of a relief.

Behind CaLarca, Sydel's hands were clasped together like a schoolgirl. Marette's smile faded. Finally, her lips stretched again, scarlet-colored and winsome.

"You do look like Joran," she said to Sydel. "Wow."

"You're Marette Lyung." CaLarca could hear the strain in Sydel's voice.

Marette nodded, casting a look at CaLarca. "I haven't used that name in a while, but -"

"You were in Kings Canyon, right?" Sydel pressed. "With CaLarca?"

Another glance over at CaLarca. CaLarca frowned at Marette. *Answer her,* she mentally chided.

"No," Marette said stiffly. "No, I wasn't involved in that. But I heard the rumors that we were in danger –"

"If you knew you were being hunted down," Sydel broke in. "Why would you dare to use your gifts for show?"

Marette let out a soft *ha!* and tossed her dreadlocks back. "I've been using it for years. To the public, it's just excellent special effects. And those on my team who know otherwise? They sign confidentially agreements."

"Someone must wonder how you do it," Sydel said flatly. "Someone will ask questions eventually. You're inviting death and destruction and fear, for the sake of entertainment."

An uncomfortable silence. CaLarca couldn't help but be mildly impressed by the girl's drive.

"And what about your sister, Shantou?" Sydel pressed on.

Marette flinched. "You've been telling her all my secrets, I see," she muttered to CaLarca.

"She's an Eko," CaLarca told her. "A Nadi, too," she added carefully.

"She is?" Marette said, surprised. "But Tehmi was an Insynn, and Joran had no skills at all. How is that possible?" She looked Sydel over with new interest. Sydel ducked her head.

Marette sighed. "I haven't seen Shantou since Kings."

Ahead, one of her bodyguards made a gesture at her. CaLarca caught the slight shake of her head in response.

"Can I ask you a question?" Sydel spoke up. "CaLarca says she gave me over to you, after my mother was killed. Why didn't you take me into your care? Why Yann?"

Marette fidgeted. "Because - because I was fourteen," she finally said. "What was I going to do with a baby? I was scared, with Tehmi dead. We made a pact, Sydel, when we found the secret exit and split off; me, Ganasan, and Yann, we made a pact to never see each other again, to never speak publicly on what happened. I kept my promise, and I'm sure they did, as well."

"You never thought to see if I was okay?"

'Why would I?" The answer sounded flippant, but it was tinged with fear.

"Maybe with you in my life, I would have learned how to control Nadi," Sydel said. "Instead of killing people with it."

Marette jerked her chin back. "Sydel," she tried, casting a nervous look at CaLarca. "I understand if you've had a difficult time. But everything will be different, now that you're finally here."

That last comment made CaLarca pause.

"I don't know," Sydel was saying, her hand listlessly lifting and dropping. "I don't know anymore - I feel like some kind of package, shuttled from hand to hand -"

"What do you mean, finally here?" CaLarca interrupted, looking in a wide arc. A circumference of staring faces, black, white and brown. Lights and flashing Lissomes. The men and women in black, surrounding the gazebo.

A sick feeling grew in her stomach.

"Kuri's here, isn't he," she whispered.

"What's going on?" Sydel asked, looking from woman to woman.

All six of the guards, having formed a perfect circle formation around the gazebo, suddenly turned on their heels, facing inward. Then they took three long steps in unison to stand just beneath the railing.

"Whose face is he using?" CaLarca demanded, hysteria rising in her throat. "Tell me!"

Then one of the bodyguards lifted his dark glasses: cleft chin, ebony skin, black eyes.

"It's a nice face," he called out. "Do you like it?"

CaLarca's teeth started to chatter.

The man laid his arms on the railing, folded over each other, and rested his heavy chin on top. He stared at Sydel for a few moments. Then Kuri Nimat pushed off the railing, and headed for the stairs, taking them one at a time, slow and deliberate.

When he entered the gazebo, he dropped to his knee, and took Sydel's left hand in his.

"I'm so sorry," he murmured. "I'm so sorry for everything. Can you ever forgive me?"

Sydel's mouth opened and closed. Her cheeks flushed a deep crimson, her right hand gripped the wooden rail behind her.

Kuri rose to his feet, his face pained. "You know, Sydel," he started. "When we were brought into Kings Canyon, we all wanted to become better people. Our intentions were good, truly. We had no control over what was done to us by your parents."

The faintest smell of smoke. Stupefied with fear, CaLarca glanced at Sydel, and at her right hand. Under her fingers, the white wood was turning a pale, scorched grey. She was burning up with Nadi. CaLarca tried to establish an Eko connection, to tell Sydel to be calm, to tighten her core muscles, to breathe, but the girl's mind was firmly shut.

"I was sorry to hurt CaLarca like that," Kuri was still speaking, in that familiar, gravelly voice. "But it was necessary, and you've performed beautifully, Sydel. You're so much better than your parents ever were. We can work together. With your help, we can put this NINE history in the past." He glanced at CaLarca. "If you'll cooperate."

"Cooperate!" CaLarca spat out, breathless.

Even with the new face, his eyes were as as dark as ever. "You've already kept me from coming onboard the *Arazura*. I'm running out of patience, CaLarca."

"That was you?" CaLarca choked. "You took the form of the detective?"

"Of course I did. I've been tracking you both for weeks. Then you made contact with Marette - what a perfect coincidence."

Her cane clattered to the floor.

Then a burst of light blinded her. The remnants of the concert crowd began to scatter, screaming, as a great shadow passed over them.

"Back off," came a man's voice through a loudspeaker. "All of you. Away from Sydel. Now."

Squinting, CaLarca made out the shimmering blue shadow of the *Arazura*, hovering above the gazebo, down-drafts crushing the flowers. A gun barrel unfolded underneath the nose of the *Arazura*, trained on the gazebo.

"Sydel," the voice boomed. "Now."

What about me? CaLarca couldn't help the thought.

Then the girl ran past her, past Kuri, down the stairs of the gazebo and into the wind. "Go away! I don't want you here!" Sydel screamed. "Leave me alone!"

She waved her hand at the *Arazura*, as if to cut it in two. For a moment, CaLarca thought she saw the ship shudder, and list on its side, before it went even again.

Then the side exit door to the *Arazura* unfolded. A rope ladder dropped down, and a thick silhouette descended, hitting the ground with a thunk that carried over the sound of the engines. Then Cohen Byrne stalked towards the gazebo, his red beard lit by the sunlight.

Stumbling down the gazebo steps, CaLarca hobbled in front of Sydel, her hand raised, trying to warn him: "You don't -"

His huge palm hit the top of her chest, and she flew backwards. Shock radiated up her spine and down her legs, replaced by pins and needles.

Through the screaming pain, tears in her eyes, CaLarca could hear Cohen and Sydel fighting. "Stop pushing me!" he was telling Sydel. "How could you just leave like that, without telling us, without at least saying goodbye?"

"The note was enough!" she yelled back. "I should have known you would track me down. That's all I am to anyone, something to collect and hide away."

Cohen grabbed her by the arms. "We are the only ones who have never tried to hurt you, or manipulate you, or use you. Don't you see that? Doesn't that mean anything to you?"

Sydel stopped fighting.

"Come back," Cohen was still talking. "Don't leave like this. We'll help you, we'll do whatever you need to -"

"I won't leave," Sydel said in a whisper. "No. I'll never leave the Arazura again."

Sydel's shadow passed. Her short tufts of hair rippled from the wind, and her path was unsteady, her hands hovering at her sides, as if keeping balance.

CaLarca struggled onto her hands and knees. Then the light grew cold.

"You." It was Cohen, looming over her, blocking out the sun. "You have a real talent for manipulation. Vyoma said you were a mother. She could tell you've had a kid. Well, that kid is better off without you in his life."

Then he was gone. The shadow of the *Arazura* lifted, and the sunset was there again, cold and pink.

She couldn't breathe. It was over. She had failed. She was alone in the grassy fields, remnants of dead petals strewn like a bruised carpet.

The gazebo was deserted. No lights, no cameras. No Kuri, and no Marette either. They had faded away, once again.

Cohen's words floated past. *Better off without you. Better off without you.*

She couldn't stop the tears from spilling, a continuous flow, burning trails down her cheeks. She couldn't control her anger, her fury at Kuri, at Marette, at the brothers' betrayal, her revenge and retribution for her family's loss.

The town of Zangari felt ghostly, after so many people streaming through its doors and alleyways. Her fingers shook as she found a public Lissome dispenser and keyed in the access code.

A rumble, and clang. Beneath the plastic drop, a small black cube lay, one inch squared. Cold in her hand, after so long in storage. But it still rippled to life at her touch, asking who she wished to contact.

Within seconds, the connection was made.

"Zangari Law Patrol."

Her hands burned away the cold on the Lissome. "I wish to report the location of a wanted criminal. I believe someone is looking for Cohen Byrne.

PART FOUR

I.

Two patrol officers were posted outside the town-house, rotating on twelve-hour shifts. Phaira watched through the mirrored window as Detective Ozias went through a series of checkpoints with the men, trading credentials, passcodes and retinal scans before the officers allowed her into the vestibule.

The doorbell chimed.

".... appreciate your willingness to take her into your custody," Ozias was saying. "Rough night?"

"Noisy night. She barely slept. Pacing. Running up and down the stairs. Scared me awake."

"An attempt to escape?"

"As tempting as it is, as her lawyer, would I really tell you that?"

The door to the sitting room opened. Clad in a white robe, Jetsun's hair was already styled in sweeping blonde waves, her complexion peachy and warm in the morning. "You have a visitor," she announced. "Take care with your words, because I'm listening."

Ozias slipped inside, dipping her head at Jetsun. From her armchair, Phaira watched the exchange. In the center of the sand-colored room, made with silken wood and covered by grand carpets, Phaira felt about two feet tall, and more exhausted than she could ever remember.

"Have you found him?" she asked Ozias as the woman walked past.

Ozias unbuttoned her jacket lapel before settling onto the window bench. "No," she admitted. "We don't know where that man is. Or who he is. Not yet."

"Great," Phaira said sullenly, laying her chin on her knee. "He could be anyone, or anywhere."

"Have you ever seen technology like that before? To take on another appearance?"

"I'm not sure, but I don't think that's tech."

Ozias frowned. "What else would it be, then?"

"I doubt you'd believe me if I told you."

"It's a strange enough situation, Ms. Lore. I might have no other choice."

That might be true. Still, she kept silent.

Ozias laid her forearms across her thighs, leaning forward to catch Phaira's eye. "The sooner you talk, the sooner the house arrest will be lifted."

Phaira scowled. "There are innocent people at risk here. I won't expose them. If it means jail time for me, so be it."

"You consider Emir and Anandi Ajyo to be innocent?"

"Compared to what I've seen in the past month? They're saints."

"Saints who left you to be prosecuted," Ozias pointed out. "Where are they now? Why don't they come to defend you?" As she spoke, the detective was looking at Phaira's hands and arms, the tiny white scars and delicate flecks of pink that covered them.

Phaira glared at Ozias until she looked away.

"How did you know Aeden Nox?" she tried.

"You already know."

"Ms. Byrne."

Her true surname. So much for aliases.

"It must have been very hard to see your friend impersonated like that," Ozias continued. "Horrifying, given the way that he died. Crushed by falling rock in the stairwell of the Kings underground base. Took several minutes to die, according to the coroner's report. Unbefitting for such a decorated hero."

Every muscle in Phaira's face strained to remain calm.

"But not your fault," Ozias added. "I wonder if you went to Kings to try and save him. I wonder if he got caught up in some unsavory business with Keller and Xanto Sava."

"How is this relevant to your case, Detective?"

Jetsun's voice startled them both. The blonde woman leaned against the doorframe, arms crossed, still clad in her bathrobe. Grateful for the woman for once, Phaira hunched into her chair, away from Ozias.

The detective exhaled with frustration. "I know more than you think, Phaira," she said, getting to her feet and smoothing down her trousers. "I'm just missing that last puzzle piece. Don't you think it would be better to tell me, rather than to let me make assumptions? You're so concerned with innocents; how better to protect them than by telling the truth?"

"Can I please not talk to her anymore?" Phaira called over her shoulder to Jetsun.

"We need a break to confer," Jetsun announced.

"Fine," Ozias said. "I'll go for a walk around the block. But when I get back, no more interruptions. I want this resolved today."

When the detective cleared the threshold, and she heard the door slam, Phaira pressed the heel of her hands into her eyes. *Stop talking,* she told herself. *Stop reacting to everything she says. It's a slope, and you're falling. You'll ruin everything.*

"Well, well, it's positively crackling with tension in here."

Phaira dropped her head back, taking in the upside-down silhouette.

"You know, as your lawyer," Jetsun continued. "Whatever we talk about is confidential."

"Right," Phaira scoffed, sitting upright. "I'm sure that you strictly adhere to all proper codes of conduct."

"Like you do, I suppose? I'm not sure why you're so hostile towards me," Jetsun said blithely. "You got yourself into this mess."

"Trying to protect the ones I care about."

"Well, last time I checked, Phaira," Jetsun said. "Regardless of intention, you're not exactly operating on the good, clean level of the world. Ducking the law, making friends with known criminal hackers, attacking officers. How are we so different?"

Phaira glared through the window, focusing on the waves of dust blowing down the street. But still, her heart hammered. She hadn't thought of it like that.

Jetsun sidled over to the windowpane, leaning one hip against the glass. "How do you know Theron, anyways?"

Phaira turned away from the woman's curious gaze. *I don't even know how to categorize it,* she thought. A memory hazed over her vision, the feel of his hands lightly framing her face, palms flush under her ears, fingertips in her hair. Remembering, Phaira let her right cheek graze the skin of her shoulder. How she longed to be back in that room, shut away from everything.

"Interesting," she heard Jetsun murmur.

"Is it," Phaira said, turning back to glare at the woman.

Jetsun shrugged, looking across the skyline. "You're not the typical pick. The last one was a thin, tall, gorgeous socialite, daughter of a longtime partner, from money and good heritage. Historically, those girls are the ones who get woven into the circle. Understand what I mean?"

Phaira resisted the urge to laugh. In a way, she respected the woman's nerve, how elegantly she just inferred that Phaira was poor and ugly and on a lower plane of existence. And yet, in a way, Jetsun's cold recitation of facts could be construed as a warning. Phaira understood both.

Then the woman chuckled. "There was a time when we were thought to be a match, you know."

Phaira made a face. "Aren't you cousins?"

"I'm adopted."

"You have the same color of eyes, though."

"Dyed."

"Really?"

Jetsun gestured at her face. "Shows loyalty to different strains of the Sava clan. And don't worry, that match wasn't going to happen," she added with a smirk. "A little too strange, over on that side of the family -"

"After his parents were killed?" The question came out before Phaira could stop it.

Jetsun stared. "You know about that?"

"So it really happened?"

"You doubt it?" The woman sounded surprised.

Phaira didn't know how to respond.

Then Jetsun pushed off the window, her cold exterior snapped back into place. "Ozias is coming back," she ordered. "You need to figure out what to say. She's persistent. You have to tell her something, or she'll never let you out of here. And I'm not in the market for a roommate, understand?"

When Jetsun was gone, Phaira paced the perimeter of the room, trailing her fingers across the cold windowpanes, the sumptuous curtains, the silken wallpaper. She went through the events of Kings Canyon, again and again, from start to finish, separating the bodies and the blame. There were only two sides to step on.

And regardless of the blurred lines, it wasn't the side of the Savas.

* * *

"I want immunity."

She made the announcement as soon as she heard Ozias's footsteps on the threshold. The detective froze mid-step, her eyebrows lifted. "For yourself?"

Phaira stood in the center of the sitting room. She'd borrowed clothes from Jetsun, who handed them over with reluctance, stating that they were old and far back enough in her closet to warrant a donation. The black jersey dress swung to her ankles, belted at the waist, and the slim-cut black jacket over the dress made her feel a little more secure, a little more contained. She looked slim and chic, by the reflection in the mirror, a slicker version of herself. "For my family."

Ozias looked at her askance. "Who is your family?"

"You know."

The woman's mouth twisted. "You know, your brothers have been just as difficult to grasp as you," she finally said. "Quite the family."

It was a relief to hear her say that, though Phaira worked not to show it. Patrol hadn't found them yet.

"If they remain untouched, I'll tell you what happened in Kings," Phaira said, her hand resting on the pink armchair. "I want the warrant removed from Emir and Anandi Ajyo, too."

"Now, wait a minute -"

"How badly do you want to know what happened, Detective?"

"This must be some story you're about to tell me, Ms. Lore."

"You have no idea," Phaira said. "Can we find somewhere private, and unrecorded, please?"

Ozias looked across the decorated room. "Are you officially waiving your right to your lawyer?"

"I guess I am." Phaira raised her wrists, waiting for the handcuffs. "I just hope you're the right call, Detective, I really do."

* * *

For ten minutes, Ozias never moved, and barely blinked. Her brow occasionally furrowed. When Phaira finished speaking, she wanted to slump back in her chipped, rickety chair. Instead she kept her back straight and watched the detective, waiting for her reaction.

Finally, Ozias exhaled through her nose with a soft *hmph*! "That woman, Huma, she had the ability to blow up the base like that? Using her mind?"

"I can't explain how, but it happened." There was no reason that the detective had to know about Sydel's existence. Huma was an easy substitute. Her words were close enough to the truth.

"And Aeden Nox was a mercenary." There was a note of disappointment in Ozias's voice. "Working for the syndicate on this revenge-mission."

"Yes. He was a good man, as good as his record. Just got lost along the way. And unfortunately, he dragged Cohen into it, too." When she said her brother's name, Phaira looked at Ozias expectantly.

Ozias sighed. "I must admit, I don't quite know what to do with this information."

"Why do you have to do anything about it? The parties responsible are dead. Close the case. Pursue that shapeshifter instead, and let us go back to our lives"

Then Phaira caught hold of her words. "Let everyone else go back," she corrected, sobering. "I'll take the responsibility. I'm ready. I'll plead guilty to whatever you think appropriate."

"Why did the military discharge you in the first place?" Ozias queried, peering across the table at her. "I read about the Macatia case, how sloppily it was handled. Even if your public behavior was questionable, why would the government give up such a valuable commodity?"

The word commodity made her uneasy. Still, Phaira said nothing.

Ozias sat back in her seat. Phaira crossed her legs, then uncrossed them, waiting.

"And who is the shapeshifter? Any idea?" the woman finally spoke.

"He was impersonating you," Phaira countered. "Don't you have an idea?"

That irked Ozias, she could hear it in her voice: "But you said he recognized you."

"I think he did." Phaira looked down at her bitten fingernails. "When you were unconscious, that imposter told me he was with Nox when he died. That he pulled out Nox's memories. He saw me in them. He wanted to rummage around inside my head for more information."

"Did he?"

"No," Phaira said. Underneath the table, she yanked her wrists apart so the hard metal bit into her skin, forcing her brain to focus on the pain. "He didn't have the chance." An awful thought occurred to her. "Did he - to you?"

"No," Ozias said firmly.

Phaira eyed the detective, and felt a tiny, sick drop in her stomach. Ozias had crossed paths with the shapeshifter before, of course she had. Who knew what had transpired between the two?

"Here's what we do," Ozias said, leaning on her forearms. "I drop the charges. I release you into the public. And you report to me."

"As what?"

"An informant."

"I told you, I'm not a Sava, and I'm not involved with their dealings." As Phaira spoke, she did a quick sweep around the space, looking for any hint of surveillance. On entering, Ozias gave her word that there was none. She continued to search.

"You're registered as a Locate-Retrieve-Protect field specialist."

Phaira waved her hand, the chain between her wrists jingling. "I haven't decided what I'm doing yet."

"Decision made. Work with me."

"On what?"

"Well, first off, I want that imposter in my holding cell. You do that for me, we call off the charges."

"You'll let me go?" This was a trick. It had to be some kind of deception, some way to expose all her connections and friends.

Ozias spoke very slowly and clearly. "I'll put out the bulletin that you've been released. The imposter will hear, and likely expose himself again. And when he does, then you contact me, and I'll respond."

Phaira's mouth opened and closed.

"I might prefer jail than living under your thumb," she finally said.

"Really?"

"I don't know where I'm going," Phaira said after another long pause. "I don't know where my brothers are, and I have nothing with me."

"I know where they are," Ozias said. "A call came in a few hours ago. An anonymous tip, saying that Cohen Byrne has been hiding out in Toomba. That's about two hundred kilometers west, in the mountain range."

"What?" Phaira cried, her panic bursting through. "Who called them in?"

"We traced the call and picked her up in Zangari, though not without a fight, I might mention." Ozias made a face somewhere between a smile and a wince of pain. "Lucky me, to have another stubborn, sullen suspect who refuses to talk. Maybe you know her?"

Ozias drew out her Lissome. A translucent screen popped out of the top, displaying a mugshot portrait, fuzzy, but the identity unmistakable.

"You've got to be kidding me," Phaira said, staring at the pixelated image.

"Name?"

"CaLarca," Phaira said without hesitation. She didn't care about exposing the woman. "I don't know if that's her surname or what. I only met her for a day, weeks ago." Her stomach twisted with hatred. CaLarca had the nerve to try and get her brother arrested? What else had she done in the time that Phaira was gone?

"See? Our partnership is already beneficial." Smiling, Ozias withdrew the projection, and snapped her Lissome shut.

"Why are you holding her?"

"For you," Ozias said. "I thought you might appreciate it."

Already working to appease me, Phaira thought with unease. *Everything is a gentle manipulation with this woman.*

"Have you already arrested Cohen, then?" she managed to ask.

"No," Ozias said. "I'd like to confirm your story with him at some point, but not yet. I'm more interested in our imposter."

She rose to her feet. "So let's go."

Phaira followed Ozias through the door of the apartment, past the single guard posted by the entrance, and into the open, against the wind and the swell of commuters. Her borrowed jacket from Jetsun wasn't thick enough, but she did her best to hold her shivering at bay. She wouldn't show any weakness to Ozias, especially with the woman so close, her left hand gripping the link between her handcuffs.

With every step, Phaira fought the urge to disarm her and flee. She could take a flying leap and grab hold of that dangling fire escape ladder to her right. She could leap from wall to wall in the next narrow alley until she reached an open window.

Then they stopped. Phaira blinked, taken back to the present. They were standing at an intersection, swarms of people moving past them.

"This is where I leave you," Ozias told her.

"Just like that?"

"Just like that." The detective reached over and grasped the handcuffs. They fell away with the smooth turn of the key.

"You must know that I will just disappear," Phaira blurted out. "You let me go, you'll never find me again."

"Perhaps." Ozias smiled for the first time. Her teeth were white, straight and brilliant. "Curious to hear the next story you're ready to tell, Ms. Lore."

And with that, the detective crossed the street and left Phaira standing on the corner. The handcuffs were gone, but her presence lingered, an invisible bind around her throat. She'd never be free of Ozias.

"Phaira?"

That low, husky, haughty voice. She knew it instantly.

In her mind, her hand shot to CaLarca's throat. Pedestrians cried out, jumping aside, calling for help as Phaira slammed CaLarca into a brick wall, squeezing with all her pent-up frustration. CaLarca scratched at her arms, yanking backwards, scrabbling to pull away her fingers away. But Phaira didn't feel anything, just sweaty, burning fury and the rigidness of her body...

"I understand," CaLarca said quietly, breaking Phaira from her vision. "I would probably have the same impulse, if I were you."

A wave of exhaustion passed over Phaira. She walked to a brick wall, leaned against it and closed her eyes. She sensed CaLarca doing the same, staying about a foot apart. In the darkness, Phaira felt the sway and pull of waves of people, sweeping past them, the world moving on. She couldn't form a solid thought. She didn't want to. But the gnawing sense of responsibility grew in her. She couldn't ignore it.

"I can't even imagine," Phaira finally spoke, "what's happened in the past few weeks that has led you to be standing here with me."

She glanced over at CaLarca. For the first time, Phaira noted the black leggings that the woman wore, how they visibly pulsed, and the silver cane in one hand. "Did Renzo make those for you?"

"He did," the woman said, staring at her feet.

"So, to say thank you, you try to get Cohen arrested?"

"I was angry," CaLarca said simply. "It was bad judgment."

"And now?"

"I need to make amends. If you are going back to your family, please take me with you."

Phaira scoffed. "I need a better reason to put up with you than making apologies."

"I owe it to Sydel to ensure her safety."

Phaira eyed CaLarca from head to toe. "What's the threat?"

CaLarca's mouth pressed tight. She didn't speak.

"Let's be clear," Phaira told her, pushing off the wall. "Getting what you want is dependant on telling me the truth - what's happened since I left, and what part you've played in it. The truth, as plainly as you can deliver it."

CaLarca's head stayed low. Finally, she nodded. "I'll tell you everything I know. At least, everything I can remember."

As they hitchhiked and hopped trains, making their way to Toomba, Phaira stopped CaLarca at several points in her story to ask if she was being honest.

At first, CaLarca was indignant at the disrespect. Then she had to stop and think. She was so used to measuring the lies in everyone; she didn't think about how often she'd laid veils over her intentions. The exercise was brutal, but merciful in a way. Going through what happened after the disasterous NINE initiative, step by step, was a process to verify that her memories were true. To prove that she wasn't a monster.

After she ran from Kings Canyon, fourteen-year-old CaLarca woke in a hospital, severely dehydrated, sunburned, and in shock. A week later, she was home. She refused to speak, or leave her bedroom. But she heard her mother and father, their whispers, shuffling papers behind her closed door. When her parents did come to see her, they radiated with fear. They could hardly look at her.

Her first words were to ask for them to send her away to boarding school. She'd found one by the East-South border, secluded and secure. They agreed immediately. CaLarca's chest twisted when she saw their relief.

Within days, everything was arranged. Soon, she stood with two bags in the threshold of a grand brick estate on its own acreage, kilometres from any town. Dense forest surrounded the school; students were expressively forbidden to leave the grounds for fear of being lost. There were rules and timetables and uniforms, as laid out by the headmaster in his office. No nonsense tolerated. None to worry about, CaLarca promised, her tone demure.

That night, she broke into his office and pocketed his display of antique rana coins. Then she stole into the night, leaving her possessions behind. There was nothing to hold onto.

The factory sector was perfect. In the old manufacturing towns in the North, no one looked closely at faces, or backgrounds; they just needed able hands and bodies. The clattering, rattling noise of the mechanics deafened her thoughts, and deadened her raw nerves. She worked until exhaustion, so she didn't dream. But the dread remained of being discovered, of being sent back, or even worse, if someone from the NINE found her. When her anxiety grew too intense, CaLarca travelled to another plant. There were always places looking for strong hands, for someone young and malleable, eager for double shifts.

A year passed. And then ten. No one came for her. Nothing changed.

Not until that one day, in the middle of her shift.

"Hey! Someone is looking for you," the foreman hollered through her earplugs. "Tell them not to bother you when you're on the job, or I'll write you up."

When CaLarca went outside, wiping the dust and grime from her face, her gloves balled into one hand, a man was waiting. He removed his cap at her approach. Dressed in wool layers, the man looked to be in his early-twenties, though he carried several fine lines around his brown eyes. Brown-black hair cut short, a haze of a beard. Though barrel-chested, he had sharp hollows in his cheeks, the remnants of starvation at some point.

"Cyrah?" he called to her.

She froze. There was something familiar about him, but she couldn't quite place it.

"You've hardly changed at all," the man said. "It's incredible."

Then it hit her. "Ganasan?"

His face flooded with relief.

CaLarca's brain couldn't form words. "I didn't realize it was - how did you find - "

"I've been looking for a long time."

"For me?" CaLarca stuttered, her body coursing with fear. "Why?"

"Because I made a promise."

"A promise?" CaLarca felt so stupid, repeating his words, but she couldn't process what was going on.

"You don't remember?" The man's expression fell.

We'll run away. I'll take care of you. Whatever it takes. CaLarca remembered every word the boy spoke, so long ago.

She finally spoke with measured kindness: "We were just children, Ganasan. In an awful situation. You owe me nothing."

"If you'll let me," he told her, his nerves showing through his voice. "If you'll forgive me, I'd be honored if you came to stay with me."

"Stay with you?" CaLarca gasped. "Ganasan, please. You're not making any sense."

"I know it sounds crazy. But we've seen crazy, and people who understand crazy should stick together. You were my only friend in Kings, CaLarca. I want to stay connected to you."

It was true: not even a glimmer of gray around him. He was being honest.

"I can't do this right now," she finally said, painfully aware of how dirty she was. "I have to go back to work."

"Can I return when your shift is over?" Ganasan asked, twisting his cap in his hands. "Can we talk more?"

"Are you alone?" she accused.

His face went dark. "Of course."

He understood what she was asking. She recognized him now. His eyes were the same as that eleven-year-old's, full of determination, and reverence.

CaLarca stared at him, weighing her options. Ten years of life in the factory sector, living on scraps and in the shadows. Ten years of being alone with nothing but her memories, and the occasional spark of Nadi in her hands.

She would be a fool to say no.

* * *

Ganasan owned a vineyard in the South, two days away by train; small, but blissfully remote, acres wide, its border surrounded by forest. He came into a small inheritance as a teenager, he explained to CaLarca, and when he turned eighteen, he took the money, went travelling and purchased the land on sight. He had been working it alone for the past four years, with the occasional help of neighbors, but mostly in solitude. He had no desire to be near the cities, or people in general. Only CaLarca had always been in the corner of his mind, gnawing at him.

So, some weeks ago, he'd left his farm and started tracking her path from manufacturing district to district. It wasn't difficult. People remembered her green streaks, her black eyes, and her youth. CaLarca still looked like a teenager, even ten years later.

But Ganasan aged normally, she noted, peering at his profile. When he glanced over, she switched her gaze to the land, taking in the greenery, the tinny echo of birds in the distance, the smell of earth, ignoring the nerves fluttering in her stomach.

That night, in the silence of the woods, by the light of the bonfire, she told him what she'd seen that last day in Kings: the blood, the screams, the hand on her head. He, in turn, confessed that during his first Insynn rush, when he had taken Tehmi's arm, he'd seen the chain of events leading to her death, but he was too afraid to say anything. In the orange glow of the fire, CaLarca watched him struggle with his shame. Her mind turned to the baby, the memory of that warm bundle stuck with her, even more than Tehmi and Joran's murder.

We harbor the same guilt, she thought. *We're both haunted by deeds not done. We are connected. We always have been.*

It was a quiet companionship. She was used to physical work after years in the factory, and quick to learn the farming trade. And she was content in the sweat and silence, the rows to get lost in, the vines a delicate latticework over the fences, how the forest enfolded the land, and it was their own entity. She even liked the little village, five kilometers to the west, with its small stores and white fences. When the weekly errands were done, she would go to the reservoir and sit on its edge, watching the water's lazy, sweeping foam patterns, ropey seaweed in clusters, still, but vibrant under the surface.

And over the weeks, she and Ganasan drew closer, orbiting around each other. They sat by the bonfire each night, like two old pioneers. He held her hand like a gentleman, and kissed her only when she said yes. One night, when it seemed like Ganasan wanted more, she let it happen. Soon, she found she craved the same. Every step felt natural, and right, and more familiar than she ever would have imagined.

Years passed. The vineyard thrived under two sets of hands, and the occasional hired worker for harvest season. Sales expanded, just enough to keep them stable. And together, CaLarca and Ganasan began to revisit their NINE abilities, prodding, testing, holding onto each other as things sparked to life. Ganasan had more control over his Insynn flashes. They only happened when he willed them to, not with any touch of bare skin. And CaLarca made knives again, and wire sculptures, and pieces of string that she would playfully drape on Ganasan's back without him knowing.

On their twelfth year together, when spring broke into summer, CaLarca couldn't shake a new, unsettled feeling. In the shadow of their bedroom, when Ganasan was away, a quick scan of her body almost made her faint: there was the tiniest halo of energy in the middle of her abdomen.

"Do you think he'll have our gifts?" she'd asked him that night. "Or more?"

"He'll have something," Ganasan said. His beard had a sheen of silver to it, those hollows in his cheeks still sharp. "But we can teach him now to use it well, whatever it might be, and to keep it hidden from the public."

When Bennet was born, CaLarca looked hard and long into his black eyes, a thousand secret fears in her brain, wondering if she was really capable of this. If she was worthy. If she would only ruin him in the end with her selfishness and solitude.

But Bennet grew, and he was quiet and curious; he rolled in the leaves and studied each intently; he was fearless and buoyant, and loved her the best of anyone. And she was content, she realized one day, truly, with her unexpected domestic life.

One day, there was a knock at the door. CaLarca was alone, picking up after Bennet's flurry of playtime. The knock sounded again.

Curious. They rarely had visitors. A quick glance out of the window showed a craggy-faced old man. She couldn't recall his surname, but he was a friend of Ganasan's, she recalled. His property was to the east, maybe four kilometers away. She had to acknowledge him.

Wiping her dusty hands on a towel, she opened the door. The man greeted her. "CaLarca."

"Yes," she said as politely as she could manage.

"May I come in?"

"If you're seeking Ganasan, he's in the fields with our son."

"Your son," the man repeated.

A shimmer came over the neighbor's face, like a ripple of heat.

Within two seconds, CaLarca manifested a boning knife in her hand, the other palm outstretched to ward him away. "Stay where you are," she commanded.

The man smirked. "You've barely changed at all. How is that possible?"

A pull in the center of her chest. Familiar voice. Something in the way he was looking at her.

"Will you please dissolve that thing? I'm here with a warning, Cyrah."

Kuri. It was Kuri's voice, coming from the mouth of the neighbor.

CaLarca stared at him. The knife in her hand trembled. Had he possessed the man? Had he killed him? Or was it an illusion? Tears crawled up her throat. "I don't want you here," she hissed. "Not here."

"I never wanted to see you again, either," Kuri told her. "But we're in danger."

"Who is we?" she demanded.

"All of us from Kings. We can't hide anymore."

Inevitable, she couldn't help but think. Punishment was inevitable. It wasn't enough that she and Ganasan had expressed their grief, that they tried to make a good, productive life. They couldn't escape who they were, and what they did in that underground base.

The door creaked open. Ganasan stood in the threshold, holding two-year-old Bennet.

Kuri eyed him up and down. "My," he deadpanned. "You've grown."

Ganasan frowned. Catching his eye, CaLarca gestured with her chin. "Kuri," she said curtly.

Bennet started to wiggle, wanting to get down, but Ganasan held firm. "Did you kill our neighbor?"

"Of course not. I just borrowed his face," Kuri said. "I knew you wouldn't let me in if I showed up as myself."

"Then take off that veil, or whatever it is," Ganasan commanded.

"No time. We're being hunted down."

"By who?" CaLarca exclaimed.

"The Sava Syndicate. Crime family in the North and East. Remember the four kids from Kings, from that day?" he added, glancing at CaLarca. "Up on the cliff? They grew up to be influential, and hungry for answers."

"So you came to warn us?" Ganasan said flatly. "We had nothing to do with them."

"They don't know that," Kuri said. "The Savas recovered all the records from Kings: Joran's files, surveillance, everything that was left behind. They know our names, our faces and our abilities. They're in the base now, making preparations."

"But you -" CaLarca had to work to keep from stammering, her nerves were so rattled. "You killed Tehmi. And Joran. And that family."

"I didn't kill anyone," Kuri objected, his face growing red. "Tehmi was an accident, I never meant -"

Then Kuri looked at his feet, taking in a long, slow breath. "I wasn't as skilled as I am now," he said quietly. "I'm in control now." He shot a look at Ganasan. "That's why I came. The Savas are putting together an army to track us down, and you're on the list."

CaLarca didn't have to look at her partner to know what he was thinking. They were so entrenched in their lives here, separate from the world, their own land, their own rules. They couldn't leave it behind and start anew in another territory. They didn't want to.

"I'm going back to Kings to investigate the threat," Kuri continued. "Maybe try to neutralize it, somehow."

"By doing what?" CaLarca challenged. Bennet began to whine, reaching for her. When she crossed the room and took the child, balancing him on her hip, she felt Kuri's eyes on her the entire while.

"There's a rumor that the baby, Sydel, is alive. And involved, somehow. If we can talk to her, maybe she can help to diffuse the situation." He paused for a few moments. "I'd like CaLarca to come with me."

"Why?" CaLarca said faintly. The baby was alive, and out for revenge against her. How had this happened?

"I think another woman's presence might help," Kuri said. "And just in case, I want someone who can defend herself. Unless you've suddenly developed skills other than fortune-telling," he sniped at Ganasan.

"Where's Shantou?" CaLarca couldn't help but ask. "Are you still in contact?

Oddly, Kuri winced. "She's – not able to travel," he finally said.

He was full of deceit. He couldn't even show his true face. CaLarca stared at him, trying to pierce the veil. It was strong, though. And despite all that she knew about him, she felt an irresistable pull. She had wondered about that baby for over twenty years. She'd been waiting for this moment. She set Bennet down on the floor, prodding him to go play.

"Wait outside," Ganasan told Kuri. "If you try to eavesdrop, she'll know."

"Wouldn't dream of it." Kuri tipped his hat, and like a spectre, he slid out of the house.

"Take my hand," CaLarca said quietly when the door closed. "Tell me what you see."

"Are you sure?"

They both glanced at Bennet, who sang to himself, pushing a wooden train along the edge of a table. Then Ganasan's warm hand engulfed hers. His fingers stiffened, gripping her, hurting her, but she made no move to step away.

Soon enough, the pressure ceased, and his breath came back. "I see us reunited," he revealed. His hand slipped from hers. "All three of us, together, somewhere by the ocean."

"When?"

"I'm not sure. It's muddled," he confessed.

"You know I have never been able to forget about Sydel," CaLarca said quietly. "If we're ever to have peace from the past -"

"It has to be resolved," Ganasan confirmed. "One way or another." He sighed. "I guess it was inevitable."

"Yes," CaLarca said, as Bennet toddled over to lean against her leg. "Inevitable."

* * *

She left within the hour, but not before taking a moment to whisk Bennet out of sight from Kuri's curious stare. She refused to let him see any trace of vulnerability, how tightly she held the boy and took in the smell of his hair, tucking it away in her memory.

One week, she thought, as the boy clapped his hands on her cheeks and squeezed. *One week.*

The next two days were a blur of travel, landscapes, and hours of silence. After so many days and nights occupied with Bennet, it was almost luxurious.

Overnight, Kuri had taken on the appearance of a young man with black hair, and angular, handsome face, close to his original appearance, twenty-odd years ago. He didn't look like that in truth, she knew it.

"Are you so afraid of your true appearance?" she asked him, as they looked over the river, crossing the channel via ferry.

"If you have the ability to choose your looks, why not?" Kuri returned. Leaning back against the rail, he looked rakish and brooding, like a great playboy. Only when she concentrated did she catch the shimmer over his features, like the skin hiding the rotten fruit.

Still, her curiosity was there. Kings was so long ago, it felt like another life, or maybe even a dream. But here was Kuri, and she was fourteen again, afraid, in wonder, and full of dread.

"Is it an Eko trait?" she inquired. "Is it about altering my perception?"

"Both Eko and Nadi."

"I didn't realize you were a Nadi."

"I've evolved. I thought you would have as well."

She ignored the insult. "How did you find us in the first place?"

Kuri smiled. "Well, you haven't changed your names, for starters. Didn't take much effort." His dark eyes fixed on hers. "Interesting that the two of you got together. I wouldn't have guessed that you like them younger."

CaLarca took her Lissome out of her pocket and waggled it in front of his face. "And what would I discover if I looked you up?"

His smirk faded. "I've made mistakes, I admit it. But anything you might find out? I did it all for Shantou. That's all you need to know."

"Oh, aren't you the sweetheart," CaLarca cooed. "You actually care about someone, not just sucking out memories and living vicariously through them?"

Kuri clenched the railing so tight that the veins stuck out.

"What?" CaLarca challenged. "What did you expect? Reminiscing about old times? I remember everything, Kuri. Nothing has changed."

"Then why did you come?"

"It wasn't for you," CaLarca said. "You're a distraction. I'm going for Sydel, and to ensure my family is safe. I don't care what you do afterwards, you or Shantou. In fact, never come anywhere near my property again. Are we clear?"

Kuri glared at her, as if to pin her to the railing. She stared back at him, refusing to break away, even as a worm of anxiety writhed in her stomach, wondering what they might encounter, wondering what form that baby had taken, and how much hatred Sydel harbored.

* * *

They took an overnight train, working their way into the center of the continent. When the engines pulsed, and the carriages were underway, Kuri pulled CaLarca into his assigned bunk. Her core flared at the intimate touch, his sharp, metallic smell, but in the darkness, he let go of her arm and handed her a Lissome, already lit up.

"Look," he said grimly. "It's already starting."

CaLarca scanned the information. Just rumors on the network, but something was happening. People had gone missing without a trace. The Savas were absent from their usual places of intimidation in the East. A string of bombings throughout the North were connected, so went several theories. And stories were leaking: encounters with people who possessed strange, undefinable powers, memory loss, the loss of free will...

In her tiny third-class bunk, curtains drawn against the hall light, she called Ganasan via Lissome. She did her best to keep the call short, as Bennet was growing upset in the background. The boy's whine was a stab of guilt in the chest.

"One week," she promised. "And nothing will stop me from leaving. Even if it's bad, if I have to leave Kuri behind, so be it. Then we will decide what to do."

She had spare rana, tucked into a hidden packet at her hip. She could travel, she could hitchhike. She'd cut off all her hair, she'd change all their names, if needed.

Really, they should have done it earlier. Why were they so careless?

The sun rose, and the train pulled into Ivo, that same old sleepy town. It looked the same as it did twenty-five years ago. Stepping down from the train, shielding her eyes from the sun, CaLarca could hardly breathe with the flush of memories. She balled her other hand into a fist, remembering the cool smoothness of the parasol handle, her fear mixed with excitement.

"Ready?" she heard Kuri's voice behind her.

They walked for hours. When Kings Canyon shimmered into sight, they took the long way around, so to observe the familiar cliff-face from afar. As they hiked through brush, CaLarca focused on conserving her Nadi. It prickled in her stomach, longing to be released, but she might need it. She had to hold onto it for as long as possible.

When they finally reached the opposite edge of the Canyon, puffing from exertion, they took in the sight of the cliff-face, jutting one hundred feet high, red and rocky, and unmistakable. The old base was in there. It should have been shut down, boarded up, collapsed, but it looked just the same. There was something strange in the air, though. CaLarca squinted.

"What is it?" Kuri said under his breath.

When she let her mind open, she saw it: the shimmer of a barrier, like a patchwork quilt, different energies seamed together and covering the cliff-face.

"Is that... Eko?" she wondered outloud. "They have Ekos in there, protecting them?'"

Kuri shrugged. "Makes sense, if you think about it. Use like to attract like. We were never the only NINE."

There was movement on the canyon floor. CaLarca's heart leapt as that secret door swung open, a black hole at the base of the cliff, where four bodies emerged. One shadow loomed over another, their words inaudible. Then the four stumbled down the rocky incline. A clicking sound reverberated. Staring at the group, CaLarca zeroed in on the single girl, with copper hair and bronze skin, prodded by a lean, dark man, who glowed a faint red.

"That's her," Kuri said, excitement in his voice. "Sydel. It has to be her."

But the girl was next to that dark man, who waved a firearm in her face. One of the Savas?

"He's the leader," Kuri hissed. "I've read about him. Keller Sava."

"And the others?" One was a young man, thick and tall with a shaved head, who remained close to Sydel; the other an older woman with a white cloak and short silver hair.

"Mercenaries, most likely," Kuri surmised. "They aren't important. Sydel's the key to everything."

"Then we need to protect her." As soon as she spoke the words, she knew it was right. It was her responsibility to make first contact, to ensure this girl was kept safe. Her redemption, twenty-five years in the making. "I'll go. You stay here."

"Go?" Kuri sputtered. "And do what? Introduce yourself to the enemy?"

"Let's see what happens."

"Have you forgotten that everyone here in Kings is bent on killing us?"

"I'm not staying here," CaLarca shot back. "I need to know if it's really Sydel."

She didn't give him a chance to respond, moving swiftly through the brush, gathering her skirts to slide down rocky paths, past disintegrating bushes. The landscape opened, and flattened. The sun beat down, but she didn't notice. As an afterthought, she tossed her shoes aside.

When CaLarca slowed, finally touching the canyon floor, she saw the aura of a consciousness arching through the air like a lazy bird, searching. CaLarca remained still as the rolling energy came to her, passed over her, and circled back. Inside, she could see the faintest outline of brown eyes, beckoning.

CaLarca kept her mind sealed. Then the consciousness disappeared.

CaLarca walked faster to the light that marked the entrance into the canyon. Her feet swept through the sand, making little arcs. She could smell sweat, and metal.

The foursome came into view, one hundred feet away. The dark one with a firearm, surrounded by red. The stocky teenage boy, vibrating with orange. The old woman, weakly lit in yellow, like a forest blocking out the sun. And the girl: small and bronzed and thin, copper braids twisted up on top of her head. For a moment, CaLarca couldn't catch a breath; all she could see were Tehmi's eyes, half rolled back into her head, her hand flopped over the edge of the bed, the sound of a baby whimpering...

A voice broke through her thoughts. *Get away from here. These people mean to kill you and your kind in vengeance.*

Surprised, CaLarca looked to the group again. The older woman looked enthralled. The man aimed his firearm at her, but for some reason, CaLarca felt no real threat.

Sydel was looking at her. The voice, soft and girlish, came down the Eko channel again. *They want to torture and use you to track down the rest.*

We know, CaLarca sent back. *These people have not been subtle, Sydel. We came for you, regardless.*

We? You know me?

CaLarca stared across the canyon floor at the girl. So young and afraid, so much like CaLarca when she was first in Kings. *I knew your parents. A long time ago.*

Suddenly, the man with the weapon grabbed hold of Sydel's arm, jerking her to his side. Consumed with anger, CaLarca's hands burned, ready to manifest a knife and stab that man under the ribs.

Sydel's voice flooded into her head again: *Please, just go! She cannot be trusted. No one can.*

Then CaLarca's own arm was grabbed. The Eko channel broke, and she was hauled back into the shadows, the woods and rocks, Kuri's voice in her ear: "Not yet. Not yet."

"Get your hands off me!" she hissed.

"They won't kill her. They'll never get the chance." She could feel his heartbeat, raging against her back.

She wrenched her arm free, just long enough to hear a cry. Sydel was being dragged into the hidden entrance at the base of the cliff. And when the door closed, there was no sign of the girl's consciousness. The rocks shimmered: the Eko barrier, reinstated.

"No," CaLarca whispered. She crouched into a ball on the sand, her hands in her hair, trying to catch her breath. Nadi burned through every pore, and her organs threatened to explode.

"Focus on expelling the Nadi," she heard Kuri's voice. "I know what to do."

So CaLarca put her hands in the sand and let go. The Nadi bled through her fingertips, pooling around her legs like a suffocating blanket, whipping at her hair, squeezing her tighter and tighter, until she thought she might pass out. The ground trembled underneath her, a tiny earthquake.

Then, mercifully, the Nadi began to disappate, as more sounds emerged from the canyon. Blurry-eyed and shivering, CaLarca craned her neck to see. People were pouring out of that same black entrance: large men and women, flashing metal, armor, whooping and slapping each other on the back. A brilliant figure in white suddenly appeared on the cliff-face, halfway between the ground and the top. There was more movement up there, a face emerging from the rocky depths her copper hair rippling in the wind. Sydel!

But then everything happened so fast. An exchange of gunfire, the sudden, silent appearance of a huge blue vessel, descending into the canyon. A mercenary crumbled, and blood shone red, visible even from a distance. One man turned his rifle on the crowd in the canyon. Throats were slashed, the top of heads blown off, a chaotic flurry of death. They were fighting each other.

Next to her, Kuri's hand opened and closed in a slow pattern.

Dust billowed through the canyon, followed by a shockwave. CaLarca covered her head with her hands. And then the world went dark.

How much time passed, she couldn't say. Shadows passed over her, grey, then black, voices, and then nothingness. Then the sun was bright, and the cold wind was whipping over her body, broken and bleeding, and all she could do was cry out for Ganasan, for Sydel, and plead for forgiveness before blackness took over again.

* * *

"And nothing more?" Phaira prodded.

"No," CaLarca said. "I don't know what happened between that day, and when Sydel found me." Just saying the words made her furious. And Marette's presence in all of this was jarring. Why would she get involved with Kuri's plans? Was she doing this on behalf of her sister, Shantou? Was Kuri holding the sisters ransom? Or was it something worse?

Question after question swirled through her head as the train slowed. They were at the base of the Toomba mountain range. Looking up, CaLarca saw no peaks, only clouds.

"Are you coming?" came Phaira's prompt.

"What if I'm a danger to you all?" CaLarca asked. "If I'm wrong about everything?"

"We already know you're wrong about everything," Phaira said, getting to her feet and pushing back her hood, exposing her jagged blue hair. "Here's your chance to change your reputation."

III

There was no way that CaLarca could walk the steep mountain path to Toomba. So the green-haired woman settled into the tiny train shelter, promising to wait there for further instruction.

Phaira didn't quite believe her. Even with her recent confessions, she still didn't trust CaLarca. But the most important thing was making contact with her family. She had no choice but to leave CaLarca behind and forge on.

Hiking through the rocks and mossy growth, it felt good to use her muscles for something other than a fight, to climb and balance and catch edges with her boots. On occasion, Phaira heard the rustle of footsteps. Did Ozias follow her here? Anything was possible, now that she'd agreed to work for her. But no one emerged from the trees.

She trudged upwards for two hours before she caught sight of steps. The woods broke open at the top of the stone stairs, exposing the purple-blue mountains on either side, and just how high Phaira was.

A flicker of movement, just behind the edge of the stone. Someone was up there.

On reaching the final steps, one hand flexed to graze the knife concealed at her thigh, Phaira eyed the old woman who stood at the town entrance, her heavy knitwear, her clean-cut grey bob and lined face. No sign of anyone else. Just a series of winding dirt paths, and great caverns in the background.

"You're Phaira," the woman called over.

Phaira's skin tensed. But she kept her stride, until she loomed over the woman. "I am," she announced.

Suddenly, the woman grasped Phaira's face between two knobby hands. Her icy-blue eyes flicked up and down, examining every corner of Phaira's face.

Phaira jerked away. "What is this?" she barked.

The woman didn't seem to hear. "You look like Lora," she was murmuring. "How strange."

Phaira's heart jerked. "Who are you?"

The woman smiled thinly. "I'm your grandmother, child. Vyoma."

"You're not," Phaira said automatically.

A wry smile came over the woman's face. "I'd be reacting the same way as you," Vyoma said in her odd, creaky voice. "Just as suspicious."

Then she put her hands behind her back, like a soldier standing at attention. "Your brothers are in my house. Just around the path, second cavern. The dark red one."

Caught up in her shock, Phaira managed one word, the first 's' drawn out: "Sydel?"

"Over there," Vyoma nodded over her left shoulder. Phaira caught a glimmer of blue in the distance "In the *Arazura*."

"Why is she in there?"

"I cannot say," Vyoma said with clear disapproval. "She won't come out. Your brothers have tried several times. So have I, and the town physician. She refuses to be seen by anyone. We don't know if she is eating, or going mad."

Her voice dropped in volume. "That green-haired one caused a lot of trouble, by the sounds of it."

"So I hear," Phaira said wearily. For a moment, she wondered if CaLarca would suddenly appear. But when she scanned the horizon, there was nothing but clouds.

"Will you tell Ren and Cohen that I'm here?" she asked Vyoma.

"Shouldn't you tell them yourself? They've waited a long time. And I'd like to - " Here, the woman faltered. "Well, have a chance to introduce myself. Explain myself."

"I don't need an explanation," Phaira said curtly. Her mind reeled with a thousand different emotions, none of which were useful in that moment. She could process them later. "Right now, I need to see Sydel."

"Are you close with that girl?"

"Not really," Phaira said as she brushed past Vyoma. "Barely know her."

Toomba held cavern after cavern, and within lay huts and houses, made of wood, something that Phaira hadn't seen before. Some smaller openings held broken-down transports, heavy with rust. Her boots crunched against the gravel on the ground. How many people lived here? Why would they choose a life so far removed?

Inside the fourth hollow, the *Arazura* stood, cold and silent. Phaira crept closer, slipping through the entry door. Her steps made small tinny echoes up the stairs.

Then her feet hit piles of trash, thrown clothes, wires snaking along the hall. The rooms had been ransacked: Sydel's alcove, Cohen's and Renzo's cabin, the common room upturned, the contents of the kitchen dumped on the floor. And inside her own cabin, Phaira could hear muttering, and movement, like a skittering rat.

Bracing herself, she hit the release. The door slid open.

The room was dark, and smelled of dust. Sydel was in the corner, riffling through Phaira's clothes.

"Sydel!" Phaira burst out. "What are you - ?" Then her voice caught in her throat, taking in the girl's hair, her red eyes, her flushed, waxy skin.

"Go away," Sydel hissed, a haunted, drawn-out exhalation.

"No," Phaira snapped. "Get up and tell me what's going on."

Sydel rose to her feet, wavering in place, like she might keel over. Her dress was heavily wrinkled, with visible stains. Her collarbones jutted out.

Then, with slow, shuffling steps, Sydel drew closer. A wave of heat went through the room. Phaira's skin broke out in goosebumps. She pressed her back to the doorframe and held her breath, resisting the urge to lash out, to stop the girl from getting any closer.

Suddenly, Sydel lurched forward, grabbing Phaira's hands. "I just want to try it." she whispered, her voice feverish and low. "I just want to forget for a while. I know you have it somewhere, I'm sorry I made such a mess, but - will you show me where the mekaline is?"

"What? No!" Phaira exclaimed. Is this what the girl thought of her? As a drug connection?

Sydel glared at her like a sullen teenager. "Why won't you share?"

"Share?" Phaira repeated. "I'm not - I don't have a stash here, Sydel." She yanked away her hands. "And even if I did, there's no way that I'm exposing you to it."

"Why? Why is it okay for you, and not for me?" Sydel accused, lifting one bony shoulder. "You do it, and you must get some satisfaction out of it."

Phaira winced, but Sydel continued to talk: "Why can't you just let me have it? What does it matter? Why shouldn't we just do whatever we want?"

Phaira took Sydel by the wrists. "What's happened since I left?" she demanded. "What's going on that I don't - ?"

"I'm waking up," Sydel interrupted, lifting her chin. "I'm pulling my head out of the sand, as you once told me."

"No, you're digging into a whole different pit," Phaira corrected, giving the girl's wrists a yank. "The Sydel I know wouldn't even think to ask me about meka."

"You don't know me," Sydel shot back. Then her lips quivered. "Do you know we're nearly the same age? Yann erased my memories," she added, with a small bark of laughter. "Seven years, gone."

Phaira did know. Yann had confessed it to her, weeks ago. But it wouldn't help to confirm it outloud.

"Now everything makes sense," Sydel continued. "Why everyone in Jala Communia, all the people I loved and grew up with, why they drifted away. I wondered for years what I'd done wrong, what I'd said to make everyone hate me so much. Now I know. They were afraid. They knew I was unnatural. Just some foolish pawn, easy to manipulate, soft, stupid Sydel." She jerked her wrists away from Phaira's grip. "Well, I don't care anymore."

Phaira took hold of Sydel by the shoulder and steered her to the mattress on the floor. When the girl sat down, Phaira slid next to her. "Look at me," she demanded.

Scorn on her face, Sydel glanced over.

"Yann was terrible to you," Phaira told her. "You're right to be so upset. But you don't ever, ever use meka. I mean it."

"But you do."

"I'm an addict."

Cold rushed through Phaira. She'd never said those words before; even as she spoke them, she was desperate to take them back.

"You hate me." Sydel's voice brought her back. "Even more than before."

"I don't – I don't hate you," Phaira said, with a sigh at the end.

She slung her arms over her knees, and looked down at her feet. "I'm really scared of you, Sydel," she confessed.

"You don't have to be"

"But I am," Phaira interrupted. "I'm terrified you'll explode again, or take over our minds, or some other awful thing."

She glanced at the girl. Sydel's mouth was in a thin line, her eyebrows knitted together.

"But you're a good person," Phaira continued. "It's obvious you're a good person. You're kind, and generous, and you're probably better than the rest of us put together." She exhaled slowly. "I don't know what to say to you. I don't know how to relax around you. Or if I ever should."

"I'm not going to hurt you." Sydel's words came out in a rush. "I'll never hurt you, or your family, or anyone. Never again. I'm not going to be that person." She looked fierce and pink, with some of that familiar stubbornness. Buoyed at the sight, Phaira wished she could tell Sydel that she believed her.

"You need to know something, Sydel," she said instead. "I met up with CaLarca."

"What?" Sydel recoiled. "Where?"

"It doesn't matter. But we spoke, and - "

"You can't believe a word she says," Sydel interrupted. "She was manipulating us the whole time."

"I know," Phaira told her. "She told me everything. She wants to make amends with you."

Sydel snorted. "I don't care what she wants. I only care about what I want." Her jaw tightened, and she nodded three times before continuing. "I want to take responsibility for the things I've done. There's one Sava cousin left; I want to apologize to him for killing his kin."

"You can't do that," Phaira said immediately. "It'll bring the world down on our head, and us, and lead everyone straight to - " Then she stared at the girl's profile. "Wait, did you do it already? Did you reach someone?"

"No. I don't know how to reach the Sava family, the grandfather, or the remaining cousin." Her head lifted, and her determined eyes met Phaira's. "I want to apologize to them."

Phaira felt weak. "Sydel, you mean well, but you don't know what you're asking."

"I can't move forward until I confess the truth," Sydel said. Her face darkened. "And you can tell CaLarca that if she wants to make amends, she'll do the same."

A quiet knock echoed through the room. Phaira and Sydel looked up. Renzo and Cohen stood in the doorframe.

"There's -" Renzo began. "I don't know how he found us, but... Yann is out there."

Sydel shot to her feet. "He's here?"

Cohen nodded. "He says he has to talk to -"

"Is he alone?" Phaira broke in.

"No," Renzo said. "He brought reinforcements."

IV.

The balding man stood red-faced and puffing, his hands on his knees. Behind him, on the final stone step of the Toomba path, his four companions were unfazed, their hands behind their backs, dressed in the unmistakable colors of law enforcement. Phaira froze at the sight.

It was only by her brothers' prodding that she started to walk. The foursome stayed close, Sydel in front, drawing closer and closer to the Communia elder. During the silent walk, Phaira stared at Sydel's back, wondering what the girl was thinking.

When she stopped, six feet away from her former master, Yann straightened. "I'm so sorry, Sydel," he croaked, his voice gritty from dehydration. "I owe you so many apologies."

"What are you doing here?" Her question was barely a whisper.

Yann moved to embrace her. "When I heard about Kings, I had to see you -"

"Hands off." Phaira's voice was half-lost in the wind, but the man caught the intent.

Yann lowered his hands. "You've changed. You've become so strong."

"Not for the better," Sydel said flatly. "Though inevitable, given my heritage. Predestined to hurt." Her gaze drifted to the four men and women behind Yann. "Are they here to arrest me?"

"Of course not," Yann soothed. "You've done nothing wrong."

Sydel's face twisted. "You excommunicated me because I was wrong, in every way."

Yann sighed. "My word," he muttered, "still as argumentative as ever." He gestured at the men and women in uniform. "They are here as escorts. If you will only listen -"

Cohen made a low growl in the back of his throat.

"Why now?" Renzo barked, his arms crossed over his chest. "A sudden change of heart?"

"No," Yann said. "New information." He glanced at Sydel again. "Kuri came to see me."

Everyone stiffened, but Yann kept talking. "And I think he's right. I think after all this time, we have to come together again, and sever the last connection to what happened so many years ago." His hand lifted to the back of his neck. "We have to remove whatever was implanted into our brains, and we need you to do it."

"Me?" Sydel gasped. "How can I do such a thing? I'm no surgeon."

"This kind of surgery is incredibly costly." He sighed again. "As crude as it sounds, we need rana. And you, as the rightful heir to Joran's estate, can provide it. You can save us all."

"You're here for money?" Phaira burst out. "After everything you did!"

"Stop," came Sydel's hushed voice. She gazed at Yann. "What do you need?"

"Syd," Cohen gasped.

"A signature, and a vial of blood," Yann said, ignoring the outbursts. "The blood to acknowledge your existence as Sydel Shovann Asanto, the rightful heir to Joran Asanto's estate. The signature to transfer ownership of the existing accounts." He smiled faintly. "You'll be quite the heiress, my dear."

"Why now?" Renzo questioned. "Why do this now, and not years ago?

"Because I didn't know about the others," Yann said. "My concern was keeping Sydel safe, not my own wellbeing. But we all want the chance to start anew, if she is willing. If she is the girl that I raised."

"She's far more than that," came a new voice.

Everyone turned. There was CaLarca, hunched over her cane, breathing heavily and glaring at Yann. A frightened hiker, her escort, was already running at full speed down the stairs, his footsteps richochetting through the mountains.

"What are you - ?" Renzo and Cohen exploded.

"She came with me," Phaira interrupted. "Stand down." It was enough to shock both brothers into silence.

Then Yann spoke, wonder in his voice. "Cyrah. You're here."

CaLarca grimaced. "Don't." She shuffled towards Phaira and the others. A crack broke through the atmosphere, somewhere in the distance. Everyone jumped, looking in all directions, but there were only birds in the air, and the sound of wind.

"I'm also here to apologize," CaLarca began, eyeing Sydel.

"I don't care about apologizes," Sydel interrupted. "Our issue goes beyond each other. We need to make amends to the survivors of the first attack." Her glare cut a line between Phaira and her brothers, pinning Yann and CaLarca. "If you do that, I'll sign the papers, and provide the blood."

Emotions passed over Yann's face: fear, disgust, wariness.

"I will do it," CaLarca said after a long pause.

Sydel turned to the man. "Yann?" Her chin lifted. Phaira felt it, that old tension crackling between them, just like in the Communia.

"If it means you'll forgive me," the old man said, "then yes."

* * *

There was no question of letting Yann into the *Arazura* to make the call. Regardless of his intentions, there was too much uncertainty, too much tension simmering between CaLarca, Yann and Sydel. Neither Phaira nor her brothers could predict what might happen, but Phaira was the one who suggested that if an apology was to be made, it should be made to the surviving Sava cousin,

Theron. And it should be made in private, inside the grandmother Vyoma's house.

"You come too," Sydel told the siblings. "I want you all to bear witness."

Then she strode past them, heading for Vyoma's red wooden hut in the cavern.

"Remain here," Yann instructed the silent officers, before following her.

"This is crazy," Renzo muttered to his siblings. "She's crazy."

"She's not crazy," Cohen said sullenly. "Stop saying that."

"Well, this is going to be a disaster," Renzo snapped at his brother. "Why are we going along with this, we should stop them."

"I don't think we can," Phaira said. "It's over our heads."

All three slowed to watch CaLarca shuffle past them. Phaira studied the green-streaked braids as they swayed in the center of the woman's back; her heavy gait, the click of metal on rock.

"How could you, Phair," Cohen said under his breath.

"Not now, Co. More has happened than you know."

"Well, I'm not going up there," Cohen announced gruffly. "You two do what you want."

Then he stalked away, his broad back disappearing around the corner.

Phaira blinked. "He's pleasant."

"You have no idea," Renzo sighed.

When they reached the front of Vyoma's house, the two huddled before the open door. The sound of footsteps on the creaking staircase wafted over the threshold.

"Why suggest Theron?" Renzo whispered.

"Better than the grandfather," Phaira said. "Trust me."

"But you barely know him," Renzo exclaimed. "How do you know that he won't command all the syndicate to wipe us out?"

Phaira lifted one shoulder. "You worked alongside him, Ren. You really think he's that kind of guy?"

"Sure, we got along fine," Renzo said impatiently, "but that was a few catastrophes ago."

Phaira shrugged again. She craned her neck to peer up the rickety stairwell, into the darkness.

Renzo exhaled, long and low. "Well," he began. "Someone has to make the introduction. Might as well be me."

* * *

There was barely any space in the attic to stand, let alone keep the safe distance that everyone wanted. Every eye checked for proximity: who looked at what, who sweated, who might be contemplating a weapon, physical or metal, and the space quickly grew awkward and overheated.

The sooner this is done, the better, Renzo thought, placing his Lissome on the foot of the bed. He quickly activated a video-screen, expanding it to three feet wide with his hands. He looked at Sydel for confirmation. She stood straight-backed, her mouth set in a determined line.

Renzo held his breath and typed. Numbers and symbols flashed across the screen, bypassing borders, sending out inquiries.

Waiting for responses, Renzo stole looks at CaLarca and Yann. They stood next to each other; surprising, given their animosity. Yann looked like he might pass out. CaLarca refused to make eye contact with anyone, glaring at the floor.

The screen went black. Renzo could hear swallows, feel how everyone was collectively bracing for sound or sudden light. A click sounded through the Lissome soundsystem. Then a voice.

"Renzo?" The audio was clear, though the picture remained dark. Theron Sava sounded surprised, though not angry.

"Yes," Renzo said uneasily. "How's it going?" For a moment, he wondered if he should add sir to the end of that sentence.

"Funny you called, actually. I was going to look you up. Had a couple of questions for you." There was a pause. "But I sense this isn't the right time." Another pause. "What's with the crowd?"

Renzo wet his lips. "Some people want to talk to you. I hope that's okay."

"Some people," the man repeated. "Your brother is well, I hope?"

"He's fine, yes," Renzo said, peering into the blackness. "Can't you activate the visual, Theron? This is weird."

"No." There was no further explanation. "And Phaira?"

"I'm here," Phaira said, though she remained in the corner, out of sight.

"You're Sydel." The statement made everyone stiffen. "The little stowaway. Back in the fold, I see. Are you the one looking for me?"

Sydel's cheeks flushed deep pink as she stared into the void.

You don't have to do this. Renzo tried to push his words into her mind. *I can shut this off in a moment, make some excuse.*

"Please, Mr. Sava, may I see you?" Sydel finally asked. "I want to ensure that you hear me."

"I can hear you. What do you want?"

Sydel took in a shaky breath. Then she blurted out:

"I am responsible for the death of your cousins."

Phaira bit her thumbnail, trading looks with Cohen. CaLarca stared at the back of Sydel's head. Yann looked surprisingly calm, his hands in his sleeves, waiting.

"Tell me how." Theron's voice was quiet, but sharp.

"I have the ability to generate energy," Sydel began, visibly trembling. "I was under duress, strangled by your cousin Keller, and I lost control of the energy. It killed your cousin Keller, and damaged the foundation of the underground base, causing it to collapse. Which your other cousin was caught in." There were tears in her voice. "I'm so sorry. And I'm so sorry for what happened to you when you were a child. You and your family."

The tension in the room heightened by a thousand degrees, as everyone held their breath.

But Theron said nothing.

"I know this is sudden," Sydel continued. "And I know you're distraught, and confused, I can sense it -"

"Sydel," Phaira warned from the corner.

"But I hope you have the capacity to forgive," Sydel concluded. "And not just me."

She looked over her shoulder at CaLarca and Yann.

"You with the green hair," came Theron's quiet voice. "You're one of the originals, aren't you?"

Renzo saw real fear on CaLarca's face as she took a step forward. "Which - which one were you?" she asked the black screen.

"Black hair. Eight years old. Red shirt." He listed off the facts without emotion.

"I was fourteen," CaLarca said haltingly. "And very scared, and trying to understand what I was involved with. I only saw your family from a distance, but I didn't actually -"

Then she corrected herself. "No, that's not right." She took in a long, steadying breath. "I should have stopped the others, or at least tried to," she confessed. "I should have told someone what happened. It's just as cowardly to keep it a secret all these years, and... I'm sorry."

Sydel nodded, relief on her face.

"But this man next to me has no remorse."

Yann started. But CaLarca plowed on, drawing so close to the screen that Renzo thought she might tumble through. "He wears another face, but Kuri Nimat was one of your attackers, and he deserves all your wrath. He can take on appearances, but I'm sure you have the resources, Mr. Sava, to track him down. I encourage the use of every single one."

Yann darted forward, grabbed the Lissome and threw it at the opposite wall. The Lissome ricocheted, just inches from Phaira's head. The screens dissolved with a burst of static. Phaira had her hidden knife drawn and flipped in reverse. Renzo backed into the corner, his hands up. Sydel's hands were fixed to her mouth.

Braced in the doorway, Yann's face shimmered. The jowls tightened, hair spread over his head, and his body thinned.

Within seconds, it was a new man, tall and lean, mid-thirties, black-haired, bronzed and handsome, looking at them with pity.

"You have to understand," Kuri said. "I wanted no violence. But he wasn't willing to listen to me."

"No," Sydel choked through her fingers. "No, you didn't."

Kuri stretched out a hand to her. "What I said outside was true, Sydel: every word, every apology, every thought of wrongdoing, they were all his. I wish he had the courage to tell you himself. But unfortunately -"

His whole body jolted. His eyes bulged, and a strangled sound came out of his mouth.

Then CaLarca stepped away from him. The knife she bore dissipated into a puff of smoke, red droplets hitting the wooden floor.

Kuri keeled over, gripping his ribs, blood spilling through his fingers.

Sydel caught his arm and helped him to his knees. Phaira went to pull her away, but she pushed off their hands.

"What are you doing?" Renzo yelped. "What are you doing?"

"I'm healing him," Sydel said resolutely, drawing Kuri down on his back.

"Syd -" Phaira started.

But Sydel's voice was sharp. "No. Not like this."

Standing in the corner, CaLarca didn't react or move as Sydel passed her hands over Kuri's heaving torso. No one spoke. The temperature in the room rose. Kuri's face contorted, and, for a moment, shimmered, before settling back into the lines. Sydel's fingers held steady over the red.

Then she sat back on her heels. Kuri drew up on his elbows, breathing hard. But there was no more wet blood, only dried brown.

Kuri wobbled to his feet, and darted out the door. They heard his footsteps on the staircase, the creak of the door outside. Phaira, CaLarca, Sydel and Renzo stared at each other.

"We have to stop him, right?" Renzo asked the group.

Phaira shook her head. "Wait." She strode across the room and snapped up the fallen Lissome, activating it again. She punched in a series of numbers.

"Who are you -" Renzo mouthed, but stopped when she spoke in a brusque voice: "Ozias, it's Phaira."

Wait, Renzo thought, his panic rising. *Wait. Ozias. The detective? Wasn't that her name? The one who was looking for Cohen?*

"Is the shapeshifter there?" came a woman's voice.

"Yes. Kuri Nimat," Phaira said, glancing at CaLarca for confirmation. "He's taken the form of a young man, dark hair, six feet, early-to-mid-thirties. But he has officers with him, or at least four who look like law."

"I can't get a handle on your location."

"Toomba," Phaira said. "In the Cyan Mountains, south of -"

"Toomba?" Ozias repeated, her voice sharp. "Those men aren't officers."

"How do you know that?"

"Don't you know anything about where you are? A patrol officer would be shot on sight if they tried to broach the border. In fact, no stranger is ever allowed up the mountain."

"But," Phaira sputtered. "I came here, I wasn't assaulted."

"Because you are family."

Everyone turned at the old, cracked voice. Vyoma stood in the doorway, her hands behind her back, surveying the room like a drill sergeant.

"Close it down, dear," she told Phaira.

With a click, Phaira snapped the Lissome into its dormant form.

"Now," Vyoma said quietly. "Let's have a talk with our visitors."

V.

Outside, one hundred residents of Toomba stood in rows, each with a firearm primed against their shoulder. Some were rusty, some were ancient models, and even a few newer versions glimmered here and there, but no barrel wavered, no eye blinked. One of those eyes were Cohen's, Phaira realized with a start; she recognized his Vaccaro rifle. While they were making the call to Theron, he was rallying the troops. The Toomba militia. And he was part of it.

Fifty feet away, near the edge of the mountain, Kuri's arm was still clasped around his ribs, as he peered from behind the four officers.

"You realize this is all for show, correct?" Kuri called out. "Should we chose to do so, every rifle will be turned back on its owner."

We, Phaira thought. *He's not the only NINE present.*

"What do you want?" Sydel's shrill voice carried through the mountains. She stalked in Kuri's direction, leading with her forehead like a ram. "When does this stop? What do I -"

"Sydel," one of the female officers suddenly spoke.

Sydel stopped ten feet away.

The officer's face shimmered, and grew pale, her dark hair shifting to white-blonde dreadlocks.

"I'm sorry," Marette began. "I'm sorry for deceiving you. We were going to tell you the truth as soon as we got off Toomba."

"How could you?" Sydel hissed. "Yann sheltered me, when you couldn't be bothered!" Her gaze shifted to the other officers. "And who are these, then? Is your sister in there?"

"No, these are my bodyguards," Marette said. "On contract to serve me and my interests, as always. And they won't hesistate to hurt anyone who approaches without warning." She looked at Sydel beseechingly. "Understand, Sydel, that I agreed to this for Shantou's sake. When I learned about her condition... I need this surgery to save her, and I'm -" Her voice broke. "I don't have the rana to make it happen."

"So you need mine, is that right?" Sydel snapped. "And you're willing to kill Yann to get it?"

"This isn't working," Phaira heard Kuri mutter.

Marette stepped back into the ranks. Long seconds passed. Fingers tensed around triggers. Energy crackled through the mountain.

"We're running out of time here," Kuri finally broke the silence. "I don't want to cause any more harm, Sydel, but -" He gestured to the Toomba residents, the hundred gun barrels aimed at his head. "Foolish for gathering in one location," he remarked. "It would be simple: just move a rock and let it fall."

A few of the Toomba men looked away, scanning the mountainside.

"You won't do that," CaLarca chimed in, finally joining them. "You'd have to divert Nadi from generating
your appearance. And you're too vain for that."

"There's no deal," Cohen's voice rang out, so loud that
it made Phaira wince. "Leave now, while you have a -"

"Cohen Byrne?" Kuri interrupted.

Cohen inched ahead of the group of Toomba militia,
his Vacarro still against his shoulder.

Kuri nodded. "Nox was so disappointed in you."

Cohen's mouth dropped open.

"You were so weak, passive, embarrassing," Kuri continued, drawing out each word. "No mind of your own.
He never had confidence in you, not in training, and not
in Kings Canyon."

Furious, Phaira glanced between Kuri and Cohen,
wanting nothing more than to reopen that stab wound
in the man's ribs.

But Kuri's right hand was moving, she realized, fingers undulating along his thigh, in a rolling pattern,
again and again. And Cohen was staring at Kuri, as if
transfixed. What was he seeing? What was he thinking?

Kuri's voice grew quiet. "Last chance, Sydel," he addressed the girl.

"Or what?" she snapped back.

Cohen's eyes bugged out. The Vacaaro clattered to
the rock floor.

Then her brother broke into a sudden, frenzied run.

Phaira's body exploded with adrenaline, but before she could scream his name, before she could stop him, Cohen was past her.

He was leaping over the brink.

He was swallowed by the clouds.

Screams echoed through the mountains. One of them was Phaira's, trailing behind her like smoke as she ran to the edge.

Somehow, Sydel and CaLarca were already there, their upper bodies hidden from view. Phaira dropped onto her knees, every muscle like stone, horrified of what she would see.

But Sydel's hands were outstretched, her fingers rigid claws. And Cohen's silhouette was one hundred feet below, his waist bound in rope, the length taut, running all the way into CaLarca's white-knuckled hands.

Cohen wasn't falling. He was floating. He was flying. They were pulling him back.

Astonished, Phaira grabbed hold of the rope (where had it come from? Why was it so hot?). As Sydel drew her hands in, again and again, as if beckoning Cohen to come, CaLarca and Phaira pulled him closer and closer. Incredibly, he was almost weightless; it was like pulling on the string of a heavy balloon. His head was flopped back, but Phaira could see his chest rising and falling. How was this possible? Was this a hallucination?

When close enough, Phaira snatched Cohen's leg, then his belt, hauling him over the edge. Finally, finally, he was slumped on the sandy floor, as Phaira threw her arms around his neck. "Are you okay?" she couldn't stop whispering. "Are you okay?"

When she felt the slightest pat on her back, Phaira forced herself to release her little brother.

Next to her, CaLarca was slumped into herself, the white rope coiled around her legs, next to her fallen cane. Suddenly, the rope dissipated into puffs of smoke. Phaira jumped, but CaLarca didn't seem to notice; she was staring at her reddened hands.

A roar of pain, and the crash of bodies on the ground. Phaira sprang to her feet. Renzo had tackled Kuri. The dull smack of knuckles of flesh echoed through the mountain. Marette leapt on Renzo's back, yanking on him, pulling his hair. Her bodyguards swarmed around Renzo. The residents of Toomba charged, a wave of metal and wool.

"Stop where you are!" The voice boomed through the mountains.

The wave stopped. The bodyguards froze, looking in all directions.

What now? Who was here now? Phaira bemoaned, searching frantically for signs of satellites or drones.

"Troublemakers."

Phaira recognized the voice immediately. But it was coming from the fourth canyon.

From the *Arazura.*

"Stand down, Kuri Nimat, Marette Lyung, and all minions," Anandi announced. "These people are under the protection of the Hitodama."

"What?" Renzo cried, pushing off the bodyguards' hands.

"Shush, Ren!" The sharp feedback made everyone wince. "Get behind the militia already. And if you make a move, Kuri, I'll take you down, both you and your girlfriend there."

What was she talking about? Hitodama? How could she take Kuri down? Reeling, Phaira helped the still-woozy Cohen to his feet. CaLarca and Sydel huddled together, backing away in the direction of Vyoma and the Toomba militia, all retreating into the safety of the caverns.

Kuri stumbled to his feet. "This isn't over!" he yelled into the mountains. "I don't care who you think you -"

"Enough!" Vyoma's voice crackled. "I want them dead or contained!"

The Toomba men and women surged forward. Simultaneously, Kuri and Marette lifted their hands, while the bodyguards drew arms.

"Don't!" Sydel pleaded to the militia as they rushed past. "They'll hurt you! They'll -"

A line of men dropped, clutching their heads and screaming. Shots were fired, booming, backfire. Chaos and flashing blue lights. Vyoma was suddenly in Phaira's face. "Fall back!" she commanded. "Take the other two into the tunnel."

"Are you kidding me?" Phaira exclaimed, drawing her blade and moving to push past the woman.

"Don't argue!" Grabbing Phaira around the arm, Vyoma hauled her under the overhang of the cavern. Shocked, Phaira stumbled over her feet, only gaining her balance when she faced a dark opening in the rock wall, with an open iron door. Sydel and CaLarca were already huddled inside.

"What is - ?"

With surprising strength, Vyoma shoved Phaira into the tunnel, cutting off her question.

"Take them deep inside," Vyoma told Phaira. "Don't come back until you get the all-clear."

"What?" Phaira yelped.

But the door spiraled shut, cutting off her cry and the light. All Phaira could hear was the sound of her loud, quickened breathing, and the shivering exhales of the other two women.

Slowly, her eyes adjusted. The tunnel was lit every ten feet by a luminescent, graying lightpod, and stretched on and on. She couldn't see the end.

Phaira grit her teeth. Why wasn't she out there, fighting with the others? Who did Vyoma think she was, putting her hands on Phaira, telling her what to do? What good would it do to go deeper inside the mountain? This whole situation was an insult.

"Come on," she told the other two. "Walk."

The tunnel was so narrow and low that they had to hunch over to walk. Water dripped on their heads as they stumbled over old rails, their hips and arms scratched by rocks.

"This is ridiculous," CaLarca's surly voice bounced off the walls. "I can't run from this. I'm the one who has to resolve -"

"Don't be stupid," Phaira shot back, scraping her leg and wincing. "You can barely walk."

"No, I'm the one," Sydel bemoaned. "He's done all of this to get to me, all these horrible things."

"Both of you, be quiet!" Phaira commanded.

The tunnel shuddered under their hands. Rubble fell on Phaira's shoulder. An explosion? Would the cave collapse on them? They were old mining tunnels, they were reinforced to some degree, but were they using bombs out there? What if they were now trapped in the mountains?

Then a humming noise grew: a wave of sound, coming closer and closer.

CaLarca and Sydel heard it too, by the way they craned their necks, their eyes wide with fear.

Phaira turned in place, searching, until the feedback hit, screeching through her brain like a malfunctioning radio. Memories and voices swarmed through her head. Her body was alight with electricity. She couldn't see, she couldn't speak.

Then it was gone, and she was panting for air, fingernails digging into the wall to hold herself. Ahead of her, CaLarca and Sydel were on their knees, clawing at the air, whimpering.

"Syd! Phair!" Cohen's voice echoed through the tunnel.

"Co!" Phaira yelled back, shaking her head to clear it, scrambling back to the entrance. She glanced back at the other two; they were breathing hard, red-faced and smeared with dirt, but pulling themselves along, following her to the outside.

The sun framed Cohen's bearded face. No smell of smoke or chemicals, just the faintest whiff of gunpowder, Phaira realized. He stretched out a hand for her. She took it gratefully.

"What happened?" Phaira asked, trying to see around him.

"It's done," he told her brusquely. "He's down. They all are."

VI.

A burlap sack covered Kuri's head. He lay on his stomach, his hands bound behind his back, and three Toomba militia stood guard.

The three bodyguards were on their knees, their hands on their heads. Their eyes were dilated, faces flushed, and they kept asking: "What happened?" Whatever spell was cast over them, it was broken now. And Phaira could see why in the distance: white-blond hair spread out across the rocky floor, streaked with red. Marette was dead, shot through the throat, by the look of it.

"You're bleeding," came Vyoma's scratchy voice.

Phaira swiped under her nose with the edge of her hand, catching a trail across her knuckles. Then she ran her thumb over one nostril, then again, sniffing to make sure the flow had stopped. The grandmother stood shoulder-to-shoulder with Phaira, surveying the fallout.

"You were impacted by that wave," Vyoma said, her words cool and clipped. "You're one of them."

"We barely know each other, lady, let's not start judging," Phaira retorted. She closed her eyes for a moment. Her head was still ringing.

"I forgot that you had some Eko in you," she heard Renzo from behind. "You all right?"

"What did you do?" Phaira asked, opening one eye a crack. He was looking at her with concern, peering at her over his glasses.

"Anandi did it," Renzo said. He glanced back at the *Arazura* with an exhausted grin. "She just flicked the switch."

* * *

The device sat in the corner of Renzo's cabin, a jumble of copper and rubber, with a thousand wires and a hundred different angles. Phaira studied it from the doorway. When her older brother was assaulted and left for dead, half of his skull caved in, she would have never thought that he could create something so incredible again. But only a year later, look at what he did. What he was capable of. It felt strangely frightening.

"Combination of a high-pitch frequency and electromagnetic pulse," Renzo was explaining. "That's why Vy put you in the caverns; I told her to, to shield you all from the blast zone. I knew it would still impact CaLarca and Sydel, but muted, at least."

Vy. The name rolled around in her brain. Were they that familiar? Was he really so quick to believe the old woman's story, just like that?

"You did this in the last two weeks?" she asked.

Renzo shrugged. "Two powerhouses living on the *Arazura*; makes sense to have a failsafe. Especially with Sydel's instability." He gestured at the device. "We have this now, so if it happens again, we can shut them down. And I'm working on a portable version."

Phaira winced. It sounded so robotic. And calculated.

"Don't get touchy," Renzo said, as if reading her thoughts. "It's just a means to disorient and negate NINE abilities. Like a larger, more targeted version of the HALOS. It's nothing permanent."

How can you be so certain? Phaira wondered. She touched the edge of her thumb to her nostril, remembering the blood.

"Anandi?" she called out. "Are you sure you should still be on the line?"

"It's fine," Anandi's voice carried through the room. "Completely secure. And the arrest warrants were dropped on me and Father. I'm guessing that had something to do with you, Phaira."

Phaira waved her hand, even though she knew Anandi couldn't see. She didn't want to get into it. "How did you know what was going on here?"

"I picked up on your conversation with Theron Sava," Anandi said. "Since we ran out of Liera, I've been trying to track you all down; had a dozen algorithms running, waiting for some identifying characteristic to register. Then the Hitodama contacted me, asking about Lander's condition, and I got to talking to a few of them, collaborated on some ideas over the past week. They were with me when you called Theron. And he wasn't doing much to guard the connection, surprisingly. We traced it, hacked into the *Arazura* and turned on the speakers to the outside."

"And when everything went crazy, and I couldn't get to the *Arazura*, she bypassed all my securities and activated the pulse," added Renzo, pride in his voice.

"How's Emir?" Phaira asked, staring at the creation in the corner.

"Better," Anandi said, her voice quieting. "It was rough for a while, but now that he's settled, he's improving every day."

"Do you think - " Phaira started, and then stopped. She looked at her brother. "You know Sydel isn't well, right?"

Renzo shrugged again. "Clearly, but I didn't know what to do about it. We kept her safe, at least. She hasn't hurt anyone."

"You want my dad to talk to her?" Anandi chimed in. "He's worked with patients who have experienced trauma. Maybe he can give her some guidance."

"Maybe," Phaira said. "When things are fully resolved." She glanced at Renzo. "But we've got a decision to make first."

* * *

The Toomba tavern was closed to the public. With shades drawn, and chairs in a circular formation, the residents of the *Arazura* sat astride, straddling, or with ankles crossed underneath.

"Ozias wants him," Phaira began. "I don't know if they have the means to contain him. But maybe we just go the conventional route. Turn him over and wipe our hands of it."

"I can't believe you made a deal with law patrol," Cohen muttered.

"I didn't have a lot of choices, Co," Phaira shot back. "And I was trying to protect you and Ren and Sydel."

"Well, I didn't ask for protection," Cohen said. "I could have handled it on my own."

Stung, Phaira glared at Cohen.

Renzo lifted a tired hand. "Can you knock it off until this is settled?"

"Kuri won't stay in prison," CaLarca declared. "Even if they build a custom cell, the other NINE may come for him. Shantou is still out there. And Voss. And who knows who else has been recruited. If they are working with Kuri, they could hurt a lot of people in trying to set him free."

"What are you suggesting, then?" Renzo asked. "That it's better for everyone if he just disappears?"

"The offer's already been made," Cohen said gruffly.

Everyone turned to look at him.

"Vy can make it happen," Cohen said. "If we ask, Kuri goes into the mountains, and he doesn't come out. Same with that blonde girl's body. They deal with this kind of thing all the time. The law doesn't mess with Toomba militia."

"What about the bodyguards?" Renzo pointed out. "What if they talk?"

"They were being controlled," CaLarca said. "They have no memory of what happened. They're desperate to leave the mountain alive. They'll do whatever we ask."

Phaira glanced at Sydel, who stared at her hands. "What do you think?"

"Is that what you all want?" came her quiet voice.

"It's not a question of want," Renzo retorted, though his voice was kinder when he spoke again. "If we don't make the right choice here, it could be disastrous."

"Believe me, I want nothing more than to never see him again," Sydel whispered. "Or see any of this again."

"Nor do I," CaLarca muttered, picking at her fingernails. "He's a thief, a blackmailer, a kidnapper. But he hasn't actually killed anyone. At least, not successfully."

"So forcing me over the edge of a mountain doesn't count?" Cohen shot back.

"Stop fighting, please."

Cohen fell silent at Sydel's voice. She looked calm, but exhausted.

"I'm done," the girl said. "I don't want Kuri to hurt anyone. Ever again. I vote for the mountains."

"It's agreed then," Phaira said, after a long, awkward pause. "We get up and walk out and don't look back."

Everyone nodded. Chairs scraped across the wooden floor as the five rose to their feet. Then one by one, they shuffled out of the door.

All except CaLarca, who hovered, leaning hard on her cane.

Then she made for the backroom.

Wedged between barrels of ale and storage crates, Kuri was bound to a chair, his head slung with a metal HALO loop, and, by his request, his head still covered by that sack. The HALO was disrupting his Eko ability, and by the look of his liver-spotted hands, his Nadi, too.

His head tilted at her entry. "Come to say goodbye?" he asked, his voice muffled through the burlap.

Her cane made a loud rap on the floor. "I want the truth, Kuri. What did you do to me in those two weeks?"

She heard snorting.

"I could just split open your head and pull out the memory," CaLarca warned him.

"Nah, you won't do that. Who knows what else you might see in there." There was something sinister in the way he said those words.

But she had to ask him. "Is my family alive?"

Kuri chortled, a slight wheeze in his breathing. "I know nothing about that. I've been with you, remember?"

"Then who burned down my farm?" she demanded. "I saw the satellite images. Was it Shantou? Was it someone else you manipulated? Why did you do it?"

His hands gripped the armrests. The wood squeaked under his fingers.

In a burst of anger, CaLarca yanked the sack off his head.

Yelping, Kuri turned his face into his shoulder. She glared at him, taking in the sagging, pockmarked cheeks, the melanoma patches along his forehead.

Then she limped out of the room.

* * *

"What do you mean, he's gone?"

"You said it yourself, Oz: Toomba has its own rules," Phaira said into the Lissome. "He's not where we left him, and no one is talking."

"Don't call me Oz. And we made a deal."

"The deal was that I would track him down and contact you," Phaira pointed out. "You chose to send no backup, no support, so don't blame me for losing him. I'll come in for debriefing, and tell you what I know."

Inspiration struck her. "And I have information on the remaining NINE. If you'll fund the expenses, I'll do reconnaissance overseas."

"What are you doing?" Renzo mouthed from across the *Arazura* common room.

Phaira waved her hand to shut him up. "There's at least two other NINE out there. I have leads. I'll uncover whatever I can and bring it straight to you."

Suddenly, Cohen was next to Phaira, bent over to speak into the Lissome. "Detective Ozias," he boomed. "I'm Cohen Byrne. Just so you know, I would have been happy to talk to you about Kings. If you still have questions, I'll answer them."

"Your sister put in a lot of effort to protect you from me, Cohen," Ozias said with surprise. "You're waiving that protection?"

"I never asked for it," Cohen said.

Phaira held her breath, and her hurt in check.

Ozias was the one to break the silence. "At the moment, Cohen, I think I have the information I need. There's a lot of processing to do. I'm glad you're willing, however."

"If you change your mind," Cohen said, "I'll be in Toomba."

Renzo and Phaira glanced at him. Cohen continued to look down at the Lissome.

"Noted," Ozias said. "And Phaira? Let me see what I can do."

"Yes," Phaira said. "Thank you."

The connection broke. All three were silent. Cohen glared at them, his back stiff, his chin held high and his arms crossed, as if waiting for a scolding.

Then Renzo's shoulders slumped. "If that's what you want, Co," he said, his voice exhausted. "Stay in Toomba."

Something shifted in Cohen. "Don't be sad about it, Ren," he said, sounding a little like his old, bashful self. "I like it here."

Really? Phaira wanted to protest. *With all these mountain men, in the cold, in the middle of nowhere?*

But she just nodded. "It's your choice," she managed. "You're an adult. As much as we forget sometimes," she added with an apologetic note.

"What about Sydel?" Renzo chimed in. "I doubt she's sticking around here."

Cohen shrugged. "She's got her own issues to deal with."

Curious, Phaira peered at her little brother. His eyes were moody and far away.

"Wait a minute," Renzo interrupted, looking panicky. "If you're staying in Toomba, and Phaira's going on a search, then it's just going to be me and those two girls in the *Arazura*?"

He looked sick at the prospect. Phaira couldn't help but laugh. Even Cohen cracked a smile under that heavy beard.

"Not me," came Sydel's quiet voice from behind. "I'm leaving."

Everyone turned. Sydel had changed into a brown woven dress, with a blue wool jacket belted over. A satchel was slung over her shoulder. Her copper hair had been trimmed, so it was at least even. Her features were sharper, more pronounced.

She doesn't look like a scared teenager anymore, Phaira realized. *She looks like someone to be reckoned with.*

"Where?" Phaira finally asked.

Sydel smiled faintly. "I'm going to serve as caretaker to Emir. And when he recovers, I'm going to serve as his medical apprentice."

"When was this decided?" Renzo exclaimed.

"Just now," Sydel said. "He called me, and suggested it. I think it's a good idea. It's who I really am. Not all of this...."

She trailed off, averting her eyes.

"I want to go back to traditional medicine," she finally continued. "And I'm officially retiring my abilities."

"You don't want to do that," Renzo exclaimed.

"I do," Sydel said. "I want to build a regular life, without Eko, or Nadi, or any of it." She glanced over her shoulder. "I just need to get down the mountain and find my way to Emir."

"Don't be silly, I'll take you wherever you need to go," Renzo interjected.

Still, Phaira saw the furrow in his brow, and Cohen's bunched forehead, even felt the tension in hers. She just assumed that in the end, they would all be together again in the *Arazura*. But what could anyone say? They were all destined to separate, at one time or another.

"Well," Phaira broke the awkward silence. "I guess we should get going."

"You be careful with Ozias," Cohen said to Phaira gruffly. He hesitated for one moment, one long moment, before he crushed Phaira in a hug with those familiar, heavy arms.

"You watch out too," she whispered into his ear. She wished she could say even more than that. She wished that he was still the boy who listened to everything she said, that she could ask him to stay with Renzo in the

Arazura, that he could see that they were better together. Safer together.

But she bit her tongue, and let him set her back on the ground.

Renzo and Cohen embraced, Renzo slapping him on the back. "Call me if you need anything," he told his younger brother. "No matter what."

Sydel was gazing at Cohen, her hands clasped in front of her, her thumb tracking the other's nail.

"We should - " Phaira whispered to Renzo, gesturing at their cabins.

"It's okay," Sydel told them. "I don't mind if you stay."

Cohen slowly turned to face her, rubbing the back of his neck in that familiar nervous gesture. "I hope you... figure out what you need," he said to Sydel. "Emir is a good guy."

"I want you to know that I'm sorry for the way I acted," Sydel said. "I was afraid, and confused, and not in my right mind."

Did Phaira see a flush underneath his beard? "Don't worry about it."

"Of course I worry," Sydel said quietly. "I never want to hurt you. Ever."

"I know, Syd. It's okay," Cohen muttered, as one boot scuffed the ground. "I'm sure we'll catch up at some point."

Sydel's face fell, just a little. Then her expression settled into calm resolution. "Of course."

Oh no, Phaira groaned inwardly. *Dammit, Cohen.*

But her little brother was already striding to the *Arazura's* exit. Just before the stairs, he hesitated, looking back at the three of them.

"Goodbye," he told them.

"Goodbye," they repeated.

VII.

The pyre burned orange and yellow, with the occasional spark of green. The body's silhouette showed through the flames. Staring into the fire, Cohen swore he could smell burning flesh. He had to remind himself, again and again, that it was an illusion.

Vyoma had suggested the mock-service in memory of his father. It was how they dealt with the dead in Toomba. There were no fancy transports or burial grounds, just the burning of the body, the smoke joining the clouds, the ashes in the wind. She showed him how they built straw facsimiles of the dead, complete with head and limbs, to serve as stand-in. It happened more often than he might think, she told him; living in the mountains often brought sudden disappearances. She was skilled in building the straw body, binding the joints with rope with her gnarled, strong hands.

"I did this for your mother," she told Cohen. "When I learned of her death. The ritual helps."

In addition to the burning, words were to be said about the deceased. But Cohen didn't know what to say.

"Then why bother with the ceremony?" Vyoma countered. "What do you care if he's dead?"

"We should have done this with Ren and Phair," Cohen muttered. "They remember more. I hardly have anything. Just the bad stuff, and their stories."

"Then I will speak," Vyoma said. She tucked in her chin as she peered into the fire.

A few moments passed. Cohen looked down at his grandmother, whose head barely passed his sternum. He knew better than to say anything.

"Dasean," Vyoma finally spoke, her voice clipped. "I expected more from you. For a long time, I blamed you for taking my daughter away. Now she is gone, and you join her. But my grandchildren found me. It's the best of the both of you, given to me at the end of my life. So, for me, your death has been a blessing. And I thank you for that."

She was crying; her face was still etched in stone, but there was a definite tear track making its way down the folds of her cheek. Cohen shifted, wondering if he could try and comfort her. Something told him it was no use. Maybe she didn't even realize that she was weeping.

So, instead, he watched the fire. In his peripheral vision, he saw some of the townspeople hovering, but not daring to approach. He turned his head to the side, as a warning. The shadows retreated. He liked the respect he garnered here.

"Now you, Cohen," Vyoma said, stepping aside.

"Father," Cohen started. "Dasean," he corrected. For whatever reason, it felt more natural. "It would have been good to know you better. To have you around. But I guess you weren't able to take care of us. I get it, and I'm not angry. But I've been lucky, with Ren and Phaira.

Because really, they're my parents. I know that sounds weird, but it's true."

He looked up at the plumes of smoke. "So if you've got any kind of presence, or power, or whatever," he added, "please look after them."

And as the fire flared, he added a prayer:

And please look after Sydel, wherever she is.

* * *

Sydel twisted the strap around her shoulder, staring at the door. She checked the room number again. It was correct. But she couldn't muster the courage to knock.

Was she really leaving the *Arazura*? All of the siblings? No schedule, no security, no familiar embrace, no cabin on the ship that she'd come to call home. Phaira seemed so wistful when they said farewell, when the *Arazura* descended into the Mac, where she was slated to meet up with Emir. Sydel wasn't sure what to do as they stood at the exit. Should they hug? Shake hands? There were a thousand conflicting emotions in the moment: strange affection, some measure of relief that she was leaving, a nagging worry in the pit of her stomach.

"Remember what I told you," Phaira told her. "No matter how bad it gets, don't ever touch meka."

"Please be careful around CaLarca," Sydel countered with a whisper. "She's not stable. I don't think she'll try and hurt you, but -"

"It's okay," Phaira said. "I think we have an understanding."

"But it's a wonderful thing you're doing, going to search for her family," Sydel said quietly.

Phaira frowned. "I'm not - "

"I know you're going to seek out the NINE," Sydel interrupted. "But I also know that's part of your mission. You're a good person."

Then, impulsively, Sydel took Phaira's hands and kissed their backs. "And don't negate what I just said with a silly comment," she added.

"Okay, okay," Phaira mumbled, a faint, embarrassed smile on her dark lips.

For the first time in a long while, Sydel felt some measure of peace; calm enough to walk away, and into the streets alone, intent on following Emir's directions to his place of recovery. But now that she was there, just outside his room, she was frozen with fear. What if she was a disappointment to Emir, as she was to Yann? She hadn't given much thought to Yann, other than sadness at his death, and the bitterness, buried deep inside her. But the memories of his disapproval still held power over her. And here she was again, going under the tutelage of a senior.

But now I'm an adult, she reminded herself. *Free and independent. I can refuse, I can argue, and I can leave whenever I want. I have a place to go home to, if I ever need it.*

Bolstered, she knocked on the door.

Emir Ajyo was sitting up in bed, the mattress tilted to a right angle. His beard was longer and bushier than she remembered, and he was very pale, but his eyes were alert. Anandi Ajyo stood next to him. Her pockets gave out little blips and beeps, and her fingers waved over her hips, shutting off whatever was going off. She murmured something to her father, something that Sydel could not hear, and then swept past Sydel and down the corridor.

Emir crooked a finger and beckoned Sydel. "Hello again."

Sydel dropped her borrowed leather satchel, with her clothes and kits, and came to his bedside.

"Hello, sir," she said shyly.

"None of that," Emir corrected, though gently. "Just Emir. And you're Sydel." He studied her belongings. "I need to ask, have you had any kind of physical examination from an outside professional? Or have you been self-diagnosing?"

"Me?" Sydel asked, confused. "I've just healed myself. Nothing serious has ever happened – well - " She flashed back to Kings, when Keller beat her. It took some concentration, but she was able to reduce the swelling.

"If you wouldn't mind," Emir said. "I'd like to run some tests. Just to confirm you're in sound physical health."

Sydel nodded. "That's fair."

"And mental health." His blue-green eyes were frank.

"Of course. I understand. I want to fully disclose everything," Sydel told the man, working to keep her voice even. "I've had traumatic experiences, and sometimes it impacts my ability to think and cope with stress. My long-term memory is damaged; in some parts, I've lost months."

"And on occasion," she admitted. "I've heard voices. But I couldn't tell if they were self-generated, or if I was overhearing the thoughts of others. So, I've made the vow to stop using any kind of NINE ability. I want to be a normal human being. I want to help people instead of hurting them."

"Not even to heal?" Emir asked. "It's quite the ability, Sydel."

"I can't do it anymore," she said, her voice strained. "I won't. Please don't ask me."

Emir held up a lined hand. "Okay," he agreed. "Back to the basics, then. You have a good understanding of anatomy, steady hands, a quick mind. You're a good healer, Sydel, but there are several holes in your education. There's a lot you can learn, but you're capable of doing so."

Sydel nodded, embarrassed at his words, but grateful for the truth.

"And when I am strong enough, I'll be seeking out independent employment," Emir cautioned. "It's a travelling life; it means we take the work as it appears, sometimes with suspicious persons. You can leave whenever you want, or if I start to bore you," he added with a smile. "But I do ask that you can take care of yourself, your physical health, your mental state, and that you tell me truthfully if you have difficulties. Is that acceptable?"

"Very," Sydel said.

Emir extended his hand. "So it's agreed, then."

Sydel took his hand. She worked to return the pressure of his handshake. "Agreed."

* * *

"You know my father will watch over her," Anandi said, as Renzo drummed his fingers on the bistro table. "And I'll check in with her, too, when I'm around."

"I know," Renzo said. "They're a good fit, really. Probably the best place for her." He peered at the tiny Lissome screen. The glowing blue around Anandi's head made her look almost angelic. "Sorry I couldn't stay and visit."

"Another time. I should get back to work anyways. I have about one hundred requests to review." Her grin faded. "Bad news on Lander. They don't know if he'll ever recover. So, the Hitodama are asking for my help. I don't think I can turn it down, y'know?"

Renzo was silent for a few moments. "He was a pain," he finally declared. "But it's still lousy to hear." He pushed his coffee from one hand to the other. He realized that one leg was bouncing from nerves, and he put his hand on his thigh, calming it.

"In that vein, Ren," Anandi said, her voice growing quieter. "There's something I think I should tell you. But

I feel guilty for it, because, well - Phaira's done so much for us."

Renzo's insides froze. "What?"

Anandi looked down for several seconds. Then her voice floated through. "When my father was comatose, when we were in Liera for that week, she would leave at night. All night, only coming back in the dawn. And she was... different during the day. Distracted, and tired, and... well, I know there's some history there with me-kaline. And she's such a good friend, and your sister, but I -"

A rush of perfume in the air. Renzo clicked the Lissome shut, cutting off Anandi's words, as golden blonde hair swung before him.

"Sorry I'm late," the woman purred. "I haven't been to this part of town before."

She settled into her wrought-iron seat, her slim leather briefcase on her lap, manicured fingers riffling through the contents. She wore a hat that dipped in front of one eye, like some kind of debutante, a long-sleeved dress with a subtle thorn pattern, and heels so high that Renzo had to stop from leaning over and peering at her feet, marveling how someone could be mobile in those.

"So," the woman began. "You're Renzo Byrne. Nice to meet you. My name is Jetsun."

"I figured," Renzo said curtly. "What's this about?"

"Right to it? Okay, then," she agreed. "I'm the le-gal representation for an investor who doesn't wish for his name to be said in public." As she looked over her sunglasses, her gaze wandered to Renzo's Lissome, cupped under his palm.

"It's not on," Renzo said, showing the Lissome in its deactivated square shape.

"Anonymous investor," Jetsun said. "For this conversation, at least. We have to be cautious. So. keep this to yourself, until you have some time to review it in private."

She slid over a black folder, an inch thick with paper. "You're quite inspiring, Mr. Byrne, with what you've been able to create with so few resources. There's a new market for inventive minds like yours."

She smiled at him. Her teeth were so perfect and white that it made Renzo uneasy.

"And you have a friend who wants to lay claim to it," he finished.

Jetsun snapped her briefcase shut. "There's cc contact information in that packet," she gestured. "Call me if you need anything explained."

Then she rose to her feet, a perfect hourglass of black, white and gold. Everyone's heads swiveled to watch as she walked away.

Renzo looked from left to right, and even up, looking for any hint of surveillance before he peeked inside the folder.

The first page was a patent: sparring gloves, with an auto-ricochet feature.

The next page was a diagram of the HALO.

And there were several pages more, and a handwritten note inside:

Renzo - Let's talk. – T.S.

* * *

CaLarca sat on Sydel's bed. The twin mattress was both inviting and terrifying, still infused with so many memories of her immobilility. But in the cold, clear quiet, with only the slightest ache in her back and legs to remind her of the devastation, CaLarca could see that the siblings had taken pains with this room. The furniture was secondhand, but sturdy. The deprivation tank was sleek and modernly designed, tucked behind that sliding door. A specially-designed refuge for someone else.

But for now, this was her home until she recovered, or Phaira returned with news. She'd asked to go with the blue-haired woman on her NINE search, but was turned down.

"I've only got funds for one, and one is better," Phaira instructed her. "One can get into places that two cannot. And you're still healing."

You'll slow me down, CaLarca heard under her words. *And you can't be trusted.*

Perhaps it was for the best. CaLarca couldn't say how she might react to the charred remains of her family's farmhouse, the blackened vineyards, years of work ruined. Or what might be found in the rubble. The workings of her mind were enough to deal with: her fears, her memories, her mournings, her burning rage to get out of this room and do something, to find Ganasan and

Bennet, to take her revenge. It was stolen from her when Sydel healed Kuri from the knife wound. There would have been such satisfaction to watch his blood soak into that attic floor.

She heard the *Arazura's* exit door clang shut. Renzo walked by her door, holding a slim briefcase under his arm. He glanced inside her cabin. "Okay?" he asked curtly.

"Of course," CaLarca replied.

"We're taking off, and going on auto," he told her. "But I need to be left alone."

"Understood."

Renzo's footsteps trailed away. CaLarca heard the click of switches in the cockpit, felt the *Arazura* come to life under her feet. When the *Arazura* lifted from its docking magnets, CaLarca stood, taking hold of her cane. The SCKAFO activated immediately as she walked into the corridor, down the stairwell, into the lower level.

Part storage hanger, part training facility for Phaira, this was a place to learn how to incapacitate and kill. Skills she sorely lacked. Something that she needed to cultivate. Her old life was over, and everything would explode, sooner or later. Kuri and Marette were just underlings. There was still the question of Shantou and Voss. And there were mechanisms at work here, far beyond what she understood. There would be struggle, and death. And she couldn't rely on these siblings and their own small problems.

The most powerful of us all, Voss called her, so many years ago.

At one time, perhaps. Perhaps again.

So CaLarca opened her Lissome to a directory of weapons, the diagram before her in a wide two-feet by three-foot projection. She studied the images for several seconds. Then she broke open her Nadi, let it run through her veins and set her muscles alight. Finally, it poured into her hands, condensing, forming and cooling into a short oak staff.

And she practiced.

* * *

"Stop in five," came the announcement.

Crammed into a window seat, Phaira rummaged through her knapsack, looking for gloves. Underneath the neatly folded layers of clothes, there was a bundle of paper, wrapped around a square, and also something thin and fragile within. Confused, she shook the package.

A Lissome fell into her lap, along with a folded pair of glasses, gray, with thin wire frames. Phaira stared at them. Then, when she was certain that no one on the bus was looking, she tentatively slipped them on.

Surprisingly, everything jumped out at her, even from far away. Every edge of every letter was clear. Cohen was right. She needed glasses.

Smirking to herself, Phaira held the Lissome between her thumb and forefinger, and then read the letter.

Renzo's handwriting was as erratic as ever, a scrawl that travelled in a diagonal.

The money from the Macatias is yours, all the information is in this Lissome. Buy some nanotube bodysuits, or a place of your own, whatever. Do what you want with it. Don't bring it up again.

The transport dinged; next stop in one minute.

Daro. An apartment building for senior living. Apartment 705. Mr. and Mrs. Nox.

Aeden's mother and father were waiting when she got off the elevator, with tea and scones and other niceties that she was heartsick to look at. She made apologizes for not coming to see them sooner. She could hardly look at their hungry eyes, their worn bodies on their faded couch; when they pushed a cup of black tea in her hand, she launched into a halting explanation on what happened to Nox, how he was a hero, going back to save those trapped in Kings, how he helped to save her little brother. What a good friend he was to Phaira, how steadfast, how quick to help her and her family. She rattled the facts off, one after another, only the good parts, the best parts of Nox.

In the elevator, over seven floors descending, Phaira removed her new glasses and covered her face with her hand.

But there was still one more visit before her meeting with Ozias.

Another bus, this time into night and poverty, and the other side of Daro. Staring through the window, equally wretched and nostalgic at the familiar, curdling sights,

the same FOR SALE and FOR LEASE signs, dirty al-
coves, abandoned shoes, faded graffiti. Home. And not
just for her, either.

She got off at the station, wincing at the sewage smell
in the air, and ducked under a security gate long broken.
Soon, the gravel turned into grass, surprisingly lush,
given its water source. The river that ran through the
city was notorious for its noxious chemical levels. Full
of shadows, with a distinct lack of police presence, the
Envoy Bridge was the place for teenagers both making
out and dealing drugs. In her youth, Phaira traipsed by
the river many times in the middle of the night, desperate to be alone.

How strange that her father had chosen this river to
have his ashes dumped into. Yes, there was a bronze memorial plate affixed to the rust-and-black fence, at the
end of an old fishing platform.

Dasean Byrne, the placard read. *At Peace, At Last.*

Was that his choice? she wondered, staring at the inscrip-
tion. It was done cheaply, the script blocky and uneven.
*Is that all he wanted, all this time? If we were around, if we let him
back into our lives?*

No. She shook her head, squinting into the wind.
Nothing could have changed. She owned him nothing.
He was gone long ago, far before his date of death. She
still felt the sting on her cheek, the burn on her arm, that
familiar, swamping, stifling fear. Strange how it rose to
the surface so quickly, so many years later.

Phaira hoisted her body up onto the corner of the railing, braced her legs against the metal, and stared across the river to the cityline. Her father's plaque was beside her thigh. She put her hand over it, the edge cutting into her palm.

A surge of cars came onto the bridge, their headlights streaking over her like a meteor shower.

Tears form in her eyes, growing cold in the wind. She let them blow away, the runaway beads streaking a path across her temples.

* * *

From her perch on the railing, they would be nearly eye level. He'd stand just between her knees, take her face with his gloved hands, and kiss her until his mouth went numb, and everything grew hazy and hot, just like every time before, when she'd pressed her strong, arching body into his, sparking a heat that ran down every limb, overwhelming the cold in his fingers and toes.

A hundred times, Theron reached for the release on the door of his black ground transport. Phaira was still there, down the embankment and on that filthy fishing pier, sitting on the corner of the railing, staring out into the water. She hadn't moved in an hour. He should just get out of this transport and stop watching, actually do something for once other than watch other people.

But CaLarca's face floated through his mind, and everything went cold. *Don't be so stupid,* his logic lectured.

There were facts to weigh. Phaira was affiliated with CaLarca; she'd housed her, healed her, and never told Theron about it, when she knew what that woman and her friends had done to him.

If she was capable of that, what else was she hiding? And what happened in Kings that she was so keen to keep secret?

He let his hand fall from the door, but kept his eyes on the dark silhouette.

Finally, Phaira left the pier, and trudged downtown. Theron followed, keeping a block between them.

Outside of the local police precinct, someone was waiting on the front steps. Detective Daryn Ozias, extending her hand to Phaira.

After a long hesitation, Phaira took it, gave it one firm shake, and then let go. Then her head turned, that sharp profile scanning the streets.

The drive back to the airport was long, silent, and mostly thoughtless, save for a call from his cousin, Jetsun.

"Well?" he barked, annoyed at the interruption. "Did you give Renzo the paperwork?"

"I did, but I'm not calling about that, Theron." He could hear the tremor in her voice. "Grandfather is dead."

Theron stared at the road ahead.

Not yet, his mind pleaded. *Not yet.*

"They found him this morning," Jetsun continued. "They think it was a stroke. I know he's been weak for so long, but still. Do you - I mean, how do you want to proceed? Sir?"

Sir.

Because he was next in line to lead the syndicate.

Theron shut his eyes and let the auto-drive take over, leaning back into the leather seat.

After several long moments, he spoke. "Make the arrangements as soon as possible. No autopsies. Inform the families. Keep the media out. I'll be in touch when I get back from my meeting."

* * *

The old man lifted his head when Theron entered the basement. Shackled to the wall, clothes splattered with blood, his one blackened, bruised eye was open enough to shine with hatred.

A tiny knock against Theron's skull. Theron shook his head, tapping the half-circle of silver looped under his hair. "None of that," he instructed.

"You can't lock me away forever," Kuri Nimat spat. "I have friends, followers, who will be searching for me. They'll find out that the militia sold me to you."

"I'm not going to lock you away forever," Theron said. "I just want to know everything that's lodged in your memory, and how your NINE abilities work."

"I won't talk," the man said with a sneer. "Beat me all you like, I won't do it."

Theron gestured to Kuri's swollen eye. "That was one of my employees, getting carried away." He walked in front of Kuri, his hands behind his back. "You should know that I don't work like the rest of my family does: messy, violent, emotional. Stupid," he added with emphasis. "I have my own ways of doing things. Of getting what I want."

He stopped at a door with a brass handle. "Guess what this is."

The door swung open. Inside was a cell, six-feet squared, windowless, the walls covered with thick fiberglass wedges, arranged in horizontal and vertical patterns.

"A padded cell?" Kuri snorted. "That's your big plan?"

"Actually, it's my big experiment," Theron said. "You and your kind, you like experiments, don't you? Well, this is a replica of the world's quietest room. I read about it in a science journal. This room is covered with sound-deadening material: insulated steel, concrete and fiberglass. When you're inside, the only sound is you: your lungs, your heartbeat."

Kuri huffed again, though his confusion showed on his face.

"Oh, it might sound pleasant," Theron said. "But in fact, the brain is not used to hearing absolutely nothing." He gazed into the room, thoughtful. "In clinical studies, the most anyone has lasted inside is 45 minutes. Usually it's far less time, before the hallucinations and general psychosis takes over. How long do you think you can stand it?"

Kuri's mouth opened and closed, but no sound came out.

Two guards appeared at the door to the basement. Theron nodded.

The men strode over, took hold of Kuri, and propelled him towards the quiet room.

"No! No!" Kuri gasped, clawing at the doorframe before the bodyguards shoved him inside, and the door slammed shut.

"Go," Theron ordered the bodyguards. They ducked their heads and backed out.

Theron took a seat, and he activated the screens that measured the room's temperature, energy output, and brain wave activities.

The sound of fists pounding on walls filled the basement.

about the author:

Loren Walker hails from Ontario, Canada, and today lives and works in Rhode Island. Her poetry has appeared in the anthologies Routes, Frequency Writers City and Sea, and QU Journal. Her debut novel EKO, the first installment of the NINE Series, was a finalist in the Half the World Global Literary Award completion, chosen as a Library Journal SELF-e Select Pick, and selected as a Shelf Unbound Notable Indie. Get publishing updates, character biographies and custom illustrations at her official site: www.lorenwalker.net

The sequel to NADI is INSYNN.

thank you:

- to my family and friends, my eternal cheerleaders.
- to my beta reader Jill Corley, whose excitement to read my first draft make me smile every time.
- to my editor Lindsay Galloway, and to Deranged Doctor Design, for making NADI look good.
- and to you, for sticking with the story.